LUNA

MIST RIDERS
BOOK ONE

Stella Fitzsimons

BUTTERFLY ELECTRIC PRESS

This is a work of fiction. Names, characters, organizations, places, events, and incidents are either products of the author's imagination or are used fictitiously. Any resemblance to actual persons, living or dead, or actual events is purely coincidental.

LUNA

Copyright © 2019 Stella Fitzsimons

Cover Design by Dan Fitzsimons

All rights reserved. No part of this publication may be reproduced, distributed, or transmitted in any form or by any means, electronic or mechanical, including photocopy, recording, or any information storage and retrieval system, without permission in writing from the author.

Published by Butterfly Electric Press

www.stellafitzsimons.com

For my husband and sons,
and the disorganized narrative of our life

LUNA

The Chronicles of Luna Mae

Chapter 1

YOU DON'T GIVE UP on dreams as much as dreams give up on you.

Grandma's predilection for riddles shone through every time she shared her meticulous bits of advice. I had heard that phrase more than once. It was her not-so-subtle way of advising me to be careful what I wished for—an uncertain dream is a dream that can never come into being.

"Dreams are a kind of magic," she said. "And magic is certain."

Outside the coffee shop window, the soft colors of sunset had begun to gather on the horizon. At just before seven on a Friday evening, the coffee shop was oddly empty. True, we were at the far end of the campus and it was Labor Day weekend, meaning most students had more interesting plans than coffee and a bagel, but still... The last customer had departed with an espresso macchiato five minutes ago.

Maura and I sat behind the counter, messing with our phones.

"We might as well clean up," Maura said as she stood.

I nodded but stayed put. I closed my eyes to calm my nerves. The prospect of a brand-new life overwhelmed me at times. I never let myself believe it was in the cards, but here I was, stressing over my future.

A sudden gust of wind swung the door open, hurling a flurry of yellow and brown leaves inside the shop. The leaves swirled and danced, becoming translucent under the fluorescent lights before landing on the floor.

"What the hell was that?" Maura said, rushing to close the door. "Huh," she said as she turned to me. "It's dead calm outside. No wind. Strange."

There's always a wind. Not one moment, not one heartbeat passes where I don't hear the sound.

I usually did a better job at keeping the wind harnessed, but the fact my life was about to take a new turn had thrown me off my game. The lapses were becoming more frequent.

It didn't take much effort to keep the elements at bay—to me such a task was a primal instinct, like breathing or blinking, but a shock to the system can even make us forget to breathe or blink for a hot second, can't it?

Maura waved a hand in front of my face. "So, will you go?" she said. "They have all those tall, blonde women there. A fiery little green-eyed brunette like you would be *très exotique* in Sweden."

Wow, stereotype, much?

"I'd be going to Stockholm to study, not work in a brothel, Maura."

"That's no fun," she said, her eyes locked on mine. "What's the verdict, Miss Collinsworth?"

I looked down at the letter as I took it out of my pocket. I had already memorized its contents as if it were a school project.

Dear Ms. Collinsworth,

We are pleased to inform you that your scholarship application to study toward the Master in Ethnology has been accepted. You are eligible for a scholarship amount of $12,000 for one full year.

Please confirm receipt of this letter either through mail or email and inform us whether you intend to claim this scholarship by October 8. If we do not receive a response by October 8, the scholarship will be offered to the next deserving student.

Congratulations and we look forward to welcoming you to the University of Stockholm.

"Well?" Maura insisted.

"I wish I knew," I said with a sigh.

"You should obviously go, Sophie," Maura concluded with a matter-of-fact tone. "Regrets and all that jazz," she added for good measure.

Yeah, what is life but an endless engine of regret? Wearing

harem pants in tenth grade, breaking up with Tobin right before our high school graduation ceremony and, most of all, leaving Grandma behind in Astoria, the small Oregon town on the Columbia River where I grew up, to study social anthropology in San Diego.

Even though she expressed only encouragement, I could always sense a sincere concern in my Gram's benevolent eyes every time I visited. Her fears felt palpable although I'd managed to stay far away from trouble.

I could only imagine the dread in her eyes when I told her I was considering going to Europe to complete my master's degree and begin research for my PhD on Medieval Mingling of Myth, Magic and Witchcraft.

If I ever had a dream, this would be it—to follow my curiosities down a path that would make me a functioning member of society, hiding out in the joyous anonymity of a small-town college professor position.

"Maybe you're right, Maura," I said the moment Rob walked in to work the evening shift. "Big Rob's here, my cue to leave."

"That's right," Maura said with a sigh. "Lucky girl. I'm here till ten."

"The lucky girl's the one who gets to ride with me," Rob said with a wink as he passed by on the way to the timeclock.

"A Rob shift is always fun," I said, tucking my letter into my back pocket.

"It's still Friday night though," Maura said, wiping

down the counter.

Rob handed me my purse and denim jacket. "I punched you out, homie. Go forth and get your youth on."

"Oh, I turned my youth off years ago," I said as I headed for the door.

The sky had turned the darkest blue. A pale moon had started to emerge, half-hidden behind a dark cloud. The breeze tickled my sandaled feet as I walked onto the sidewalk. I curled down my toes and huffed.

"Don't F with me," I scolded the taunting breeze as I hurried down Caesar Drive to catch the bus.

Streetlights came on one after the other as I moved past them. They hung brightly above flower beds and trees like hovering fireflies.

I watched in astonishment as the bus drove off. Just my luck. Of all days, today was the day that the perpetually late bus ran on time.

That left me with two choices, and both pissed me off: wait for the next bus for thirty minutes or walk home, which would probably save me a minute or two.

Or I could go for option three and cut through Mission Park. That would save me more like ten minutes, but it would also mean I'd be walking through a very active collection of flora at dusk.

This would not concern a normal girl, but I was anything but normal. As a rule, I didn't cross big parks after sunset as there were always too many elements to appease at once.

I was definitely in no mood for multitasking.

In the end, impatience won out. Not to mention that if I ever wanted to live like a normal person, I would have to start acting like one.

I peeked up at the darkening sky. The nearly full moon was partially obscured by hastening clouds. Chances were that the lunar energy field wouldn't be overwhelming.

"Just relax," I told the grass as I stepped onto the path into the park. "I have this under control."

The vegetation all around began to hum. It was a subtle, benign murmur but, at the same time, impossible to ignore. With a sigh, I stepped onto the grass, letting it brush softly against my toes through the sandals.

A pulsing sensation ran up my leg as I stepped on a dry, yellow leaf.

I hastened my gait, leaping from leaf to crunchy leaf, timing my breaths with every crackle and snap of my landing feet.

There was not a moment to blink. With every footfall, my powers swelled and broke like an ebbing wave. It was like surfing a frantic tide, rising and falling in tandem with the moon's whims.

The vibrations underneath my feet surged unexpectedly. I quickly veered back onto the gravel path, so as not to wake what would best be kept in peaceful slumber.

I pricked up my ears when a low, guttural sound cut through the dark, its source way too close for comfort.

Was I too late? Had some unsavory beast banished from the Deep Down sensed my maturing command of Earth elements and decided to come out to play?

It was not something I cared to find out. I accelerated into a trot when a tall figure across the park caught my eye. His dark overcoat and long-tailed hood stopped me cold.

The man lingered as well. The hood hung low, concealing his eyes in shadows. All the same, I could feel the menace of his gaze fixed on me.

Any deliberation as to how to proceed ceased when I sensed the shallow breathing of a second hooded man behind me.

"What the hell is going on?" I whispered as I spotted a third man standing under a tree to my right.

A triangle. Nice touch. No shape in nature is stronger. Each of the four elements is represented by the symbol of the triangle.

I closed my eyes for a brief second, trying to stimulate the protective shield hidden under my fingernails even though using it was forbidden in the *basic* world. I didn't feel an etheric field. That meant these men, whatever they wanted from me, were mere humans—*basic*, as my kind called them.

In perfect synchronization, they closed in on me, barely leaving an arm's length of free space around me. I swallowed to steady my frenzied nerves.

"Yeah," I said, "so what do you want?" A thousand possible unwelcome responses flooded my head.

The tall one smiled, revealing a set of crooked teeth. "What we want, my pretty little thing, you have aplenty," he said, reaching out to wrap his fingers around my throat. "Plenty for all of us."

Chapter 2

THE MAGIC RACED TO my fingertips, gliding through my etheric field to heat up my palms. I struggled to control the current's raw power. Magic was as hard to resist as any instinct—all efforts to suppress it gnawed at my human core.

Struggling to inhale, my nostrils filled with the man's foul breath as his fingers tightened around my throat.

My hands flew up and jolted his hands with enough magic to loosen his deadly grip. My gut twisted after that burst of forbidden witchcraft.

The thug shook off my zap. Locking his sinister eyes on mine, he slipped a hand underneath my shirt. My lungs stopped working when the second goon slathered his hands all over me from behind, feeling up my thighs and hips.

Disgusted, I pushed back against him but found it impossible to budge his massive body even a bit. I was trapped between two vicious goons, feeling their intrusion at the center of my being, crushing me, annihilating my spirit in more ways than one.

My mind melted into a state of incoherent thought. Anger sparked.

"That's the spirit, lass, I can feel you warming up," one of them hissed.

His casual tone made me shiver. My vision blurred as blood pounded inside my skull. Another thug closed in, shoving his partner aside to get his hands on my chest. His hood fell back, exposing his cruel face.

I got a quick glimpse of the hard lines across his forehead and his dark, heavy eyebrows. There was something wrong with the way his eyes glimmered in the dark—yellow, stark, inhuman.

"You dimwit," the man behind me snarled as his accomplice quickly put the hood back on his head.

I knew it was my chance and took it, delivering a quick knee to his groin.

The man moaned and cursed. I whirled my body, lashing out on instinct, and managed to pull myself free from the unholy trio of miscreants.

I sprinted away only to trip and fall, rolling onto the soft grass.

Again, the tall men closed in on me. "Mess with us, little slut, and you'll pay the price," one of them said. "You've no idea who you're dealing with."

My eyes rose to the sky. The clouds had drifted north,

unveiling the Moon in its full, luminous silence. Still on the ground, I scurried backwards on my hands and butt.

The moon beams finally remembered me, surging into my pores, filling me with their silver energy.

A single spinning leaf hovered next to me, offering up its elemental core, as I slammed both palms on the grass, stifling my senses. The roar of the grass split my eardrums in half.

My assailants moved toward me, hearing nothing.

I raised my eyes to them as fury overtook my features. "No, it's you who have no idea who you're dealing with," I muttered, rising to my feet.

Six hands reached for me. I stomped my right foot on the ground, unleashing my energy field from its tethers.

"Run!" I yelled as the energy swelled into a purple fireball.

"Girl, what you..." was all I heard before the unbridled force shuddered along my spine and tendons and detonated.

The energy blasted out of me, colliding with the ground, sparking and howling as it began to envelop the thugs on all sides and above their heads.

The hapless men ducked down and ran off, disturbed to their cores, exactly as I had willed it to be.

That felt good, even glorious, to use the full force of my magic again, something I had only done before in controlled environments underground. The Lunar Order wanted to keep all the training sealed up in the dim chambers and ancient catacombs of the Deep Down.

For the first time, I had engaged my true nature in the basic world. My brain felt finely tuned and my skin glistened with health. To bring out my magic under the full moonshine, to use it in a fight and to win—God, that was something new, a sensation like no other.

Then the gravity of what I had really done hit me like a ton of bricks. I had been forced to use magic in the *up above*, or what the *basics* knew as the *real world*. I didn't even know how many rules I had broken at once, or the punishment I would suffer if my actions became known to the Lunar Order.

There were few extrasensory orbs left in the hidden lands of the Deep Down and even fewer in the up above, but those that remained could record disturbances of equilibrium in the elements from great distances. Nothing came free. Every use of energy we initiated had to be drawn from somewhere in nature.

That which is expended cannot be replaced.

Even so, I had used a minimal amount of magic. With a little luck, my energy strike would slip by unnoticed.

I ran. Leaving the scene of the unfortunate events seemed prudent. The witches of the Lunar Order were spread thin across the globe. Maybe my little blip would dissipate before ever registering with any of them.

I'd call Grandma to ask her to glance into her orb when I got home. She would surely discover any disturbances in the elemental power fields. I'd rather have a gentle Grandma scolding me than a couple of random magistrates of magic showing up at my door.

My lungs filled with air for the first time when I neared the side street that would take me out of the park and toward home. A few more quick steps and the Mission Park incident would be a memory.

The passage to freedom was interrupted by a tall, powerful figure that materialized in my path as if from thin air.

A chill cut through me.

Why can't I catch a break tonight?

This man was different. I knew it the second I laid eyes on him. I could feel his power, palpable and potent, pulsing with menace.

He was also the most impressive-looking man I had ever seen. His eyes were dark yet somehow blue like the ocean deep. He had broad shoulders and a sparkling about him like a shimmering aura. Leather jacket, boots, lips that seemed freshly minted, almost feminine.

Was it my own magic that had summoned him? If so, how could he get here so fast? There was no way this dude lived in my neighborhood.

The aura shone brighter as he neared. I backed up but then hesitated in order to better study his face. He was more than handsome, he was hypnotic.

I debated whether this spell was cast by potent magic or superb genetics. Either way, his essence was irresistible, a beacon to every woman or man entering his orbit, be it witch, sorcerer, mage, shapeshifter, faery, healer, slayer or basic human. They would all drop their defenses and follow this unparalleled man through eternity.

Dammit, Sophie, you need to snap out of it. Your defenses are weakening.

My fear that someone in the Lunar Order would sense my unauthorized behavior blinded me to the real threat, the possibility that my magic would be felt by a powerful hostile.

His magnificence did not fool me for long. In my gut, I knew that this being's aesthetic attributes were pure danger.

From my very limited options I chose once again to run. The man would not dare follow me out into the streets among the *basics*. At least, I hoped he wouldn't. Certain things were forbidden to all of us.

I found an angle and bolted for the road. With the slightest twitch, he knocked me clean off my feet with a powerful undercurrent. His energy struck my calves, flipping me a few feet above ground. I landed with a twisting thud that shot pain through every joint in my body.

The green world stopped rustling, its sudden stillness whooshing through my ears as I fought to maintain mental clarity. I planted both palms on the grass underneath me as the man advanced toward me with long strides.

Elemental power coursed through my veins, strong and willing. I felt it swell and sizzle on my palms. The energy ball I hurled at my opponent was made of pure force, capable of knocking out a pack of elephants. He deflected it easily, like it was nothing much, *poof*, a thin veil of mist that fell to the ground.

He circled me, urgent and unfeeling. "You're good at party tricks," he said. His deep voice echoed in my head. "Now let's see if there is anything substantial inside you."

I summoned a new wave of power. He crushed my magic before it left my hand. Searing pain ripped through my ribcage and twisted my heart.

I screamed.

With a snap of his wrist, a levitation force lifted me, ever so slowly, and left me suspended twenty feet above the ground.

My whole body hurt as if I was clenched inside a giant hand.

All my bravado from vanquishing the three hooded men had vanished. The man in front of me was beyond my powers. It would be pointless to continue the fight. I had already attempted what Gram would have advised, to back down and run, but failed at that as well.

The grass anticipated my fall, expanding and softening to cushion my plunge as the man released his hold. Considering that he had bonded the trees to his magic, keeping the leaves still, so I was unable to absorb their energy, it was a wonder he hadn't controlled the grass. He could have turned it hard like cement if he had so desired.

So, his cruelty isn't absolute. Nor does he want me dead.

Not yet anyway.

My adrenaline surged the second the ground began to

shake under me. Springing to my feet, I ran as fast as I could, ignoring the excruciating agony that burned through my body.

An invisible whip lassoed around my left ankle, yanking me off my feet.

I expended an incredible amount of my magic to latch onto the earth, as his greater force dragged me to him, breaking my fingernails. In my heart I knew my resistance was futile, but I would at least stall for time.

As bad as the encounter had gone so far, I was in no hurry to find out what happened when he got his hands on me.

"Did you really think you could hide from me?" he said as my body rolled onto his boots.

With a wave of his hand, he propped me up on my feet, then knocked me back down with a blow of air that felt like an iron fist. My mind spun. What was this creature? The depth of his power was unfathomable—and I had seen some absurdly powerful witches at work.

"Who in the fucking world do you think you are, measly witch?" he went on, locking in his glare.

The words oozed from his lips like poison. What beef did he imagine existed between us? Would it matter if I told him I had no clue what in the hell he was talking about?

As drained as I was, I managed to force a thin layer of protection around me that could maybe buffer whatever was coming next.

It was a big maybe, the biggest maybe of my life.

"Did you send those creeps?" I managed to say. "How did you cloak their energy fields? They felt human."

"You might as well be human, as weak as you are."

His aura turned dark purple as his eyes hardened. Instead of an answer to my question, he summoned a tangle of energy fields which shattered my shield and cut through me like a hot bullet. I was on fire, my insides burning, lungs gasping for air. I coughed up bile and blood.

I wanted to ask for help, but no one would hear. The park was empty this whole time. It made sense now. My magic hadn't summoned him. He was already on my trail and had controlled everything that had happened since I stepped onto the park path. His magic had sealed the scene from the outside world.

Screw this guy. I decided to lift my head while I was on all fours. I stared at that smug bastard, defiantly. I could barely breathe, but I persisted. He rewarded me with one more blow of energy that struck between my eyes.

I felt my front teeth cracking. Blood flowed from my ears and nose.

With trembling hands, I reached out to search my forehead for blood.

A word formed inside my head, a fiery, unwelcome word I had been taught to fear since childhood: *Immortal.*

And then all went black.

Chapter 3

I BLINKED TO MAKE sure I wasn't dreaming. I was lying on a four-poster bed, under a burgundy canopy, in an unfamiliar room. The walls were covered by dark wood panels dotted with round paintings of seascapes. Heavy drapes hid the only window in the room. A single lamp leaked a dim, sickly orange light.

My shirt and jeans were still on me—dream or no dream, that was good. I craned my neck to search for my jacket and shoes. They were gone. Memories flooded my fuzzy head. I missed the bus, walked through the park and was beat down by some psycho dude's powerful magic. Yet, I felt no pain, no fatigue at all.

If it wasn't a dream, maybe I had been fixed up by a skilled mage healer. Grandma thought their kind still existed, though no one had seen one in the basic world in centuries.

I didn't care to find out, to be honest. All I wanted was

to run but quickly discovered my hands were tightly bound to my sides. I felt the restraints, but I could not perceive anything visible restricting my wrists.

Panic surged in my chest. Whoever managed to make this spell invisible to a lunar witch was packing some serious sorcery. Like all witches of the Lunar Order, I had been trained since birth to divine spells. No standard enchantment could hide from us no matter how elaborate or rare. We spotted magic designs and could extract incantations and verses from the air more expertly than most other factions of magical beings.

And, as any witchling could tell you, a spell must be seen to be broken.

The door swung open, and my heart leapt. If the blue-eyed villain had looked formidable under the moonlight, right here, in this strange room of dim, orange light, everything about him had become astoundingly majestic.

He was tall and powerfully cut. Black dress shirt and black jeans. His sharp features were perfectly symmetric beneath his short, dirty blond hair.

He made no effort to hide his etheric field. His aura oozed out of his hypnotic blue eyes. He obviously couldn't care less if I read his energy capacity, which I easily did. My captor was definitely not a mage healer.

So, the guy had an accomplice or two, maybe a whole evil crew.

He studied me from head to toe. "You're awake? Finally,"

he said as he shut the door behind him.

This guy. I was not a fan. What was he exactly? His aura helped me determine what he wasn't but revealed nothing about what he was. Did he really beat me down with magic and then have me healed, or did he have suggestive powers? Was it all a dream planted in my head? And why did I feel certain it was morning?

He snapped his fingers, releasing the binding spell around my wrists.

I stared at him with defiance as I rose to my elbows. When I tried to move my legs, I noticed my left ankle was chained to the bedpost.

What sick game is he playing?

The bastard sighed as he started to pace. Back-and-forth he went, shaking his head. He came to a stop in front of a dresser.

Where did that dresser come from? It wasn't there a moment ago.

When he turned to face me, his magic flared about him, betraying more of his etheric essence. I shivered.

I was just a college girl from Oregon. This was way outside my safe space.

The forbidden word came to me again. Somehow, I knew my initial impression of him was correct.

I imagined the legendary tattoos on his muscled body. I was certain they would be there: the bronze star at the base of his neck, the flame serpents on his forearms, the double-headed eagle across his chest.

I could smell it on him now. My bloodline's old enemy.

Be thankful if you never have to meet one.

He saw the confusion on my face now. I knew Immortals possessed inhuman strength and speed and were lethal with an enchanted sword. I knew they could block most magic effortlessly and as efficiently as they blocked technology, but they could not wield elemental magic unless they were gods. And gods were rare. They did not walk among mortals.

Gods were elevated Immortals, the legend went, divine beings as old as time, living in the mystical eternal halls. They had witnessed more, experienced more and learned every single trick. They were able to generate magic from within their undying cells. They were here when basics slept in caves. Survival of the fittest applied not just to humans, but to Immortals as well.

The Eternals as they called themselves wouldn't make plants grow or rivers flow like the most skilled among witches. They would not enhance or nurture life—they had long since left such trivial matters behind. In troubled times, they used magic to control masses, to wage war and to annihilate. They were the most feared souls among the magic kind.

Was this Immortal standing at the feet of the bed an Eternal god? That was an idea as preposterous as me having to fight him.

"I'm not a god," the Immortal said, the whole time rubbing a small blue bottle he took out of a pocket, warming it between his hands before uncorking it.

No, for real... he could read my mind now? If that was true, I was straight out dead. It meant he already knew I was a lunar witch. To Immortals we were the worst of the witches. Our power came from the Moon and the elements and we channeled starlight to manipulate gravitational forces. When our numbers were at their peak, we were strong enough to challenge the Eternals themselves.

Immortals had hunted my kind through the ages.

"Are you hearing all this?" I said, licking my dry lips.

He raised his brow. "How do you mean?"

"Nothing. Where am I?" I asked, not expecting an answer. "Is this like where you take your victims? You know, your panic room?"

My questions bored him. He approached, yanked my head back by the hair till my neck bent so much I thought it'd break. With the other hand, he forced my mouth open and looked inside.

My heart stopped as my jaw began to ache.

With one hand still gripping my hair, he lifted the blue bottle to my lips. I screamed and tried to twist away, but all that did was hurt my neck more. The hot liquid poured down my throat.

"This will buy us some time," he said as I coughed, spitting up blue drops of the nasty stuff.

"Time for what?" I said, gagging.

I could not feel my magic. It was as if this room was

restricting access to elemental energy.

"I'm a senior Magistrate for the Seventh Council of Eternal Beings," he said, his deep voice resonating as if from an echo chamber. "I expect forthright answers."

A dark shadow entered my heart. The Seventh Council initiated the 1765 plague on lunar witches in Ireland that left hundreds crippled, maimed or catatonic. The Seventh Council was behind the 1828 famine in the rainforests of Sierra Leone that wiped out an entire generation of forest mages. The Seventh Council triggered the white-magic rebellions of 1937 that claimed the life of my great aunt Adela in Hungary where she was in hiding, according to Gram.

If the Seventh Council had found me and knew what I was, then I was taking my final breaths. There was nothing I could do. I was damn sure not going to answer any questions from this aesthetically perfect asshat. I would rather sign my own death warrant.

"To what Order division do you belong?" he said, his gaze penetrating deep inside my skull.

"*Order?* What's that? I'm a graduate of San Diego State University."

Defying him was a death wish, but my hatred trumped my fear. A grin lingered on his lips. That was new. Was it wrong that I found his smile mesmerizing?

"Fifth division Lunar," he said. "If memory serves, the almighty Fourth were annihilated in the glory days of the Great War."

My hands burned with the desire to slap him. What I wouldn't give to be in the woods, under a clear night sky, with the Moon full, so I could gather a rippling wave of lunar force that would burn the smug features off his face.

"And your mother... when was the last time you saw her?"

"Excuse me?"

"I spoke clearly."

Every bad word I knew flooded my brain. *Oh, the choices.*

Instead, a compulsion to answer began to well in my stomach and rose into my throat. He was doing this, this spell. No, it was that potion he forced me to swallow. *Bastard.*

"You know where she is," I said in a low voice, buying myself some time. "I bet you are responsible for it, and this is part of some sick game."

His face turned ice cold. "I can assure you, I don't play games and I had nothing to do with whatever happened to your mother."

"Maybe not directly, but..." Sweat fell from my forehead and my throat felt like sandpaper. I struggled to enunciate. "You wield dark magic. You're an obvious assassin."

"That is the one thing I am not. I am Chief Magistrate. I take my duties seriously and I speak only of serious and necessary matters."

My head pounded as I struggled against his potion. "I couldn't give a fuck. And you sound like an evil Lorax."

An invisible hand struck my left cheek. I felt heat

spreading across the skin as capillaries burst.

The Immortal moved to the side of the bed. "What's your ritual name?"

"Screw you," I said. "Do you need me to spell it?"

"You have a mouth on you, I'll give you that. A vulgar side effect, no doubt, of mingling with basics."

He lifted his hand, merely slapped the air, and yet I felt the sting. He did it once more, but harder. That next blow loosened a tooth and left me breathless from pulsating pain. I could taste blood in my mouth.

He bent down. His face was next to mine, our lips just inches apart. "What is your ritual name in the Lunar Order?" His gaze was stone cold, telling me in no uncertain terms that he could unleash much greater violence.

I was nothing if not stubborn. I spit blood to the side and summoned the last vestiges of my defiance. "Sophie," I said. "Sophie Collinsworth."

His eyes brimmed with anger and maybe a tinge of perverse satisfaction at all the sadistic displays he could no doubt show me.

He straightened his body to stand at his full height, at least six foot two. "I'm feeling generous tonight, so I will give you another chance. Your bones are delicate. I suggest you answer. What's your ritual name?" His voice came out flat, almost resigned. He did not expect me to relent.

I surveyed his face. Time crawled as I calculated my chances. "And what would change? You'll kill me or turn me into a vegetable, like they did to my mother."

The blow he delivered hit me everywhere at once. His magic mercilessly tortured me, pressing and pushing against vital organs.

My voice spat my name out weakly, "Luna."

The invading force vanished from my bloodstream.

I gasped. My ears rang. I had been defeated.

A lunar witch's name is only known within the Order. A lunar witch's name must never be known outside the Deep Down. A lunar witch's name is a dangerous thing in the wrong hands.

I learned this as soon as I could speak.

"There. That wasn't so hard."

Was he mocking me? I no longer found his smile one bit appealing.

Hours ago, my only concern was studying abroad in Europe, a pleasant, contained human concern. Now everything had gone to shit. Even if he spared my life, I'd always be broken and defeated. I would always be marked.

"Get your rest," the Immortal advised. "The rest we'll discuss later."

My eyes felt suddenly heavy. One more blink and I was gone.

Chapter 4

THE DISTRESSING IMAGE OF a red, hot needle piercing my eardrum formed behind my closed eyelids as the buzzing grew louder. Right now, it didn't make much sense that I had chosen a bumblebee ringtone, but then again, not a lot was making sense in my life.

My eyes shot up to my SpongeBob wall clock. Half past eleven. A pounding headache ripped through my skull. I held my eyes closed, hoping for relief that did not come.

Tobin made that misshapen clock for me back in eleventh grade when we started dating. I wasn't sure why I still had it on my wall. It was ugly, but it connected me back home.

The ringtone mercifully stopped, but the pressure behind my temples continued to intensify. I clenched my fists. Blood and elemental energy surged to my fingertips, causing tingling sensations, as if my hands had fallen asleep.

I crept to the bathroom, an uncanny feeling of déjà vu

rising inside my chest. An unrest nagged at my very core, but I couldn't put my finger on it.

The mirror reflected my truth. I saw the image of a girl who had survived a harrowing ordeal and had barely slept: hair so tangled and frizzy a brush would have trouble sliding through it, dark circles under eyes so puffy and big they looked like quarters, lips cracked like dried figs.

A flashing light zipped across the sheen of the glass surface of the mirror, followed by a blurry image emerging from its silver depths—the handsome, hypnotic face of a powerful Immortal glaring right at me.

I gasped and backed away, leaving the bathroom, icy terror crawling along my spine and the back of my head.

What in the seven hells was that?

I racked my brain for a plausible explanation. Had an apparition followed me back from my dreams in the land of Morpheus?

I tiptoed back to the bathroom to inspect the mirror. I sighed when I saw only me there staring back. I ran my hands over my face, searching for bruises and lacerations. There were none. I opened my mouth wide and stuck my fingers inside to count my teeth one by one. Such a relief to find all thirty-one expected teeth. The only absentee was a wisdom tooth that had not yet come in and likely never would.

My ears swooshed with the sudden hum of a thousand flower beds and bushes blooming all at once.

Was it true then?

I let the water run, filling the sink to the brim. I grabbed the razor from the medicine cabinet and shuddered. I was doing the last thing I should be doing, using more magic—especially magic I didn't completely understand—but I wasn't ready to ask for Grandma's help.

My trembling right hand struggled to grip the razor firmly, but I managed to prick my left index finger with the corner of the blade, letting a few droplets of blood fall in the water.

Wrapping my wounded finger in a blue washcloth, I watched my blood disperse into fading ribbons of pink, sinking to the bottom of the sink.

I clenched my teeth as a sequence of memories flooded the water in fast-forward mode, so vivid I felt the burn and sting of the Immortal's energy blasts all over again.

He was real. The icy feeling in my gut could not be the product of a dream or even a nightmare. Only memory can cause such physiological anguish.

My breath caught in my throat as I reached into the sink to pull the plug, watching the pink ribbons spiral into the drain. By now, there was a good chance this blood magic would have sent a reverberation beyond the walls of my second-floor studio apartment.

Sooner or later, I would have to answer to the Order about this. I would have to confess that I had revealed my name to an Immortal, and who knew what else. My memories lacking clarity would not save me.

There weren't many of us left in the basic world, but

others in the Lunar Order should be told that Immortals were out hunting again.

The story of our rivalry went back to the 14th century, the time of the Great War among magic factions that lasted thirty years. The Fourth Lunar Division led the witch resistance. In the end, they were defeated. The surviving witches of the Fourth and the mages and wizards who assisted them were herded into buried prisons before being executed one-by-one by Immortal Magistrates.

To come upon one of those bastards seven centuries later was rotten luck, but to encounter an Immortal Magistrate whose power felt old enough to have been around since before the Great War, well, that was truly cursed.

This guy might have been judge and executioner of my ancestors. And now it could be my head that he removed with an ax and my headless body that he tossed into a blue bonfire.

I didn't know what to believe. I didn't know what had happened exactly or, worse, what was yet to happen. I couldn't even be sure what day it was.

A crippling doubt overtook my scattered thoughts. Was the fractured memory of this brutal magical attack an actual event, or had the Immortal overtaken my head to make me believe it happened?

His great power could be the power of suggestion. That would be better, that would be the best-case scenario. Because if his dark magic had truly reached that height of mastery, if he could control elemental energy and had healing powers, just how dangerous could he be? And maybe he wasn't the only one, maybe all Immortals had leveled up.

I leaned back against the wall, trying to pull myself together. Since birth, I had been instructed to stay clear of supernatural factions that didn't answer to the Deep Down, never use substantial amounts of magic in the basic world and avoid drawing attention to myself. The slightest slip and I could be inviting someone truly powerful to come for me.

Well, now someone more powerful than I had ever imagined had come for me and I compounded that a hundredfold by betraying my true name to him. In betraying my Order, I had compromised the safety of my grandma and of everyone else who knew me.

A text arrived at the exact moment someone knocked on my door.

If U R not here in the next 20, U R fired. Can't miss 2 shifts in a row, certainly not on a MONDAY MORNING, without so much as a call. Ugh.

Two shifts? So today was Monday. That was three days I couldn't account for. The thought creeped me out even more.

What did he do to me?

The knocking on the door became louder, persistent, intruding. Fear knotted my stomach.

Surely, he wouldn't knock, Sophie. A beast like that would blow through the door and claw at your throat before you could even blink.

I opened the door a crack, clinging to my sanity. A guy in his late teens stood there with a broad smile on his lips, a basic algebra textbook in hand, and a backpack strap around his shoulder. He was high-school thin and of medium height. He wore his hair in a cool, tight fade and there was a bare-ly-there silver stud on his left ear. His face betrayed intelligence but lacked in confidence and, most importantly, seriousness.

"Yes, can I help you?" I said as he seemed in no hurry to speak.

"I don't know," he said with a nervous laugh. "I just had to find you."

"What? I don't see a package."

"Yeah. I don't have one. It's that... I had a dream... several dreams, actually... about you."

Oh boy. Exactly what I needed. A freshman working up the nerve to knock on my door. More proof I no longer belonged on campus with the undergrads.

"Dude, not cool. Never knock on this door again," I said, rolling my eyes, before shutting the door in his face.

"Hey, it's not that," I heard his protest through the door. "We have people in common."

"I'm busy," I yelled. "Go away! Shoo!"

I waited. I could feel him there, on the other side of the door.

"I had to come here. You missed the last two shifts at the coffee shop."

Stalker, much? Sheesh.

Against every instinct in my body, I opened the door a crack.

"You're crossing every line," I said, unsure of anything at this point.

"What? You never crossed lines before?" He wiped his mouth and made no attempt to push in the door. "I mean, being in this world, isn't that already crossing a line?"

Our eyes locked. I decided to trust him. I grabbed his shirt and pulled him into my studio apartment, kicking the door shut.

"Spit it out. What's this about?" I said, my face inches away from his. From his stunned expression, I knew I must have seemed crazy.

He straightened his shirt and took a step back. "I don't know exactly. All I know is this is where I need to be at," he said. "It's never clear. My life is one big blur. Answers are scarce. I just go and now I'm here, you dig?"

"No, I don't dig. You're acting like a stalker."

"*What?* No. This ain't that. You not my type. No offense."

I raised an eyebrow at him. "Really? So, what's your deal then?"

"I mean you fine and all, but I'm not about girls, you dig?" he said as he started to move around to check out my apartment. "I'm Faion. That's my name, Faion Trice. I don't know you, but I know of you... well, our grandmothers, they know each other."

"Ah! Grandma? Of course. Mystery solved," I exclaimed, throwing my hands in the air.

"Huh? What mystery?" he said. "Your gran didn't send me."

"Then who?"

"My gran... wait, are you being tricky right now?"

"You'd know it if I was being tricky," I told him, then walked to the door, never letting him out of my sight. "If you don't have answers, I don't have time."

"Wait, okay? Damn, you ill-tempered. I'm a diviner."

"A diviner?" I felt like I was losing my mind all over again. "You?"

"Yeah," Faion said, put off. "What am I supposed to look like?"

"No... I mean, yeah, a diviner, sure. What's that to me?"

"I'm just messing. Everybody reacts that way. I'm supposed to look mystic, all wisdom and no humor, someone old and crusty. Am I right? Or maybe I should look freaky like Will Smith in that Aladdin movie."

What the hell was he on about? "Is all this ever coming to a point?"

"The point is I saw something in a dream that..." He paused, regarding me with sad eyes. "Something that... I shouldn't tell you."

"Oh my god, dude, for real?"

There was something like horror on his face. Horror and guilt.

"Did someone send you?" I said. "Because I'm not buying this. You can't be a diviner. I don't sense a magical aura and I'm pretty good at that stuff and you're pretty bad at whatever this is supposed to be."

"You wouldn't sense an aura, not in here. I'm protected." He reached inside his shirt to retrieve a triangle amulet hanging from a silver chain.

"Life and light," I said, recognizing the ancient divining symbols.

"Yeah. My gran don't play. She has my shit covered. It works best in small spaces," he said.

"710 square feet," I said. "It's not the Taj Mahal."

He relaxed which made me laugh. I could be scary to young men.

"Okay, suppose I believe you, Faion. Suppose I don't start slapping you around all the way to Sunday. What was this dream of yours about?"

"Yeah, okay," he said, taking a deep breath. "You're in trouble, Luna. And it's about to get much worse."

And just like that, while everything seemed to be slowing down all around me, Faion the diviner slipped past and darted out my door.

Chapter 5

Lunar shadows caused by dark side rotation dictate dominance levels in battle. What did that mean? It was obvious I was on the wrong path. I had discovered a tattered copy of *The Book of Night Rituals* at my local library. The book was full of answers, sure, if you knew what questions to ask, but I had no idea.

According to various Order documents, hidden clues on how to scan for material waves—in other words, how to determine what's real and what's not—were scattered throughout the book. So far, I'd discovered exactly none.

I never excelled at decoding magical text. There was a good chance I'd mess up the interpretation even if I did find the clues, but someone without a clue needs to find one and, at that point, I was willing to try anything.

"Why are we meeting at the library?" Lily said.

I slammed the leather-bound book shut, turned and fell

into her arms, hugging her so tight she had to fight herself out of my grip. Finally, something was real in my world again. Lily was real. Her soft skin was warm like hot chocolate with marshmallows, her hair was awash with the scent of green apple and aloe shampoo—everything about Lily was sunny and reassuring.

"Wow, Sophie, I get it that I'm irresistible, but that's embarrassing," she said, amused yet cautious.

"It's been a tough few days," I said with a sigh.

"Apparently." She glanced at the book in my hands.

Instinctively, I covered the title with my left palm, worried it could give away my secrets. "Life happens. I'm over it."

"Because you're a total badass," she said. "But if there is anything you need to tell your best friend, must we do it in a library? My entire motivation for graduating was to never study again. You know this."

I did know that, because it was like her catch phrase the past two months. And, of course, there was tons I wanted to unload on Lily, but I couldn't for obvious reasons.

"I have news," I said, returning the book to a random shelf.

"*Pues, dime, chica.*"

"My Spanish is rusty."

"So is mine, but I have that Nicaraguan blood so don't tell Lucia. I'm literally getting worse every year."

Lily always called her mom Lucia for whatever reason. Lucia was a brilliant, petite lady from Nicaragua and a professor of languages. Besides English, she spoke Spanish, Portuguese, French and Guarani fluently. Lily had always felt pressure to learn multiple languages, but it was never her thing.

"Do you want to hear my news?" I said, shaking my head.

"Of course. No, wait, holy shit. You got accepted?"

"*Sí.*"

"Sophie? Oh my god. That's insane!" She wrapped me in her arms and a sudden burst of emotion choked me up. I couldn't remember the last time a hug had felt so good.

"Well, it's not insane. I worked my ass off."

"You say it like it's a good thing. You're Yin and I'm Yang." She released me from her arms. "Stockholm, right? Wow. That's the one in Sweden?"

She always made me laugh. "Yes, Lily. Sweden."

"And I thought the East Coast was too far. You'll be like a billion miles away and surrounded by tall, blond guys. No variety."

I rolled my eyes. "I'm sure all hair colors will be represented."

"Are you sure about this? It's a big choice."

"As sure as I'll ever be," I said, and for a moment, I believed it. I believed I could just walk away from my mess, get on a plane, fly straight to Sweden and never look back. "It'll only be for a year, maybe two."

"Yeah, unless you mate with a huge, Viking beefcake and bear him seven sturdy sons named Sven."

"I'm pretty sure that won't happen, and Sven is a Norwegian name."

"Right, as if you'd turn down Chris Hemsworth."

"That's an Australian guy, and already married."

"You're a total dork, you know what I'm saying."

"Yeah," I said with a sigh. "You're going to miss me."

"Of course, but you'll miss me more," she said.

She was right. While Lily would still have everyone, I'd have no one and that's when I needed her most.

Lily turned her back and covered her face. "No fucking way."

"What?"

"It's Rocco. That's what," Lily muttered through her fingers.

"Who? Where?"

"At the computer in the corner. Don't look."

I looked. Rocco Barnes sat browsing the library database which was odd. He had graduated two years ago when Lily and I were juniors, and had left town shortly afterwards, but his legacy persisted on campus.

Rocco had been a college football star for the Aztecs and a hot, wild, legendary personality on campus. With my own eyes, I had seen drunk girls throw bras at him when he showed up at private parties. Personally, I thought he was too much—too loud, too smug and too masculine.

"You're still crushing on him?" I whispered, knowing the answer. "Well, there you go, fate has intervened."

"Screw fate, he'd laugh in my face."

Lily Herrero was a classic beauty with full lips, big brown eyes and more curves than any statue of Venus.

"Is this where I have to tell one of the most beautiful women in San Diego that she is, in fact, beautiful?"

"Best friend vision is like Mom vision," she said. "Biased A.F."

We'd been friends since my first days in San Diego, nearly four years ago, and became best friends within weeks of meeting. Her outgoing nature was a perfect antipode to my reclusive nature. She made me feel normal.

She deserved better than Rocco and she deserved better than a friend like me who kept so much of my life hidden from her.

Lily hurried toward the exit, almost knocking over a chair. I followed.

"He's just a washed-up ex athlete, Lil," I said. "Don't run into a wall."

Lily came to a halt outside the library. Gray clouds gathered overhead. It was the warmest part of the day and humid.

"Where were you this weekend?" Lily said, suddenly serious.

"Why, did you try to call?"

She stared at me perplexed. *"Did I try to call?* Who asks that? I left you two messages."

Oh. "I lost my charger. My phone was dead." Yet another lie.

"I called you Friday night," she said, studying my face as if a new idea had just occurred to her. "Then I left a text message Sunday morning."

Friday night. I was either unconscious or getting my ass kicked by an Immortal who dragged my identity out of me. "I was feeling beat up and slept most of the time."

"You bitch," Lily said. "Did you hook up this weekend?"

I did not expect that. "You're an idiot."

"You did, didn't you?" Lily continued. "Who is this mystery man?"

"You're right," I said, playing along. "I was busy making the sex."

She giggled as she took out her car keys. "If only that were true."

"If only," I said.

"Weren't you supposed to be working today?"

"I called in sick."

"Wait, you lied?" she said in awe. "Is that even a possibility? Can princess Sophie actually lie?"

"Yes, you'd be surprised," I confessed.

Usually, it amused me that people thought I could not tell a lie. Not today.

"I have to run," Lily said. "Lucia needs help executing her latest garden reimagining. Such bother. Lattes tomorrow?"

My bones ached and hummed at the thought of a beautiful garden in bloom. The sheer amount of fresh, pampered elemental energy always stirred my life force.

"For sure," I said, "hit me up."

As soon as Lily was out of sight, I ran back inside the library to grab *The Book of Night Rituals*. I tucked the tome inside my hoodie best as I could and walked through the security sensors like a boss. I did not believe that a magic book that didn't officially exist would trigger the alarm.

Faion's visit was still on my mind. I shouldn't have let him walk out of the apartment like that. I had to find him and make him tell me more. I needed to know all that he knew.

I heard voices behind me and hastened my gait, pulling the book out from under my hoodie. My fingers trembled with nerves and sweat. The book slipped through them, tumbling onto the pavement with a thud.

That thing was heavy enough that it would certainly be damaged if it were a normal book. It wasn't.

A stranger stepped past me and plucked up the book in one scoop.

"Hey!" I said, startled.

He gave the book the once over, arching an eyebrow. "You're into magic?"

I froze. Why would he ask that? "I'm into all things medieval," I said, then snatched the book from his hands.

He was a few years older than me, fit, and had a fresh, sporty scent. My eyes landed on his now empty hands. He had big palms and long, lovely fingers that ended with evenly clipped nails.

I raised my eyes to his and saw a sliver of gold inside warm hazel irises, his thick brown hair brushed back casually. He emanated strength and self-assurance. His pecs were visible underneath his tight sweatshirt, and a few sweat beads glistened on his forehead. I noticed the running shoes on his feet.

Oh god. I had forgotten to say a word. I was just looking, drooling really, over a tall, square-jawed stranger while my future and the future of my kind lingered in great peril.

"Well, thanks for the help," I said and turned to go in full blush.

"Hold on a second," the man said. A pleasant grin threatened to fully form on his sensual lips. "If you go, I might never see you again."

"Yeah. Is that a problem?"

He stepped toward me. "A big problem."

"How so?" Those words escaped my lips in a whisper.

"I want to learn about magic," he said.

My heart surged in my chest. What was happening? I knew it wasn't magic, but I was completely under his spell.

"You think you're charming?" I finally said, as if he wasn't.

He opened his hands, feigning helplessness.

"It's a small world," I said. "Maybe we'll meet again."

My feet couldn't carry me away fast enough.

As soon as I turned the corner, I took my phone out to collect myself. It was past time to call Grandma. If I was right and the Immortal had sealed the scene at the park, the orb would be clear, which meant *I* would be in the clear with the

Order for now. That would give me needed time to figure out what the hell I was facing.

"*Sweetheart, I've been waiting for your call.*"

"You have?" I said, cautiously.

"*Of course, I'm making waffles, you always call when I'm making waffles.*" Grandma's melodic voice warmed my insides instantly.

"With cinnamon sugar and spring yellow butter?"

"*You bet.*"

"Maybe I can be on the next flight."

"*Wouldn't that be wonderful? Is everything okay, Sophie?*"

"Gram, please, don't use your spider sense."

"*Dear, I have no bond with spiders.*"

"I know, Gram, never mind. Just tell me if the orb is clear today."

There was a long pause, too long, or maybe my anxious energy was stretching time in my mind.

"*Give me a moment.*"

I heard something new in Gram's voice that didn't feel right. An urgency or a resignation—or maybe an urgent resignation, a pallor of doom or futility.

My paranoia peaked as I waited for her return. I felt irrationally sure that the end of the world was nigh and there was nothing to be done.

I picked at my teeth with my fingernails.

"*Sophie?*"

"Yes."

"It's clear. The waves are undisturbed. Zero reverberations."

I exhaled, quietly. "Good to know," I said. "I love you, Gram."

"Oh, sweet girl, I love you, too."

"Well, I love you and I love you AND I love you."

This always pleased her to hear. I could feel her grin through the phone.

"You would tell me if something was wrong, wouldn't you?"

"Yes, Gram. Don't worry. I will see you soon."

The second I hung up, I regretted not asking Grandma about Faion and his grandmother. Maybe it was for the best. That would have been one oddity too many for a single call. Everything was happening too fast. I needed more information and I needed to collect it carefully.

The Book of Night Rituals might guide me towards that path. I'd read every word in it as many times as it took to unravel the hidden clues.

As I reached my building, magic rippled through me, warning me of an irregularity in the etheric charge around my home.

A light drizzle began to fall, tickling my face. I stood still, wondering whether to stay and fight or take off as fast as I could.

I glanced up. The door to my apartment opened.

"Welcome home," the Immortal said, his massive presence filling up the door frame. His hair shimmered gold in the waning sunlight. A twitch above his left eyebrow made his gaze even more intense than usual.

The Hemsworths had nothing on this guy.

My heart slowed. The sweat forming on my hands, mixed with the humidity, made my palms suddenly clammy. The tip-tap of the fast-descending raindrops resounded off the spine of *The Book of Night Rituals*.

I realized I was not surprised to find him there. Without resistance, I climbed up the stairs and followed the Immortal inside.

Chapter 6

THE IMMORTAL PACED ABOUT the cramped spaces of my apartment. His disdain was as clear as his intense gaze. Maybe it was the shabby, mismatched furniture that offended him or maybe the general lack of tidiness—shirts folded on tables, books splayed out on every surface—or maybe it was the tight confines: a single room that served as kitchen, bedroom and living room—it was the world *after* the walls had closed in.

I slipped out of my wet hoodie and plopped down on the loveseat. It was the first time I saw his features fully lit. I cleared my throat and tried to calm my breathing.

Everything about him suggested power. His balanced stance was poised and ready. His hulking chest strained the fabric of his linen button-up shirt. His arms and legs were striped with strong, lean muscles.

His exquisite bone structure was flawless except for a few

fine wrinkles across the forehead and at the corners of his eyes. His unblemished skin would have made you think he was in his early thirties. I knew better.

I had no doubt he was fully aware I was taking in his every detail, but he could not care less. A man like that had been savored every day of his life.

He spoke first. "You shouldn't be surprised to see me. I think I made it clear we'd be continuing our conversation."

"I'm not surprised," I said.

"At least you didn't run back to your grandmother," he said, almost reflectively. "You saved me a trip to Oregon."

I said nothing, waiting to see what exactly he wanted. My eyes wandered to the white moth orchid on the coffee table, the closest thing in the room to a replenishing source of elemental energy. If I was fast enough, if I touched the fragrant flower for a mere second—

"Resistance will be met with pain." He, too, had spotted the white orchid. He casually opened his hand to create a luminescent current of energy that shielded me from access to the coffee table and the flower.

"Yeah, I remember," I said, unimpressed. "You're a dick."

When a smile might form on his face, it quickly became a hard scowl.

"I'm whatever I need to be," he said with a sigh.

"And you needed to send men to assault me?"

He shrugged. "Let's call that a test."

"A test? That's sick," I said. "Well, did I pass your sick test?"

My insults could not touch him, the arrogant bastard.

He twisted his hands to send a blinding flash of translucent energy to encircle me and force me to my knees. I tried to resist the invisible tethers but found it impossible to move. The Immortal had again cast an immobilizing spell that I could not see.

He resumed pacing, his contempt growing stronger with each step.

"Your test went as predicted. Failure to restrict reverberations while using magic – check. Failure to recognize immortal threat – check. Panic when faced with unbridled magic – check. Failure to activate energy shield – check. Ignoring protective steps as outlined in the Lunar manual when fighting more powerful Immortals – check." He stopped to lick his lips. "You were unable to meet even my lowest expectations, Luna Mae."

He was in possession of my full Lunar name, but I didn't have the energy to make sense of that. His patronizing tone was starting to piss me off.

"Happy to disappoint."

"Get up," he said, freeing me from his spell. "It's time for you to fight me."

Was he serious? "I think I'll pass," I said with a fake yawn.

He barely gave me a second to finish my sentence. A blue blaze glowed bright in his right hand. He shook his arm and the hissing blaze leapt forward and struck my left forearm with an intense blast.

It all happened so fast I didn't realize the heat had cut deep through skin and muscle. My flesh sizzled. It hurt like hell. I put pressure on the wound to stop the gushing blood, fighting off tears.

As soon as it began, the pain subsided and the wound vanished. I wiped away the blood as best as I could. Where there was raw, devoured flesh, now there was nothing but healthy skin.

The shit is getting to be too much.

I locked my gaze on the Immortal's as I climbed to my feet. "How do you do that?" I heard the words escape my mouth.

He rewarded my curiosity with a second, much harder blow. My flesh melted away like molten metal, exposing ravaged tendons and bone.

I cried out unable to hold back the tears. Why was he doing this? What was the end game to torturing a college girl?

Screw him and screw his end game. Those eyes that I once found mesmerizing were now the coldest daggers in all the realms.

Screw the Seventh Council and all they represented throughout all the centuries of history. Screw generation upon generation of Immortals.

Enough. I resisted the confrontation he was trying to force. With every fiber of my being, I resisted. I wanted nothing to do with him or his plans.

"Your guardians have failed you, Luna Mae," he said and then gently blew on the wound. His breath cooled my burning flesh, filling the open gash with a protective white mist. "You have no skill to wield weapons of any type, do you? Any stray being with a speck of magic in them and a good sword would pummel you."

By now, my anger had swelled beyond control. I was seething mad and hungered vengeance. "A *sword*, old timer? I hate to break this to you, but the rest of us left the Middle Ages behind long ago."

My injured arm tickled as damaged skin and tissue bonded, restoring my strength and concentration. The magic under my fingernails swelled, feeding off my fury and the smell of my own blood. My fingers flared a transparent purple aura as I hurled a quick bolt of ice, sharp as a dagger.

So, I can't fight with weapons, huh?

The Immortal raised his palm casually to meet my attack, crushing the ice bolt in midflight. The exploding ice dissolved into thin steam.

How could he anticipate my every move?

The rain pitter-pattered against the windows, and the sky loomed darkly with gathering storm clouds. Lightning flashed. The thunder that followed shocked my senses. The salty taste of rain teased my palate as a sudden downpour roared outside and echoed in my ears.

The Immortal stepped towards me. I closed my eyes and

slowed my breathing. *The rainwater is power*. I remembered my training.

I opened my arms, absorbing vitality from the natural world into my own life force. I could feel the energy rising in every cell of my body.

The rain broke through the window glass, shattering it into a thousand pieces.

Razor-sharp shards lined up and hurled themselves at the Immortal. He threw up an energy shield fast but not fast enough. Not this time. Hundreds of my blurry-fast shards punctured his skin, cutting deep holes on his perfect face and neck and hands.

So, Immortals do bleed.

He stared at his blood-drenched hands, fascinated. He felt his bloody face with his bloody fingers. Bits of glass stuck out from a hundred fleshy wounds. From his expression, I gathered he was stunned.

He had not seen that coming.

This was not a case of him letting me win.

No. I did that, all on my own.

Wow.

He leveled his gaze back at me, leaning forward a little. I took a step back, rattled. A sinking dread replaced my confidence. I remembered that this man was more than powerful, he was unpredictable, deranged.

"So, there is some life in you after all," he said, almost pleased.

He wanted me to hurt him? I gave up trying to guess his motives.

"What do you want?" I said, deflated of all purpose. Drawing a little blood, or even maiming him, barely caught his attention. He was an ancient warrior who had mastered the dark arts. He could not be killed by any known method in the basic or the magical world.

I doubted he even had a conception of pain.

"You are a lunar witch. Do you really need to ask?"

"Well, that's just stupid," I said, the words spilling out before they could be stopped. "You lived all those years and you still don't have a mind of your own. You just hate an entire magical faction because some ancient law you learned a bazillion years ago says you should."

His flesh began expelling the glass. His wounds faded by the time the shards hit the ground. He didn't even flinch.

The Immortal brushed his hair back, staining a few blond strands with blood from his fingers. "I never learned those laws, Luna Mae. I wrote them."

I shot him a menacing glare. "Stop calling me that."

He raised an eyebrow. "But it's your name."

"You know that naming is essential to a lunar witch's craft. It's intricate and precise. It affects our very etheric essence. It's a high insult to misuse it."

He chuckled. Who knew he was capable of mirth? "That's the fun of it."

My spine stiffened. I had been mocked enough for one

day. "Why won't you people leave us alone? You've already reduced our numbers to next to nothing. Last time I checked, there were less than—"

I caught myself. That was not information to reveal, especially to him.

"Less than two thousand lunar witches remain in the Deep Down, I know full well. Nothing is hidden from my eyes."

Message received loud and clear. I was the mouse. He was the cat. He'd play with me for as long as it pleased him. "So, do you have a name as big as your ego?" I fired back, sick of his arrogance. "Because it seems like you're trying too hard."

He walked to the fridge and took out a bottle of water. "Here," he said, tossing it to me. "You're depleted of electrolytes."

Yeah, that happened when I overplayed my influence on water. He knew the basic biology of elemental magic as well. He was well versed. I'd give him that.

"Fattening me up for the slaughter," I said. "Does that mean you're not killing me today?"

"It's still early," he said with a sigh. "But seriously, as tempting as that sounds, I cannot kill you. I need you to do something for me."

Okay, what? Me doing something for *him?* Dude was crazy. "What exactly in your whole approach would make me now want to lift a finger for you?"

He pounced, pinning me against the wall with one

forearm to my throat, the other across my stomach, for the first time using plain physical superiority to overpower me. My magic simmered inside. I felt it hissing along my spinal cord and tingling inside every nerve in my body, willing me to fight back.

The Immortal sensed it, too. He pressed harder against my throat, cutting off my oxygen supply. My vision blurred, the violent spasms in my chest extinguishing the rising magic.

He put his mouth to my ear. "You're going to help me, Luna Mae. You're mine to command now. You're going to help me in the deep down and the up above – together we will uphold Immortal Rule."

Ha! Fat chance.

He reduced the pressure gradually. I coughed. I gasped for air. "I'm a measly witch, you said so yourself. Even if I wanted to, how could I even—"

He grabbed my shoulders and shook me. "You owe me your life. That's something you should never forget."

The Immortal let go and walked out the door.

My heart raced. I rubbed my throat and coughed up a bit of mucus into my hand. *The asshole.* My anger grew until my hands balled into fists.

I would make it my life's mission to bring that bastard to his knees and when he least expected it, I'd cut out his heart and feed it to the piranhas, at least, you know, metaphorically.

Point being I was quite pissed.

Chapter 7

The bell above the door jingled cheerfully as a young couple strolled into the coffee shop holding hands, not a care in the world, flaunting their happiness.

I glanced at Maura, pleadingly.

She nodded. "I got this."

Grateful, I glanced down at the acceptance letter in my hands, which I must have read forty times by now. Time was running out. I wondered if it'd be considered bad form to request the scholarship money right away.

The course wouldn't start for another five months, but if I had any chance in hell to get out of the country in one piece, I'd have to leave soon. Without the scholarship money, the prospects of that happening looked grim.

My options were limited. I'd sit down to write my response at lunch and post the letter after work. Digital correspondence was out of the question. I couldn't rule out the possibility that I'd been hacked.

"A penny for your thoughts."

I knew that voice. Faion Trice. He smiled, content to have caught me by surprise.

"Ah, *the diviner* himself," I said, sneeringly. "Or was it *the chicken*?"

I expected him to be thrown off, but instead he chuckled. "Yeah, that's right, I ran. My momma never raised no fools. I don't hang around when a woman gets pissed off, okay? I thought you needed some space."

"Space? That's what that was? You just tell a girl her life is about to take a nosedive and then you jet?"

"I'm not about to mess with no LW, not when she has that scary look."

He had a point. I had done my best to intimidate him.

The lovely couple beamed as Maura handed them their coffee cups. They headed for the door, arms around each other. Their laughter echoed off the small wooden tables and pastel-painted walls.

Outside, the guy planted a kiss on the girl's cheek. I envied the simplicity of their happy lives. It reminded me there was more than thieves, slayers and Immortal thugs in the world.

"Apology accepted," I told Faion. If I was to get any help from him, I had to make him feel comfortable. "And so now you show up here, at a public place, where you'll be safe... but why?"

He scanned the tranquil surroundings. "We need to talk."

Talk about the understatement of the year. "Okay, follow me."

I led him behind the counter and to the break room in back. I closed the door and, against my better judgment, cast a simple binding spell to fuse the lock so nobody could open it from the outside.

I was getting bolder with my use of the gift, but when in Rome, right? Small tricks would likely go unnoticed. At this point, I had nothing to lose.

My name was no longer secret, nor was my lineage or allegiance. It was only a matter of time before the Immortal used my name to enhance a scouting spell that would lead him to the Order's location.

Faion noticed the pictures tacked to a cork board on the wall, a random selection from work gatherings, personal trips and Halloweens past.

He focused on a picture of our manager, Doug, standing among a herd of llamas up in the mountains. "Where was that picture taken?"

I shrugged. "Peru, maybe."

His face lit up. "Man, I'd like to ride a llama. I'd go to South America just for that. It's like I look into their llama eyes and can read their minds."

"Are you nuts?" I said, then thought of it. "Wait, can you actually read minds?"

"Nah. That's the telepaths' game. We diviners only sense stuff."

"Right."

He pursed his lips. "You still don't trust me?"

"Trust takes time, Faion. These are strange days."

"Yeah, they are," he agreed, reaching into his shirt to take out his amulet with the triangle divining symbols for life and light. The playfulness vanished from his features as he handed me the amulet. He became almost solemn.

The silver charm blazed a bright orange when it came to rest in my palm. I shuddered. Green sparks swirled above the ancient symbols. My very core was affected. A tight grip of power clenched my gut before dissolving into a quivering energy that tickled through my limbs.

"Okay, so let's say I trust you," I said, deciding to take a leap of faith.

His etheric essence was true enough and beggars can't be choosers.

I retrieved my backpack from a wall hook and pulled out the worn edition of *The Book of Night Rituals*.

Faion's eyes widened as they landed on the brown leather cover engraved in gold. "That's a magic book! You must be out of your mind. Why do you have that? You can't be carrying around a book of spells. And a *night book?* If that book gets in the wrong hands—"

"It won't."

"That's it? You just say *it won't* and now the rest of the supernatural creatures of the world can just chill, even though you out here slinging around a world-destroying artifact like it's a Horchata Latte?"

"I needed answers. I need to understand material waves to determine what's real, what's magic, or what's just in my head. I think I figured it out."

He furrowed his brow. "You figured out what's real?"

"Yeah, an Immortal is after me."

Faion's face went pale as if King Yan had ridden in on his White Horse.

King Yan was a legend of the Deep Down, one of the early Immortals who had gone mad. He rode a massive white steed which, when cloaked in magic, appeared to be transparent like the mythical mist horses of the ancient mist rider stories. King Yan rode at night, hacking human and animal heads off with a scythe, igniting panic wherever his legend spread.

The legendary mist horses traveled so fast that those who blinked missed seeing them entirely. They would appear in the middle of a heartbeat and disappear just as quickly into the morning dew. The mist riders shared the vaporous effect as they raced their beasts like ghosts along the horizon.

No one controlled magic or the elements more efficiently. When mist horses and riders found each other, their combined energies were the greatest the world had seen.

Of course, no one could say with any certainty that the mist riders or their horses ever truly existed.

"You mean an *Immortal* Immortal?" Faion said. "Like the faction assassin Immortals? Those crank-ass Seventh Council war wagers? The *darkness that seeps into your nightmares* dudes? That kind of Immortal?"

I was impressed. Faion Trice was the real thing. "Yeah, those guys."

He bent his face. "How can you be sure?"

"Let me count the ways. He kidnapped me, kicked my ass with unfamiliar powers, healed me so easily I questioned whether I was ever hurt, he returned to make obscure threats, and then hurt me again before saying I had to help him with something which, of course, he never explained."

"Okay, shit, yeah—fuck, that's not good." Faion snatched my backpack and stuffed the book inside. "We need to get your crazy butt to the Deep Down pronto. I know a gate. Terra Mar Point on the beach in Carlsbad. It's walled-in, safe, shielded by the ocean."

"It's just right there on the beach?"

"On the Point, yeah, you just have to know precisely where and how to open it," he said, motioning me to remove the door spell. "We need to talk to the mages, the elders, even the clairvoyants. We'll need their counsel."

I took the backpack gently from his hands. "I can't do that."

"It's not optional. We go or all is lost."

"Faion, I can't involve the Deep Down. He'll follow me. It's probably what he wants. I'd be jeopardizing the lives of every single deep dweller, the lives of all my people and your life, too."

He looked at me with his mouth agape. "You mean...?"

"He knows my Lunar Order name. It'd be only a matter of time before he found a way to bind it to a spell that would betray my location in the Deep Down and unlock the magic in my blood. I can't run from this. And I won't be the one to beckon an army of death-thirsty Immortals to the Deep Down."

Somebody tried the door.

"Everything alright, Sophie?" Maura said from the other side.

I squeezed the fusing spell with my hand to keep the door from budging. "Yeah, all good," I said. "I need a moment."

"Okay, but it's getting busy. And that boy's too young for you."

Faion chuckled. I covered his mouth with my hand.

"I'll be right there," I said, glaring at Faion.

Faion waited before continuing. "So, what's the plan?"

"I wouldn't call it a plan. I need to stand up to him and I have no idea how to do that. I'm like a fly in a hurricane with him. His power exceeds mine exponentially. I also have no clue what his motives might be, or from what source of energy he draws his magic."

Faion clenched his teeth. "I could help, maybe... a little."

"Hey, I'm all ears, but you really should walk away."

He flashed me a crooked grin. "I'm not badass like you lunar witches. I can't blast shit left and right, but I have my own set of skills. Under the right circumstances, if the undying dude doesn't sniff it out, I could forge a temporary connective path between him and me that would enable us to monitor his moves."

I chewed on what he said. "That's a real thing?"

"It's a reciprocal thing, usually shared between diviners, but it can potentially be applied to outsiders if their core energy is overflowing."

"Whatever that asshole may or may not be, he's definitely overflowing with dark energy," I said with tapered enthusiasm, "but this sounds like a suicide mission. Have you ever actually done this before?"

"Not exactly, but I've done a lot of reading. We just need to exchange something very personal, something that contains traces of our magic, like amulets or skin particles or blood."

I rolled my eyes. "Let me stop you. I can guarantee you right now that's not going to happen. He'll never volunteer anything like that."

"I didn't expect him to just hand it over, Miss Thing," Faion said, searching in his head. "How about hair? That's possible, right? If he's packing as much magic as you say, there'll be traces of it in his hair."

"And if we manage to pull it all off?" I said, losing patience.

"Well, once the exchange is complete, I'm on live with all of his sensory experiences. I'll have extended glimpses of what he's seeing and hearing."

He sounded too confident. It was too good to be true. "Wouldn't he be able to do the same to you?"

"Not unless he's a diviner on top of everything else."

Anything was possible, but it was a risk we'd have to take. "Okay, let me get this straight. I need to get some of his hair, and we'll mix it with your hair?"

Faion shook his head. "My magic core is not strong enough to sustain the connection outside of my blood."

Lovely. "Alright, let's do this."

I got down on my knees to rummage through the bottom cupboards until I found what I was looking for—a stack of sealed urine collection cups that were used for pre-employment drug testing.

He frowned. "Really?"

"It's sterile," I said, shrugging.

With a growl and a huff, he lifted the triangle amulet and began chanting.

I removed the lid from the cup and held it over the sink. Faion placed his hand inches above the cup and slit the skin near his wrist with the sharp edge of the amulet. His blood spilled into the cup.

The current of power that was released from his bloodstream flickered brightly in the cup before I screwed the lid on tight.

I held the cup to the light. Faion's blood bubbled up like cherry soda.

"Now what?"

He tapped his forefinger on his chin. "You'll need to apply it on his skin so it can be absorbed at a cellular level. The ideal spot would be the center of his chest, the sternum, but anywhere on his torso would work."

Oh, that's all? This was getting ridiculous. "So, not only do I have to pluck hair from his head, I also have to get him shirtless and slather blood on his chest? How do you suggest I do that? Seduce my immortal archenemy?"

"Would you?"

I threw him a stare so arctic he froze in place.

"Chillax. I'm kidding, obviously."

"You better chillax."

My glare must have been lethal. He backtracked so fast he stumbled. "I'm totally going to do that. I'm sorry. My sense of humor is not one of my powers."

"Apparently," I said with a big sigh.

"Listen," he said. "If anyone can find a way to make this happen, it's you. You're a lunar witch and you obviously have your charms."

"Easy now, Faion. You better be talking about my magic."

"Sophie, I learned my lesson. No more jokes. I'm down with the *Me, Too* thing. I'm woke to that. I just mean that you're our only chance."

"That's your pep talk?"

"Also not one of my powers," he said, a sparkle returning to his eyes.

Not proud, but I started to wonder if Immortals and witches could even mate. *Yuck.* What was wrong with me?

"Moving on," I said, trying to get my mind on a new path.

"What happens if he sees the blood and washes it off?"

"The spell forces the blood into his hypodermis quickly and then quickly evaporates the rest, leaving no trace. The whole thing won't take longer than ninety seconds. You think you can distract him that long?"

Diverting his eyes for ninety seconds, *check*, I could make that happen.

Faion refastened the amulet around his neck. "Call me when it's done," he said, handing me a folded piece of paper with his number.

I nodded. "If I survive, sure. Oh, and Faion, not a word of this to anyone, especially your grandmother."

"I feel that."

I waved my hand and Faion opened the door. He stepped out, stopped and stepped back into the break room. "Dude, it's really busy out there."

"Oh, shit, *Maura*!"

I rushed past Faion to take care of the first of my tasks for the day. Serving baked goods and coffee was something I knew how to do.

Now finding a way to summon my enemy before stealing a hair from his head and rubbing Faion's blood onto the ripped Immortal's naked sternum without resorting to sex... that was way outside my lane.

Chapter 8

STANDING IN FRONT OF the mirror, I quickly stripped down to my underwear. My skin prickled as wind and moonlight crawled through the open bathroom window to greet me.

The magic had to be swift and powerful enough to cause ripples through the night skies above the city, across tall buildings and electrical wires, in order to reach the Immortal wherever he may dwell.

I had to expose my skin to receive the most natural energy. My magic also had to be strong and sophisticated enough to obscure its origin from the orbs.

If he needed me as much as he claimed—and the fact I was still alive suggested that he did—he would be listening. I had to believe that.

There was not a moment to waste. The longer Faion's blood sat inside the cup the less potent it would become.

I didn't have the luxury to wait around for Mister Sadistic Sizzle Chest to show up. I had to summon him by any means necessary.

The power rushed into me. I let it stream through my veins. The energy jolt spiked at my fingertips. It had been years since I had summoned the totality of my resources, using direct lunar energy to replenish them.

I shut my eyes, overwhelmed by the gathering force. A torrent of white energy pulsed in my palms. If I let it loose, it would detonate, sparking out in a hundred directions, imploding my apartment into oblivion—and me with it.

Drinking in a hefty dose of lunar energy, I evoked the Immortal's face to my frontal lobe. Words in my mouth turned into an incantation—*ancient, enemy, obey, magistrate, potent, succumb, assassin, immortal, arrive.*

Again and again, the words thrust forth, louder each time, until the chant and the elemental energy blended, driving the summons to a climax.

As my magic locked itself inside the mirror, a sharp ache beat within me until some powerful being intercepted my spell. I could not be sure my target had been engaged, but I could feel a sudden pushback. I pushed harder to deliver the spell, but the resistance grew too strong.

The magic dissipated in electric spirals and I collapsed onto the floor, panting so hard I thought I would pass out, but the Moon shone down to heal me with its pale light.

"Thank you," I murmured, brushing my hair away from my face.

I quickly found my clothes and dressed. I sat on the sofa, counting my breaths. *One, two, three, inhale, four, five, six, exhale.*

All I could do was wait. I immediately doubted the plan Faion and I had concocted. There were way too many variables involved, plenty of ways it could turn either pointless or deadly.

I mean, how smart was it to piss off an Immortal Magistrate who could obliterate San Diego with one hissy fit?

That's rhetorical.

When the timer on my phone warned me it was midnight, I lifted my legs onto the sofa and closed my eyes. I drifted away breath by breath. My neck muscles let go, allowing my head to sink deeper into the cushion, when, out of nowhere, an arctic gust blasted through my door, shattering the lock.

I barely had time to get on my feet before a hand grabbed my throat.

There we go again.

He glared at me. "Why the fuck would you use unsealed magic?"

I grimaced to remind him he had to let me access oxygen to talk.

He reduced the pressure but kept his hand around my throat.

"Practice," I said with a hoarse voice.

He did not believe that for a moment.

"I'm in the game now," I insisted. "I have to get stronger."

"Cut the bullshit. You were provoking me."

He released me completely now with a huff.

I massaged my throat. "What if I was? Do you expect me to hang around like a sitting duck, waiting for your next attack?"

His face turned predatory. "You think you've been attacked? There would be nothing left of you if I attacked."

"Exactly my point," I said.

"Are you always so tedious, Luna Mae?" He touched his hair as if to straighten it, but it was already perfect. "Just to be clear, as I explained to you quite plainly last time, you've been recruited and are under my command."

I snapped. "I'm not yours to command, psycho. I'm not helping you and your buddies take over the world. I'd rather fight you now."

Please, don't let him take me seriously.

He looked irritated. "Do you have a mental impairment?"

"Wow, I realize that back in whatever year you were born that might not have sounded completely chauvinistic," I said, walking to the door, "but in this world, it's really lame. Now, please, get out."

I tried to act defiant by holding open the door that had already been blown off its hinges. I knew my plea for decency had fallen on deaf ears when an unseen restraint wrapped tightly around my upper body.

"What is this? I've never heard of Immortals wielding such magic," I growled a second before he removed the restraint. "Who taught you?"

He moved toward me with an icy certainty in his blue eyes. "Whatever game you're playing, I choose to ignore it. Fighting you would be as useless for me as it would be deadly for you. Your weakness will always be met with pain in any and all the realms. I merely illustrate that in haste as I have not time for such feeble resistance. Listen to me and make no mistake, you will help me."

"Screw you," I hissed. With both hands, I struck his chest as hard as I could, again and again. He might as well have been made from stone. His bulky pecs did more damage to my hands than I did to them.

I was not sure what I was doing, but I had to do something. I growled and smacked his right cheek with the back of my hand. He didn't flinch.

Physically drained, I plopped onto the sofa. Hot tears ran down my face. They were tears born out of frustration, but he didn't know that.

He stood there, uncertain for the first time. "What is this petulance? You are a daughter of the Lunar Order. There should be at least a hint of grandeur in your DNA, some pride. An ego, at very least. I'm not here to hold your hand."

"My hand? Ha! You'd rather cut it off than hold it. You have no soul."

"Soul?" He laughed. "I've lived too long to need such a human crutch."

I kept my head between my hands, summoning what was left of my elemental power, drawing on moonlight and starlight through the open door.

He took a sharp breath in, sensing what I was doing. With a wave of his hand, he struck the door shut, the lock miraculously fixed. Next, all my open windows slammed shut one after the other.

My eyes peeked ever so slightly toward the kitchen. His gaze followed mine in a flash to spot the five-gallon water bottle near the fridge that I had bought earlier just for this occasion.

"Oh, no you don't," he said.

I could not help but grin when he locked in on the bottle. No matter his strength, he could not match my influence on water or any elemental source.

The water cooler burst, cascading out in torrents to re-form as a thick pane of glass suspended in the air. With a flick of my index finger, the flattened fluid slid across the room before I released it from my spell just above the Immortal's head, drenching him.

His hair stuck to his forehead like he had been licked by a cat. His black button-up shirt clung to his pecs and six-pack, but the most pleasurable result was the dumb expression on his stunned face.

I expected sudden vengeance, but once the initial shock

passed, he seemed almost amused. "Checking to see if I would melt?" he said, shaking off water all over my carpet.

The devil got hold of my tongue. "Maybe I want to get you out of your clothes." Holy shit! What was I saying?

He flared his nostrils. I had surprised him.

"I'm kidding, obviously," I blurted out. "I can extract the water with a simple spell."

He grabbed my wrist. "No more tricks, do you hear me? You will not draw any more attention to yourself, not while you're under my command. I've cloaked the magic reverberations, but there's a limit to my patience."

"Okay, okay, I'll use a blow dryer. Jeez. Just give me the shirt."

He started to unbutton. I turned to give him some privacy. It was hard to believe he was doing exactly what I told him. Somehow, I had happened upon the perfect plan without being entirely aware of what I was doing.

I reached just inside the bathroom to grab a towel. Keeping my eyes averted, I walked over to extend my arm. He took the towel and replaced it with his wet shirt.

Returning to the bathroom, I laid the black shirt flat over the sink and picked up the nearby blow dryer. It was a stroke of luck he preferred dark colors, possibly in contrast to his whole Nordic look—blond hair, blue eyes, pale skin. A light color would have made my newly forming plan impossible.

The hot air wafted over the wet fabric as I moved the blow dryer from side to side. Careful not to interrupt the droning hum, I reached under the sink to retrieve Faion's blood.

My heart thumped in my chest as I evenly coated the inside of the tight shirt with the dark red liquid. If caught, I'd be toast.

This better work, I whispered to myself, wiping sweat from my face.

I found him sitting on the sofa, bare chested, the towel heaped on the carpet near his feet. The raw power of his physique was nearly as awe inspiring as his magic. The golden tattoo of a regal double-headed eagle on his chest shone like amber, its spanning wings curving over his pecs. I leaned closer to admire the flame serpent tattoos on his forearms.

Wait. He was holding *The Book of Night Rituals*, leafing through the centuries-old pages.

"Put that down," I said sternly, handing him his shirt.

Keep looking at it, please. Take all the time you need.

He took the shirt and shook out the wrinkles.

"It might be a little damp," I said.

He ignored me as he slid one arm through the sleeve, then the next, his abs dancing about like they had a life of their own. Suddenly I became aware I needed oxygen. I needed to breathe.

I sat on the chair across from him, unable to look away.

His eyes returned to the book, taking no notice of my rapt attention.

Ninety seconds, Faion had said, ninety seconds and the blood would absorb into his perfect skin, leaving no trace.

I rubbed my neck and yawned. I let a sigh escape my lips.

"What are you trying to do?" the Immortal said, eyes still on the book.

"Trying to read your mind."

"Impossible."

Yeah, I know. You have like a million barriers. "I find simple minds are the easiest to read. Give me a minute and I'll know your life story."

He shut the book and looked at me. "You're covering."

"I don't even know what that means. Is there like an urban dictionary for evil Immortals I should be studying?"

"Now you're really covering."

"Okay, fine. You're kind of hot and it's annoying. You should be the ugliest man in the world, if we're going by content of character."

He got up. *Shit.* I still needed some of his hair.

I leapt to my feet and wrapped my arms around him. "If I help you, will you protect me?" I laced my fingers behind his neck.

The look on his face was one of violation. I never felt more like a stalker in all my life. I had just said he was hot and now I had jumped his bones.

"Get off of me," he said, bristling. "I am not your intimate."

He picked me up to remove me, but I held on, grasping at the hair on the back of his head, yanking a couple wet strands from their roots.

I dropped his hair to the carpet, instantly ridding myself of the evidence.

My hope was that a small level of pain would not register with him. The gamble paid off. He felt nothing, especially while fighting off my unwanted and very awkward advance.

"What has possessed you, girl?" he growled. "What possible romantic interest would I have in a meager young witchling like yourself?" He adjusted his shirt and patted down the hair on the back of his head.

I searched for some bullshit response. "I'm sorry, I don't even—"

"Yeah, you don't, because you're a mess," he said, tiring of me completely. "I'll give you this one warning. I don't have a good side or even a human side. Fuck with me again and I'll make sure our adventure will be your last."

Okay, but today might have been my last adventure, so I was surprisingly okay with his scary new threat. Today, somehow, I kind of, sort of, *won*.

Well, maybe not *won*, but for now at least, it was mission accomplished.

Chapter 9

Something paranormal was on the bus. I felt it the moment I sat down. Maybe I was too tired after a long shift and constantly stressing about the return of the Immortal. Maybe all my senses were shot.

I shifted in my seat. *There*, I felt it again. I also now picked up a scent, the unpleasant scent of a foul being, a creature neither good nor *basic*.

There were seven other passengers on the bus. I examined them one by one—an elderly lady staring out the window, a young mother playing with her prattling toddler, a middle-aged man in a suit, and three hunched teenagers minding their phones, occasionally murmuring obscenities.

None of these were the foul being.

Was it the driver? From where I sat, I couldn't get a clear view, so I rose in my seat to take a better look. Yeah, just a dude. Definitely *basic*.

What was that sinking feeling then? And that smell?

I tried to use my phone as a distraction, but the sensation drew closer like a hot breath on my neck. The hairs on my arms stood on end. I sprang to my feet. I couldn't shake the certainty that something sinister was on the bus.

I got off at the next stop and stood in a daze to watch the bus drive away. Why had I gotten off the bus to walk home in the dark? Had I been compelled by some force, some whisper, some fiend?

The last time I walked home it did not end well.

I began walking fast. I gathered my powers under my fingernails.

Something hissed behind me. I turned to look but saw nothing—just a penetrating darkness. I took a few uncertain steps on what felt like the emptiest sidewalk in the world.

I stopped cold when I saw two yellow eyes gleaming out from a dense thicket of vines. I strained my eyes to glimpse glistening fur and razor-sharp claws. The creature came into full view, standing on two legs. It was about four feet tall. Deep scars cut across its triangular face as if chunks of flesh had been gnawed away.

I startled, afraid to move. If I moved, I was certain to be devoured. The small, deformed, bear-like beast measured me with its shining, lemon-drop eyes like I was food.

Using every ounce of my elemental energy, I sprang forward, making a beeline for the nearby shopping center.

My heart leapt against my chest, striving to escape the teeth and claws of the beast behind. I weaved through cars, trying to be hard for the fiend to grasp. Two frightened people stepped back as I darted past them and plowed through the first door I could find.

I did not look back to see if the couple outside had been devoured. I bent over to catch my breath before realizing I was inside a packed sports bar.

The dim lights gave the place a shadowy, otherworldly feel. My ears pulsated with the muffled sounds of roaring stadiums and drunken banter.

The couple entered. They were alive and unmauled. When they walked past, they were leery of my presence and put off by my heavy breathing.

I sensed sinister eyes staring at me through the stained-glass panels of the door. I imagined my bones melting and becoming hot liquid.

Quickly, I disappeared into the crowd and leaned against the back wall. Sweat poured out of my every pore. I didn't have any fight left in me. That hideous face with the yellow eyes bore so deep into my center that I was left feeling hollowed out and hopeless.

"Are you alright?"

A smooth, velvety male voice.

I opened my eyes. There was something familiar about the smiling, handsome face in front of me but I couldn't place it.

He leaned forward to speak into my ear. "Do you need anything? You're shaking."

His breath tickled my ear.

Where had I seen him before? The lush brown hair, the clear hazel eyes, the way he smiled like it was Christmas morning... it rang a bell, a faraway bell, somewhere in my mind.

"Are you casting a spell?" he said, putting his hands in his pockets.

Wait, what? Don't tell me this nice guy is another deep sider.

"The magic book," he said, noticing my confusion. "We bumped into each other. You dropped your book."

Right. The guy outside the library. I pulled myself together enough to form a few syllables. "I'm fine, thank you."

He raised an eyebrow. "Okay, but you seem rattled. Have you had too much to drink? I'm not asking that, you know, in a creepy way. I'm not trying to take advantage. I'm the good guy, a good guy. Shit, I sound like a dick."

False alarm. This guy was clearly basic.

"No, you're fine," I said, forcing a smile. "Listen, can you do me a favor?"

"Anything."

Okay, that was a little too accommodating. "Would you, being a good guy, spend some time with me? Just hang out and chat until I feel better?"

"Consider it done."

He took my hand and led me to a corner booth. I realized I must look like hell, all sweaty and red-faced from exertion and anxiety.

"What about your friends?" I said. Surely, he didn't come here alone.

"No worries," he said. "They'll hardly miss me. They're here for the game and the booze."

It's always a game with men. War. Domination. Supremacy.

"Emmet."

"Excuse me?"

"My name, it's Emmet. Emmet Groshek."

I exhaled, trying to relax. "I'm Sophie."

"Cool," he said. "Sometimes, shit gets too real. I get it. If there's anything you want to talk about, anything at all I can do to help relieve stress. Again, no creepy innuendo intended in that."

"Maybe stop using the word *creepy?*"

"Right, you're right," he said. "Good note."

The waitress showed up to take our order.

"Water," I said. "I'll have a glass, no, wait. What's the biggest container of water you have? I'd like a lot of water."

It took her a moment to process my strange request. "I'll bring you out our two-liter carafe," she said. "I'll put a rush on it."

"Yes, please do," I said, overly grateful.

"The girl's thirsty," Emmet said, instantly regretting his word choice. "Just a beer for me," he said. "Sam Adams."

"Make that two Sam Adams," I said, thinking a beer in my hand might help me blend in. "But bring the water first."

The waitress raised her eyebrows and walked away.

Emmet grinned in the way men do before they attempt a joke. "Need all that water for a magic potion?"

"Actually, yes," I said, playing along. "It's a Mermaid spell."

"Nice. Mermaids are hot, and what man doesn't want to date a sexy witch?" he said. "Combine the two and that's some fire. *Muy caliente!*"

"Careful what you wish for," I said.

He laced his fingers on the table. "I'm a careful cat. For the record, you don't owe me any explanations. You do you. No judgment."

A server arrived with our beers and the oversized carafe of water. He set three glasses on the table, two in front of me.

"Thank you," I said with a big sigh.

The server emptied his tray and darted off. I filled a glass with water and gulped it down.

Emmet raised his beer. "To lucky encounters and mermaids."

We clinked our beers and drank straight from the bottles. The cool water and the alcohol hit my bloodstream. The rest of the water in the carafe began to simmer and hum. Only I could hear it. I began to feel it as well, binding with the elemental magic in my blood.

Suddenly, the urgency of the water's call became too intense. I couldn't hold out any longer. I needed the energy that was freely offered to me, the persuasive, all-encompassing power of a strong elemental source. I had no idea how the night would end, but I knew beyond the shadow of a doubt that I had to be prepared for all eventualities.

I rolled up my sleeve and sank my arm in the water. I closed my eyes as the energy shot up my arm all the way to my ribcage. It felt like an electric jolt to my heart, spreading potency into every cell of my body. An aching hum hit my nervous system, but the sharp tinge of pain felt extremely satisfying, like an intense endorphin rush.

I quietly thanked the water before I opened my eyes and pulled my forearm out of the carafe. Emmet looked stunned. He offered me his napkin.

"You said no judgment," I reminded him.

"No. I couldn't even begin to judge you."

His tone was somehow reassuring. There was zero duplicity about him. Emmet was that rare man who knew himself so well that he seemingly always spoke his truth.

I leaned in close. "Do you know how to get to the back door?"

His lips parted ever so slightly. He looked straight into my eyes. "I do," he said. His unblinking gaze had such a calming effect on me. "I can show you."

We left the table and our drinks behind. Navigating the

crowd, he reached back and took my hand. I didn't know whether it was the taste of booze or the abundance of elemental energy or Emmet's gentle grip, but I felt like I was floating as we weaved through a bright yellow service kitchen.

When suddenly we clanged out through an EXIT door into a dark alley and were standing next to an ancient green dumpster, he let go of my hand. Reality raced in and with it the rancid smell of discarded booze and bar food.

The alley was unpaved, just dirt and the scant remains of crushed gravel. Taking a few deep breaths, I did not sense any foreboding presence or malicious intent in the air.

"Where to?" Emmet said.

I gave him my full toothy grin. "You're a total prince, but I think I'm good."

He touched my shoulder lightly. "Are you hiding from someone, Sophie?"

I didn't know how to answer that.

"Listen," he said. "That's not my business, but I'm not about to let you walk home alone."

I considered his offer. Emmet's aura was a light blue, very human, too faint to even matter. Not only was he no threat to me, he was also no threat to any manner of beast that would come for me. Yet, I didn't mind the company.

"Okay," I said. "We can walk, but there's nothing after me. I'm just having a day, the kind of day I don't want to talk about."

On our way to Reservoir Drive, Emmet talked incessantly. I only caught bits and pieces as he enthusiastically gesticulated narrative details. I did learn he was an intern at Sharp Memorial Hospital, training to be a doctor of sports medicine. He also worked part-time as a trainer at a gym. He was twenty-seven and hailed from Rhode Island.

He was pleasant enough and easy on the eyes, to be honest, but no one could have held my attention that night. Two blocks from my place, I grabbed his arm to stop him. I wasn't about to lead anyone else to where I lived.

"This is it," I said, offering my hand. "Thanks for your gallantry."

"Oh, yeah. Not a bother," he said. "My mom raised me right."

"I agree, she did."

Awkward silence.

"So..." He hesitated. "Would it be out of line to ask you out?"

"I'm not sure," I said. "Maybe you should try."

"Right. Ah, Sophie, would you—"

"Emmet, I'm just messing. Yeah, we can see each other again."

"Really? Cool. That's cool."

"The only thing is, as you can see, my life's a little crazy just now."

He took out his wallet and found his business card. "Here," he said, handing me his card. "Anytime you need a lunch buddy, think of me."

I read his card. *Dr. Groshek.*

Okay, that's hot.

It was just my luck to meet a total gentleman/doctor/dashing chill dude when I was not even close to girlfriend material. I was a little busy either becoming a slave to a sadistic Immortal Magistrate or escaping to Sweden or being eaten by roaming, otherworldly beasts. My dance card was overfull.

"Who has time for lunch?" I said.

His defeat instantly hurt my heart.

"Emmet, did you not see the crazy girl in front of you tonight? I mean, dude, I stuck my arm in a carafe of water. I'm nobody's dream girl."

He nodded. "I think women say that, but what they really mean is that the man they are talking to is not their dream man."

This guy. I didn't know why, but I suddenly kissed him.

Shit. I'd completely lost it. "You see, I'm crazy."

"I'm not complaining," he said.

"You are a pest," I said. "Really, and you have horrible timing."

"Timing's never been my strong suit."

"Listen, I occasionally take a lunch," I said. "And I won't tear up your card. That's all I can say in my current state."

He lifted his hands in surrender and started to back away.

"Can I just confirm that that kiss just happened? I didn't dream it."

"What kiss?" I said. "Now go, and be safe, Emmet Groshek, or I'll use my magic to turn you into a toad."

He grinned so wide he looked like a boy, then turned and disappeared into the San Diego night. I waited a few strides before running the rest of the way home, fumbling with my keys, then falling to my butt on the other side of my locked door.

Chapter 10

Faion held the Immortal's hair up to the light.

I stepped closer to get a better view. "Do you think it's enough?"

"It's not a question of quantity but quality," he said, bringing the hair to his nose to sniff it like a hound.

"Oh, you're doing that now," I said, doubts rising.

He shushed me, then shoved the hair in his mouth and swallowed.

"What the hell?" I said, quite astonished.

He washed the Immortal's hair down with a glass of ice water.

"That's... disgusting." I didn't know what else to say.

Faion rolled his eyes. "It's an ancient way and the only way. Don't be a magic snob. I can do what you cannot."

"I'm not a snob," I said. "Far from it, but you could have warned me about the hair. It's not like I grew up in the down below, I grew up in Oregon."

"We both grew up in Oregon, but I have this kick-ass divining blood that is already honing in on his energy core."

"I'll take your word for it."

"Yes, thank you," he said, closing his eyes and breathing deeply.

"You think this will work, Faion?"

"Not if you keep pestering me, it won't."

I stopped pestering and let him do his thing.

Afterward, we lit my Moroccan, green-glass lantern and sank into my sofa. Faion made me watch three consecutive episodes of *BoJack Horseman* on Netflix. It was weird as hell, in a good way, but during the third episode I must have crashed, because next thing I knew I was startled awake by a high-pitched scream.

I sat up, realizing Faion had somehow made that high-pitched voice. His eyes gleamed like he'd gone mad.

He pushed my feet off his lap and sprang up. I almost rolled off the couch.

"What's happening?" I said, rubbing my eyes.

"I got that son of a bitch," he shouted, pumping his fist. "I'm in. I'm all up in his physiological hard drive. The F train did this shit."

I dared, for the first time, to feel hope. I hadn't let myself believe this plan would ever work. I climbed to my feet to hug Faion, but he quickly squatted down, crossed his legs and closed his eyes.

He began murmuring an iterative chant, not the meditative *Om*, but definitely a reciting tone of some type. His lips created vibrations that I could feel bouncing off the walls of the apartment.

I held my breath as his aura became visible, a soft yellow that hung in the air around him like a phosphorescent mist. I'd never seen anything like it but presumed he was entering an ectoplasmic trance.

Faion's eyes darted about under his closed eyelids. "He's awakened."

A quick shiver swept over me. That was not even Faion's voice.

"He walks," Faion's new voice added.

It was two in the morning. Did Immortals ever sleep?

Faion snatched up my hand and held it tight. "It's dark here. Cool. Sticky, wet footsteps. A subterranean walk."

A spear of fear split through me. "The Deep Down?"

"The deep is not down. The down is not deep."

"Okay, how about his thoughts," I said. "Can you read them?"

His head shook quickly, just once. "Feel the thoughts, not hear them. Guarded thoughts. Layers. Barriers. Go too deep, all will be lost. He will glimpse the blood intruder. He will see. See and destroy. Must stay calm in the blood, must wait to see what his eyes see, hear what he hears."

I clenched my jaw. I suddenly had a bad feeling about this.

Faion fell deeper into the transcendental state. He released my hand. His breathing grew heavier, his sentences shorter. "Voices," he said, "faint echoes. Energy shields. A barrier, maybe. A ward, maybe. Dim light. Torches. Long corridor ahead. Heavy legs. Tired. Descending now. Narrow stairs."

Oh, shit. The deep, the deeper deep, the true dark of the under realm.

"Arrived. Open space. Auditorium. Elevated stage. Orange electric lights. Feet meet carpet. Long court bench. On stage. Carved eagles in gold."

Faion opened his eyes and flared his nostrils. "The Seventh Council," he said, regaining his natural voice. "The Magistrate Court. We've found them."

I tried to take his hands because I felt like I might collapse, but Faion started pacing and his hands flew about as he talked.

His speech accelerated. "No protective barriers here. They're deep underground. They feel safe. Four magistrates behind the bench, two females, two males. There are more around I can't see. Their expressions are severe, their brows pensive and creased. Oh, damn. Your guy. He most definitely is not like the others. You did not tell me everything. Your stalker is hot. He's not even candy, girl, he's ice cream."

"How do you know that? How can you see him?"

"I'm not sure. The material everything is built with seems reflective. The bench, the walls, even the ceiling. Sometimes I can see a hundred of everyone."

"Don't fall in love, Faion, he's a killing machine."

"Someone called out to him," Faion said. "Strange name."

I must have bugged out of my skull. "You heard his name? Like his Immortal name?"

"No, his online gamer name. Of course, his Immortal name."

Knowing the name of an Immortal without their permission was a slippery slope. Their names didn't carry the power of the lunar names, but you gained insight into their etheric essence. If they ever found out you knew their original name, you would become hunted and the Immortal would not rest until you were gone.

"Well?" Faion said. "Do you want to know or not?"

"Tell me already, we've come this far."

"Shit, you sure? It's dangerous knowledge."

"More than that, I know—it's deadly."

"That's my ride-or-die-bitch," Faion said. "I feel that."

"Yeah, yeah, now tell me, damn it."

"Okay, chill. It's Winter. That's his name. Winter."

I repeated the name in my head. *Winter*. It suited him. I imagined his cold heart was covered in frost. Like an arctic wind, he raced through the ages, freezing everything, covering the greens and blues with white death.

"Winter stands before the magistrates, holding a scroll." Faion's face went cold. "I'm going to tell you what they're discussing, but you need to keep your shit together."

"My shit's together. Now tell me."

In no way is my shit together, but whatever.

"The Council will take a vote," Faion said.

"What vote?"

"A vote on whether to kill you or not after your mission."

Perfect. The Seventh Council was in on this whole thing with Winter. They endorsed his perverse little games. They all believed I could help them, but how, exactly? Something to do with elemental energy, no doubt. And the bastards wanted to express their gratitude by killing me. Great. I wanted to drink down all the world's resources, walk into their chamber and explode, taking them all to hell with me.

Faion's voice reached me as if from far away. "Sophie, that dude's standing up for you. For real."

"Wait. What dude?"

"Your dude. Winter. He's defending you."

That can't be true.

"He says that an asset now will be an asset later. I think you're the asset. Or, maybe, he likes your assets," Faion said, grinning. "There's more. He says a show of goodwill could make for a useful alliance with the Deep Down. Blah, blah, blah, now, in the future and so on. A little redundant, but not bad."

"What's his game?" I said.

"Don't know, he seemed to be passionate about that message," Faion observed. "I don't know how well it tracked with the others, though."

"That's it," I said. "He knows that argument won't win, but now he can pretend he's the good guy."

"Wait, the Magistrate in the middle raises his palm. Stocky guy, ash-colored hair. He says the secrets must be protected over all else. You will have seen too much. He does not think you should live after witnessing the rebellion."

A rebellion? Now we're getting somewhere.

"Winter says he'll bear full responsibility. He guarantees your obedience."

Well, how magnanimous of him who would make me a slave.

Faion's face distorted. "There's whispering behind the bench. The magistrates, they are a grim crew. Winter steps closer. He says that he will be responsible. A vote is not needed. And there's something about him boiling the hearts of any who would so much as touch you."

"Is that the way to kill Immortals? Boil their hearts?"

"I don't know," Faion said, "maybe it's one of their expressions, but by their reaction, they all seem to take him at his word."

Faion's mouth contorted unnaturally. His body started to shake, then it got worse—he started having a seizure.

Not knowing what else to do, I tried to wrap him in my arms, but he was too wild. I managed to usher him to the couch where he fell onto the cushions and shook uncontrollably.

When his eyes opened, an expression of horror crossed his face. His mouth gaped wide open and his lips quivered. "I cut the connection."

"Faion," I said, unable to process.

He looked gravely into my eyes. "Sophie, something dark, something so horrible I could feel it in my bones, stared straight into my eyes."

"Was it Winter? Did he discover you?"

Faion sprang to his feet and walked to the window. "I don't know," he said, peeking through the blinds. "I felt it as much as I saw it. Deformed. Or malformed. Sophie, I don't know. It was animalistic. It had fur, but those eyes, it was like they could see through my soul. It wasn't human. It wasn't an animal. It wasn't from the Deep Down or anywhere else on this planet."

Heat flushed my face. My monster. The one that chased me. I tried to remember but I didn't want to remember. His beast, my beast. It had to be more than a coincidence.

My encounter was bad, but to be stunned out of trance like that, with those devouring eyes staring at you, must have been worse.

"It's okay," I said, hugging him. "We're in this together."

"It's just, it was all so much like my dream."

My throat felt like dry sand. "The dream you had about me?"

He nodded. "It was in the woods. The moon was full. The silence didn't seem real, like a million beings were some-where hiding and holding their tongues. You were there, lying naked on a bed of wet leaves. A creature, not animal, not human, not magical, was licking at your toes. A second creature, bigger, stronger, uglier than the first, beheaded a third creature with an ax."

"That's really fucked up," I said.

"You haven't heard the crazy shit yet," Faion said, glancing back at me. "Maybe you should sit down."

I took his advice.

"You climbed to your feet," he continued. "You were wet and naked. You spoke an incomprehensible language." He took a break to collect his thoughts. "Everything changed. The moon turned gray. The creatures wailed. And then they attacked, they chewed big chunks off your belly and lower back. Strangely, you were cool with it. You laughed like a madwoman. You kept laughing even as your bloody body slowly dissolved into smoke, yet somehow you still had teeth and you..."

"Faion, what?"

He turned to me. "You ripped out their hearts and ate them."

Whoa. "I ate their hearts?"

"Yeah, you did, and it amused you."

There was awe in his eyes.

"It was a dream, Faion," I reminded him. "I don't go around eating the hearts of yellow-eyed, deformed beasts."

He stepped back a little. "How did you know about their eyes?"

"I saw one, I think," I said. "In a wooded area near campus."

"Why didn't you tell me, Sophie? I thought we're in this together?"

"I wanted to pretend it never happened."

He opened his arms and I walked into them. I lay my head against Faion's shoulder. "Are we any better off now?" I wasn't sure we had learned anything useful, besides that the world was scarier than any nightmare.

Faion smirked when I looked up to him. "Winter... he's hard of hearing in the left ear."

"How's that possible? Don't Immortal bodies just mend?"

"Guess not. They're not invincible. These guys can be brought down."

"Sure, you just boil their hearts like Winter. Piece of cake."

"True, and that bad boy S&M hottie who's been stalking you would boil hearts to save you, that's not nothing."

"To keep me alive for his own designs, Faion, don't even play."

"Maybe we should forget about a trip to the Deep Down. Let's go to a beach resort, instead. How about Cancun? I don't think that's a big hang for demons, beasts and Immortal motherfuckers."

I closed my eyes for a moment. "I wish, Faion. How I wish we could."

"I know. Sometimes I envy the basics."

The basics have their own challenges. A rebellion among Immortals may not reach CNN, but if it expanded to include magical factions, it could bring down all the worlds at once. For now, it would be best to let Immortals handle their affairs without interference. My hope was that it stayed contained.

I had my own fight and it was mine alone.

Fear had paralyzed me too long. I wasn't helpless. I had been born with a power and a destiny. I had been trained to use it sensibly, but I was done being a victim. Winter had a vulnerable side. I would find it and exploit it.

That night Faion slept peacefully on my sofa. I climbed onto my bed fully clothed. My tired back was warmed by my fluffy comforter. I wanted to stay like that forever. I wanted the future to stay away and never find me.

Chapter 11

ALL NIGHT, I FELL into dark voids and became trapped underwater. I swam frantically in a fathomless ocean and, no matter how hard I tried, I could not make it to the surface. I didn't even know which way was up.

Suddenly, the water tossed me into the sky. I was falling now, endlessly falling toward a shore that was falling faster. The water was gone and now the oxygen was gone, too. I was choking, suffocating. My feet and hands tingled. My stomach lunged. I thought I would die until I awoke gasping.

I scuttled to the sofa. "Go!" I told Faion, shaking him awake. "He's here."

Faion ran down the hall to the far stairs. I closed the door and waited at the kitchen counter, taking deep breaths.

Winter banged on the door.

After everything I'd witnessed, I should have been furious but, instead, found myself grateful he waited outside the door rather than blowing it off its hinges.

I looked through the peephole before I opened the door. "Who knew you could knock?" I said.

A strange feeling of satisfaction swelled in my chest. Having him here gave me a chance to measure his behavior up close.

"You're not surprised to see me? Progress."

"Should I be? You're like a bad penny."

He nodded, perhaps getting used to my attempts at lame humor. He wore a long black coat and black boots that had dried mud on the soles.

"Something's off," he said, giving me the once over.

He nudged me aside and walked through the door. He examined every detail of my studio apartment. He noticed the Faion-sized dent in the sofa and the heavily wrinkled comforter on my bed.

Yeah, I had a rough night.

"Someone just left," he said.

"Give the man a cigar."

He locked his eyes on mine. "A sexual liaison?"

Not even close, big guy. Your sensors are trash.

"Boundaries, dude."

He lost patience, grabbed my wrist and led me to the kitchen.

"You work at a coffee shop," he said, taking a seat. "Make some coffee. I need you to wake up."

"I bet you're a big hit with the Immortal ladies," I said. "It's every girl's dream to be thrown around like a sack of potatoes."

He laughed. "And you are an expert on romance?" he said. "I know you did not have sex last night. The man slept on the couch. I wonder, is it only your magic you never had a chance to use?"

Relax, Sophie, relax. Do not give him the satisfaction.

I decided not to smack his smug face for that vulgar insinuation. Instead, I calmly took out a box of instant coffee from the pantry. My gram bought it when she was in town junior year. It was almost certainly expired by now.

"All I have is instant," I said.

"Of course," he said.

Don't smack him, don't smack him, don't smack him.

I put two mugs of water into the microwave.

"Timer set at two minutes," I said. "It'll feel like an eternity."

"Said the witch who has barely yet lived."

"And what have you done with all your extra years, old man, besides avoiding good manners, abusing baby witches and kicking puppies?"

"My accomplishments are beyond your understanding," he said.

"Yeah, because I'm not a sociopath."

The microwave beeped and I got busy mixing the coffee.

"What do you take, oh great Magistrate?" I said with the sweetest smile. "Milk? Sugar? Cyanide? Perhaps the blood of innocents?"

He reached out. I handed him his coffee. He drank down the entire scalding mug in two quick gulps.

"I guess it's true what they say about those who take their coffee black."

"Drink," he demanded with an impatient glare.

"Total psychos," I said, finishing my thought.

He got up, spun around and drew a sword out of his coat. He touched the blade with one finger. I didn't know much about swords, but I could tell this one was quite impressive and very old.

In a blink he swung the sword up so I was face to face with the tip.

"You don't have to immediately prove my point," I said.

Just as quickly, he flipped the sword upside down, tip to floor, and offered me the hilt with a sort of a half bow.

Not knowing what else to do, I took it. Better I hold it than him.

In a blur, he shifted his weight and a second sword swooshed into his hand out of nowhere.

Where's he keeping these things?

His sword was longer and heavier than the one in my hand. With not so much as a sound, he brought his blade metal-to-metal against mine.

"*En garde, prêt, allez!*"

"No thanks," I said and then clanked his blade away with mine. "First with the monster and now with the sword battle and, what was that, French?"

He considered my words. "How American of you... of course that was French. You're stalling, what nonsense are you concocting now?"

"Me? This is all on you, Mr. Black-coffee-drinker. Don't play dumb. You sent a big ugly demon bear to stalk me Thursday night. Luckily, I managed to throw it off my scent. I suppose it was a test. What, did you want me to use my magic on the beast? Then again, you tell me not to use my magic, so which is it? You'll have to tell me, because I'm over these bullshit tests."

There was a visible shift in his expression. My words had resonated. "The beast was not my doing, but I'll look into it. Scent demons hunt magic. Those excessive spells better not have been yours."

"Oh, in case I wasn't clear... I'm so over your threats, too."

Provoking him was playing with fire, but it felt good. I no longer ruled out the possibility that he meant me no harm. He had, after all, defended me in front of the Seventh Council of Immortal Magistrates.

The only certainty was that my life wasn't in immediate danger, not while I was of use to the Immortal Magistrates.

"Raise that sword," he said. "I will teach you to defend yourself without conjuring unsealed magic."

"Because one lesson is all I'll need to defeat all comers."

I didn't plan on following through, but when his sword came down hard, I put mine forth instinctively and blocked the blow. I stared at my own hands, mystified. How could they handle Winter's superior strength?

He spun, the sword whizzing in the air as it came full circle, aiming for my throat. I stepped back quickly. If I was sure of anything, it was that he had no qualms about inflicting pain, and I wasn't in the mood for a beat down.

"You're crazy," I yelled as he took another swing at me. I dove to the side to dodge the blow, but I was too slow. He knocked the sword from my hand and pressed the hilt of his sword against my chest.

"This is a valuable lesson. You'd do well to pay close attention."

"I have the bruising part down," I said, pissed off. "I'm all up to speed."

He pressed harder. "Anger is your adversary, not I. It's your biggest weakness. The energy is there, at your fingertips. Use it."

"Wait, I thought not using magic was the whole point."

"You don't have to project your magic out into the open air where other charmed beings will sense it and the beasts will smell it. You must channel your energy straight into the sword, turning it into a contained extension of your arm. One energy, body and object."

I had no idea what he was talking about. Nobody had ever taught me how to Inspector-Gadget myself to inanimate objects. There had been no mention of such strange magic during my training years in the Deep Down or my conversations with Grandma.

It was most definitely not a lunar thing.

Winter released the pressure slowly, found my sword on the floor and returned it to my right hand by squeezing my fingers tightly around the grip.

"It's all here," he said, tapping on my fingertips one by one. "All the power you need. Use it to forge a connective path and infuse your sword with magic."

I stared down at the sword. "One energy."

He raised his sword above my head. I visualized it falling strong and fast, splitting me in half. There would be no coming back from that.

And then it happened—the sword fell. I ducked to shield myself with my blade, then kicked Winter in the groin before spinning away. My balance and instincts felt superhuman. My sword met his again, a violent collision, purple and green sparks sizzling across my blade as I screeched my lungs out.

Every blow I delivered buzzed up my arm all the way up to my skull and down my spine, jolting me into action. I had an intimate sense of the sword as if it were my own hand. My brain, nervous system and magic streamlined and created incredible power and speed that allowed me to hold my own and defend myself against Winter even though he was stronger and faster.

I grew confident and lunged at him one more time,

summoning all that I had and sending it straight into the sword.

Winter stepped back. *Wow.*

"Not bad for a novice, huh?" I said, breathless.

He grinned. "You'd perish quickly facing an Immortal swordsman but against unsuspecting mortals? You'd kick their ass and no one would know there was magic involved."

Sweat tickled my eyebrows and I had not yet caught my breath.

Winter circled me. "Most magic is futile against Immortals. Bullets are futile. We disarm tech through sheer intellectual will. But a sword in the right hands can create a variable that might help mortal users of magic like yourself survive a limited confrontation with an Immortal. Does this possibility interest you? To stand toe-to-toe with an Immortal adversary?"

I plopped down on the sofa. Adrenaline burned through me. "Getting in sword fights with Immortals sounds like a bad career move. Why would I want that to happen? I need answers. What kind of help do you need exactly?"

Silence ensued.

"Is that the question you want answered?" he said finally. "Because I will answer one question only."

I sighed. "Yeah, what help is a lunar witch to you?"

"It's right in your naming. You can command the Moon."

I shook my head. "Command? It's more of a partnership. The Moon must be willing to oblige."

"You know better than that, Luna Mae." He locked his eyes on mine. "Have you ever heard of Chaos?"

"As in the opposite of order?"

"Not the word, the Immortal. He is the leader of a rebellion."

"Chaos is his name?"

"His name, his plan, his everything," Winter said. "He intends to take control of every Immortal Council and then proceed to subdue or destroy every magical faction dwelling in the Deep Down."

He was trusting me with details of the rebellion? This was beyond anything I had hoped to draw out of him. "It must be bleak," I said cautiously. "To tell a witch all this and a baby witch at that."

Winter opened his hands, almost helpless.

"This Chaos dude," I pondered with a laugh, "I assume he's ancient, shouldn't he have been inspired by his extremely on-the-nose name before?"

"This amuses you?" he said, furrowing his brow.

"Sorry, no, I'm just worn out."

He walked to the window. "It took him hundreds of years to build allegiance with enough renegade Immortals to attempt this insurrection. Some say he has two hundred with him, others say he has as many as three hundred with the extra hundred hiding among the faithful. He'll need more, but how many more we do not know."

"So, stop him now before he finds more renegades."

"We will need your help."

A disturbing thought. "You're not going to sacrifice me or some shit?"

"Or some shit."

A knock on the door.

"Expecting anyone?" he said.

I shook my head. *Please don't be Faion.*

"Sophie?" Lily's voice came through the door as she tried the lock.

"Shit, she has a key," I whispered, springing to my feet.

Winter nodded, giving me permission to open the door.

Lily became transfixed with Winter the moment she saw him.

"Oh, my bad," she said. "I didn't know you had company."

"Old family friend," I said, but then I remembered. *The swords!* I scanned the living room and found nothing. They were gone, probably back inside the Immortal's coat. Finally, he was good for something.

"On my way out," Winter said dryly, walking by Lily to the door.

She pinched my arm, forming a silent *wow* with her lips.

"Nice to meet you, too," she shouted after he had closed the door.

I rolled my eyes. "Very mature, Lil."

"You got your Viking already? He's fucking hot. Order me one, too."

"Gross, he's old and like an uncle and not a favorite uncle."

"Really? He'd be my favorite uncle," Lily said, batting her eyes.

"You're such a tart," I said, grinning, as I headed to the kitchen.

Lily followed. "What's his name? Is he from Oregon?"

I shrugged. "He knows my grandma, friend of an uncle from way back. I don't know where he lives. He just stopped by randomly."

"He's not a relative and he just stopped by? He's into you."

"C'mon, Lily, he's like thirty-five." *More like thirty-five hundred.*

"So?"

"Changing subjects, sort of. I've actually met someone and he's a bit more age appropriate."

She arched an eyebrow. "Viking hot?"

"I'm not honoring that question. His name is Emmet Groshek. He's a medical intern at Sharp Memorial Hospital and a fitness trainer."

Details always help when you're trying to be elusive.

Lily frowned. "Emmet Groshek? Well, I guess if he's a doctor and fairly hot, he doesn't need a name. When will I meet him?"

"We haven't even had a proper date yet," I protested.

"Shut up," she said, excited. "Did sweet little Sophie have

a one-night stand? Do I smell sex in here?"

"I swear, Lil, your mind is a total cesspool."

"You say that like it's a bad thing," she said, happily. "So, I'm here on Lucia's behalf. She'd love to have you for Sunday dinner. Bring Doctor Emmet."

"No, not Emmet, but mind if I bring someone else?"

"Yes, on the mystery guest. You know Lucia cooks enough for an army."

"Tell your mom I'll be there," I said.

Chapter 12

EMMET DROVE UP IN a silver Toyota Camry, dressed in a lavender polo and black cargo shorts. He knew of a quiet beach near Silver Strand, hidden from the road by a row of live oak trees.

I never thought I would contact him, but I kept his card. For two days, I resisted the urge to text him. This morning I gave in. I told myself that going out with him would mean what I had told Lily wasn't a total fib. His response was instant.

Ed Sheeran played quietly in the car as Emmet turned onto the oceanfront drive. I slid my window down to fill my lungs with fresh sea air.

"I needed this," I said.

He grinned as he turned into a parking area. I took in the sky-blue ocean expanse with hungry enthusiasm. Speaking of hunger, on the way to the ocean Emmet stopped at

Monello to pick up a preorder which included grilled chicken, Fettuccine Alfredo with diced tomatoes and spinach, four-cheese calzones, freshly baked bread and Italian sodas.

I watched lazily as he spread out a beach towel and then splayed the food cartons out on it with surgical precision.

He plopped down onto the sand. I did the same. When he shot me one of his radiant smiles, my heart skipped a beat. His smiles were dangerous.

Emmet had picked the loveliest spot. I could hear the waves crashing—ocean breezes kissed my neck and played quietly in my hair. The total chill of it all was such a comforting change from the turmoil of my last few days.

That beach, that boy, they made me feel safe and strong.

"We're safe here," Emmet said, handing me a napkin.

Did he read my mind?

"Safe?"

"The other night at the bar, I felt you were frightened."

I shrugged. "Oh, that, I can be a stress monkey sometimes. Thanks for saving my night. That was cool. I'm good, Emmet. All good in the hood. Good and boring and safe."

"Glad to hear that."

"Actually," I said, "I should be upfront about that."

"About what?"

"My dirty secret. I'm boring. Just a prisoner of my bullet journal. One task and then another until bedtime. Spontaneity be damned."

Emmet grinned. "Well, I made it through med school. I

haven't exactly been living with wild abandon."

I decided I liked him. "I guess that makes us boring compatible."

He grinned again. "Works for me, although my life wasn't always such smooth sailing. My early years were a little more ragged."

"Ragged how? Parents? Parties? Drugs?"

"I touched all the bases of a troubled youth. Drugs, sure. Running away from home, unhappy parents, hanging with the wrong crowds."

"That's hard to believe," I said, incredulous. I shook my head. "I would have guessed you were the perfect boy-next-door."

"Sounds like you never went next door," he said, reflectively. "Looks can be deceiving."

No argument there. "Well, you've turned it around nicely, Dr. Groshek."

He bit into a calzone. "Still warm."

I grabbed a calzone and gave it a good chomp. "Mmmm," I moaned.

He chuckled. "Hungry?"

"Almost *hangry*," I said with my mouth full.

We chewed and smiled for a while until he handed me a water bottle.

"*Agua*," he said with a wink.

So, I'd never live down the water carafe thing at the bar.

"*Gracias*." I wiped my mouth and studied his face. "So,

Emmet, what do you want?"

I could see a thousand thoughts behind his eyes.

"In a global sense? We're not talking about… now? Like in my life as a whole?"

I laughed. "Yes, in the grander scheme."

"I knew that," he said. "I want to do some good. Be an agent for positive change in the universe."

"Did you remember that from your last pageant?"

"I'm serious," he said. "I was still a kid and I just drew a line in the sand and decided I would not be a pure consumer, swimming in the techno wonderland until death, a slave to pleasure and escapism."

"Good God, Emmet," I said, wildly impressed. "You really dig in when you answer a question."

"I know it sounds pretentious or whatever, but I want to add something to this world, not just use it all up as I'm using up all my precious time."

"I feel like I should clap," I teased him. "But really, I loved that. We can't always hide our words and deeper thoughts for fear of judgment."

He laughed. "That's kind of you, but I immediately regret saying that."

"Don't, you might have even scored some points, don't worry."

"I'm totally worried. Those words won't age well. I'm hearing that video game sound where you go over the cliff and lose all your points."

Is this guy real?

"In a video game, you can always start the level again."

"If only life were that way," he said.

"Oh, no," I said, firmly. "Most of my levels I wouldn't want to do again."

Emmet found a pebble and threw it hard enough to reach the water.

"That's my story," he said. "Now yours."

"That was totally not your story. There were like zero specifics. That was barely even broad strokes."

He chuckled. "You noticed that, huh? Okay, broad strokes then."

"I see you, Groshek. You're kind of smooth. Duly noted."

For the first time, we just looked at each other, without hesitation. We were forging a deeper connection and, to be honest, it was exciting.

"Sophie's broad strokes," he said, softly.

I filled my lungs with ocean air. "Okay, I might as well get it out of the way. I'm leaving for Europe after the holidays."

Assuming I'm not dead by then.

He squinted his eyes. "After the holidays?"

"Yeah," I said, reflecting his disappointment. "Graduate school."

"Wow," he said, taken aback.

"It'll be a year. At least a year, rather."

"What are you studying?"

"Ethnology."

His eyes glimmered as he took my hand. "Not the end of the world," he said. "We can get a head start on your studies. Isn't ethnology the study of relationships between people?"

I bent my face. "That's simplifying it a bit. It's comparing peoples as in large cultural groups, not really meant for one-on-one kind of analysis."

"You see, that's where you're wrong. I'm here representing all the boys next door of the planet Earth."

"Cute, but let's be real, long-distance relationships are not cool."

Did I just use the R word? I half expected him to suddenly remember he had an urgent meeting and run for his life.

Instead, Emmet Groshek shrugged. "Maybe I'm not cool."

"You know you're cool, but we would be connecting to the idea of each other and not actually to the real person."

He picked up a plastic fork and faked a stab in his chest. "Your wisdom cuts deep," he said with a chuckle, "so let's put an expiration date on it. We'll just throw it out like bad cabbage when you leave."

"There's that smooth Emmet again," I said. "You forget that I see you. I know you know that's bullshit."

He laughed and stared at me in that way that makes a girl blush, like I was a pastry he was about to eat. Instead, he jumped to his feet, startling me.

"I forgot," he said before sprinting to his car.

I knew it, there he goes, running for the hills.

He returned holding a small bottle of Merlot. It was too obvious to think he was trying to get me drunk, but if he was, I might just let him.

He splashed a little wine into two plastic cups. I picked up mine and took a sip, savoring the sweet, fruity flavor.

He winked before tasting his wine.

"This stuff is good," he said, then took down a huge gulp.

"Remember, you're driving."

He took the cup from my hands and leaned in close enough that I caught a scent of the Merlot on his breath.

As his eyes intensified, gold sparks glistened in them. It reminded me of the first time I saw him, but more magical. I could swear those sparks were more than *basic,* but I sensed no etheric energy about him. Maybe basics possessed a magic all their own, a magic called radiance or charm.

"There is a little-known legend about this area," he said. His eyes turned dreamy. "A story from before the time humans walked the Earth."

I felt intoxicated and it was not from the wine. His voice swam into my ears in ripples. Strong and soothing yet soft as a whisper.

"Tell me," I urged him.

"An ancient nymph lived here in Silver Strand when the world was still quite primitive. She was the first sentient being. She drew her essence from the stars. Being alone, she grew lonely. She wished for a companion. The stars made it known that a price would be exacted. Her life. The nymph wandered for weeks before coming to a decision. She threw herself in the ocean and sank. Her body absorbed water until her arms and legs sprouted into roots that stretched out and shook up the dark depths of the sea, and from her sacrifice came life, first in the ocean depths and then above on land."

I shuddered, having my own affinity to the stars. I hoped my fate would be less sacrificial.

"The nymph didn't ask to be a martyr," I said. "Doesn't make sense."

"Legends rarely do, but your delicate grace reminded me somehow of the lonely nymph. You might be her direct descendant, a star child."

Bullshit artist.

As his lips met mine, warmth slid down my spine all the way to my toes. I hesitated, trying to decide whether to push away or close my eyes and receive his lips eagerly with a proper kiss.

He kissed me so sweetly before I could make up my mind. I didn't want him to stop. I pressed against him. Exhilaration coursed through my veins as our tongues playfully tangled. The sense of flying mixed thrillingly with a primal, irrational fear that I was doing something very wrong.

Yet, all I wanted was to linger inside his embrace, to stay wrapped up in all that exhilaration and warmth until the end of time. To grow dizzy in the spell of his fresh-shaven scent and in the safety of his strong, gentle arms.

He pulled away, placing a quick kiss on my nose.

"That's all I have for you," he said. "If you want more, you'll have to go out with me again."

Oh, the nerve. I rolled my eyes, emphatically. "That's extortion, and otherwise not cool, Dr. Groshek. Next you'll tell me there's a co-pay."

His eyes grinned. "Funny. Let's call that kiss your co-pay."

"Let's not," I said, then pinched his arm.

His laughter, like everything else, was growing on me. This was not smart, this was horrible timing, this was completely reckless.

I couldn't wait to see him again.

Chapter 13

LUCIA'S POT ROAST SMELLED so mouthwatering I feared I might drool. It had been such a long time since I had enjoyed a decent homecooked meal.

Faion spooned some of the tender meat into his mouth. "My goodness, that roast melts on the tongue like warm butter. This comes from God's kitchen," he told Lucia. "If I was ever to date a woman, you'd be her."

Lucia turned to me, disbelief on her face. "You can bring your sweet-talking friend to dinner anytime."

"Don't say that," I said, shrugging. "He'll just show up at your door."

"Gay or straight," Lily said, "men always talk shit."

"Lily!" Lucia said. "Faion is company."

"Nah," Faion said. "She right. Men are bullshit artists."

"Yep," I said, "we can toast to that."

We all lifted our glasses of Cabernet to seal the toast.

Lucia could have been mistaken for thirty. A flattering linen floral print dress clung to her petite frame, her dark auburn hair pulled back and braided into an elegant bun. Her huge silver hoop earrings jingled as she laughed and turned her head to attend each of her guests.

She spent her childhood in the Nicaraguan highlands, chasing her friends through rolling coffee fields. Lucia and her family immigrated to the States when she was only four-teen.

Lily shared an apartment on campus with two friends but spent half her time at her mother's place, a ranch style three-bedroom house with a large backyard and a lush, wild garden that was Lucia's pride and joy.

Lucia was also a sublime cook. The rustic wooden dining table was overflowing with delicious offerings. The puffy bread rolls were freshly baked, the nacatamales were still steaming and the orange juice had been squeezed only moments before being served. Lucia could have been a world-renowned chef.

"Damn, Lucia, these tamales are banging," Faion said, still chewing.

"They're nacatamales," I corrected him. "A Nicaraguan dish."

Lucia gently patted Faion's shoulder. "Thank you, Faion. If you ever need an adoptive mother, you can show up on my doorstep anytime."

Lily turned and rolled her eyes at her mother. "I've long

suspected that you've been trying to replace me."

"Oh, honey, I couldn't do that," Lucia said. "The laws wouldn't allow it."

This amused everyone, even Lily.

Lucia turned her attention to me. "Lily tells me you've been accepted for your master's degree. Stockholm. How exciting, Sophie."

Faion coughed, immediately covering his mouth. "Europe?" he said, locking eyes with me. "You sure that's prudent?"

I kicked him under the table, a bit harder than intended.

He winced and rubbed his calf. "Okay, yeah, Europe, cool."

"Why wouldn't it be prudent?" Lucia said, her maternal instinct piqued. "Is there something holding you back, Sophie?"

I gulped down an entire glass of water, taking my time. "Like we said, men do like to talk smack. And for Faion, it's something of a specialty."

"Rude," Lily said, gently elbowing my ribs.

"Wrong girl," Faion said, avoiding my gaze. "Sometimes I get my white female friends mixed up. My friend Tara, she a mess right now."

Um, not convincing.

"How's your mother, dear?" Lucia asked, inquisitive look on her face.

My least favorite subject.

"No change."

"I've been reading about alternative treatments for catatonia," Lucia said.

"Oh, mother, no one cares about your reading," Lily said.

"No, it's fine," I said. "My grandmother reads about that, too. I am sure she's tried everything. Send me the link. Trust me, she'll check it out."

Strange that she would bring that up now. Lucia was usually discreet, preferring to dive into less personal, more obscure facts, like a newly discovered uncontacted tribe in the Amazon Jungle, or how Ecuador gave *nature* constitutional rights.

"It must be tough for you," Lucia said.

"Honestly, I was too young to remember," I said. "For me, my mom has always been like this. It's been normalized. I'm not harboring hopes."

"Oh, you sweet thing," Lucia said. "I do wish your father had been around at the time. It helps to have another hand to hold."

I smiled. Lily could tell I needed a subject change. Little did either of them know I'd spent most of my life lying about my mother and avoiding the topic of my father about whom I knew little.

Mom wasn't catatonic in the strictest sense. She was under the influence of a potent, cruel spell that kept her trapped inside her own mind, unable to move or communicate but painfully able to think. I was four at the time.

The most skilled witches in the Deep Down had never been able to identify the spell, let alone reverse it.

This was not a basic-friendly story. Instead, we told everyone she was being treated for catatonia in a facility in Oregon. The magic world and the basic world must never intersect under any circumstances.

I shivered, getting pins and needles in both palms. A numbing sensation rushed through me and exploded into an unsteady current inside my belly.

What I sensed was a magic ripple, but how? I wasn't its origin. I was in control of my magic. Was it Faion?

I reached out to touch his hand. It wasn't him either. His etheric field was steady and calm as usual. He squeezed my fingers, once, twice, then three times.

Whatever this was, Faion sensed it too.

"Guess who I saw at the farmers' market?" Lucia asked Lily, thankfully changing subjects.

"Tom Hardy," Lily said before Lucia could finish. I swear, Lily mentioned Tom Hardy's name multiple times a day.

"I saw Cynthia Barnes," Lucia said, undeterred.

Lily sighed, disapprovingly. "Mamá, how very not exciting."

"Did you forget? Cynthia is Rocco's mother."

Rocco Barnes. Right. Lily had mentioned in passing that Lucia was acquainted with Rocco's mother.

Lily put a big piece of bread in her mouth. Her cheeks bulged out.

"She said Rocco's in town, and we should visit for old times' sake."

What was it with Lucia today? Why did she go out of her way to bring up topics she knew perfectly well we didn't want to discuss?

Lily swallowed and put her fork down. "Old times? I barely know them."

Faion leaned toward me while our hosts exchanged barbs. "You feel that?" he whispered.

I nodded.

"Would you two like some dessert?" Lucia asked. "I think we could all use a change of mood."

"Is Kanye crazy?" Faion said. "Hell, yes, I want dessert."

"I guess I could find room," I said with my hand on my belly.

"Right answer," Lucia said, the sparkle returning to her eyes. "We have lemon cake and pecan pie and homemade vanilla ice-cream."

Faion considered his options. "I'm going to need all three."

Lucia smiled and reached out for her daughter's hand. It would have been the polite thing to help, but I needed the time to talk to Faion.

As soon as the two women stepped inside the kitchen, I turned to the window. Darkness had descended while we ate—the night shadows loomed, gathering power and menace. The moon was out of sight, but I could feel its silver energy hidden behind the passing clouds.

"Do you think one of those scent monsters is out there?" I said, the memory of the deformed animal haunting me most at night.

Faion shook his head. "Whatever, maybe, but it's not out there, Sophie, it's in here."

"You think something followed us here?"

Magic creatures usually stayed clear of basic homes and businesses. It had been that way since the beginning of man. It was the reason coexistence had been possible for all these millennia. Even Immortals avoided openly messing with the real world, but these unknown demon-animals might have had different rules altogether. The thought of that was chilling.

"No." Faion pointed at Lucia's seat. "I think it's the mom."

My eyes almost popped out of their sockets. "I've known Lucia for years. She's basic, Faion. You're crazy. You and Kanye."

"She just happens to have a wild garden and food to die for... let me guess, she's good at everything."

I was not willing to concede anything to him. "You're wrong. Period."

He stared at me, tenderly. "Okay, maybe someone or something is plugged into her. Maybe, but I doubt it."

"That makes more sense," I said. "She has been acting strange."

"Be careful, Sophie," Faion whispered. "Wishful thinking is a mistake only basics can afford to make."

Lucia and Lily returned to the dining room, carrying trays with offerings almost too good to be true. Dare I say, *magical.*

Was Faion right? Had my friendship with Lily thrown off my senses and left me unable to see what was in front of my eyes?

I reached out and took Lily's hand. Her face was radiant and clear as usual—no signs of etheric energy about her. In fact, Lily's aura was the clearest and lightest I had ever sensed. *Ever!*

Why did everything suddenly feel so suspicious?

If her mother had any dealings with the world of magic, Lily had been shielded from it completely, but what else was being shielded?

Lucia would not have been the first basic to have been tutored by a wielder of magic. Although strictly forbidden, there were plenty of rumors about basics learning to use some form of witchcraft or other in a limited fashion.

Unfortunately, those stories never ended well.

Chapter 14

WHEN I GOT OFF the bus, it wasn't my intention to catch the next one to Ocean Beach Pier, but as the first bus pulled away, the second approached. I felt an overwhelming urge to connect to my elemental sources. I needed to sort through the mess in my head.

In one weekend I had gone from: *a)* fighting with a sword, to *b)* learning of a rebellion led by an Immortal named Chaos, to *c)* going on a date with a guy I really liked, to *d)* suspecting my best friend's mother of learning forbidden magic that might end up killing her.

Only two weeks ago, I had opened a letter that promised a new life, a life for which I had planned and hoped. How did it all flip upside down so quickly?

A half-moon lurked above, waiting for the night creatures to return.

I walked a few steps onto the empty pier. The dark waters

below sparkled with distorted moonlight. It dawned on me that Winter had not only been testing me since that first day at the park but also training me. He wanted me to join the fight against Chaos. Why was I not running for my life?

A chilly gust of sea air went right through my white cotton cardigan, making me shiver to my bones. Turning around, I rubbed my arms and decided to walk the beach instead. The sand jumped up to tickle my toes.

As I started to relax a little, a tall man suddenly appeared in my path. He wore some sort of a black mask that covered the top half of his face. He stared into my eyes as his lips worked at a spell.

Despite appearances, he felt basic. If he was supernatural, he was doing a superb job hiding his etheric field.

I looked around to see if we were alone. It was just the two of us. Even if he had brought an army, it would not have mattered. I was not the same girl from that park two weeks ago. Now a bunch of such goons would have been little more than a light practice.

Channeling my powers, I took a step toward the masked man. I knew that spell on his lips. He was chanting out a fire-ring spell meant to encircle me in flames.

Seriously? Fire spells? I hate fucking fire spells.

I raised my hands, turning my palms to the sea.

"Salacia!" I whispered.

Drops of saltwater flew across the dark beach to meet my fingertips.

"Relido!" I ordered.

The drops fell to the ground and misted, washing away the ring of fire before it could build.

I stepped over the dying flames, my eyes fixed on the man. His pupils glowed red for a moment and then he began working at a new spell. I was hardly in the mood to break spells all night long, so I stretched my fingers out before recoiling them tightly into fists, gathering pure energy.

Challenging me next to the largest ocean in the world was a big mistake by any being, but by a basic human it was a total farce. No matter how many spells he had, I had infinitely more.

I didn't have to learn magic, I *was* magic. Young witches were not taught how to conjure magic, they were taught to control magic already growing inside.

The stupid man showed no signs of fear. The sizzling energy blasts I was about to hurl at him would teach him otherwise.

Right before dispensing the brutal lesson, I held back my magic. Winter's warnings echoed in my head. The bastard could be useful at times. I quickly threw a containing shield around me to prevent any magic reverberations from escaping the scene.

Finally ready to attack, palms aflame and eager to devastate, I heard a strange galloping sound. I spun around to find a huge wolf charging.

I noticed the beast's gray fur had been burned in spots

as his long, drooling fangs readied to snap shut around my neck. A breath away from decapitation, I remembered I had gathered power into my palms and blasted the wolf on the snout, spinning him back through the air.

The wolf hit the ground hard. He snarled at me, foam oozing out of his mouth and nostrils. This was no ordinary wolf. The deep scars on its face and hide, its sick lemon eyes and their otherworldly gaze, all told me this was no typical scent beast—it was a demon from the darkest hell.

Behind me, the man chanted a paralyzing spell. The demon wolf found its feet and came for me again with its shining fangs and maddening bloodthirst.

I wanted to avoid using potent magic, but I had no choice.

My legs felt suddenly heavy—the paralyzing spell's effect. I stomped my feet to get some feeling back and ran back onto the pier. Blood pounded in my ears. I needed the Moon. I looked up and called for its powers.

Caught between two enemies, I removed my cardigan, letting the moonlight spill into the skin on my arms, loading me with silver energy.

The water rose as man and monster made their way to the pier. I shuddered. Waves crashed against the pier, spraying me with more power.

The wolf raced toward me as the man resumed chanting while opening his arms wide to the sky.

I clenched my teeth, growing more pissed by the second.

The fools, thinking they can take me, a daughter of the

Moon, servant of Selene, at the witching hour, with an ocean of water surging at my feet.

I formed a ring of my own, a tight line of swirling magic that scattered into a purple magnetic field that swept the wolf off his feet just as he tried to launch into me. I had to duck as the wolf flew over me and into the sea.

The wailing of the monster echoed off into the night.

The man kept chanting that paralyzing spell, faster, more urgently, but it soon became clear, even to him, that the task was beyond him. Whatever magic he thought he knew had come completely undone under duress.

Moron.

With my eyes closed, I summoned total control of the water, creating an ice spear in my right palm.

The man gasped, losing nerve for the first time. I sliced his energy spell into shreds with my spear, barely missing his throat.

Then I leaped over the railing in pursuit of the demon wolf.

The white-hot magic of the saltwater singed my skin as I hit the surface. The wolf turned for me, snarling, his legs churning wildly under the water.

I aimed the tip of the spear at him, feeding it a contained stream of magic, just like Winter had instructed me, and then hurled it at the demon, twisting my torso as hard as possible to generate maximum thrust.

The spear pierced the monster's chest, then shattered into

a thousand sharp spikes that lodged themselves inside arteries and veins to reach every organ and... *explode!*

It was a horrible thing to watch. A shudder ran through me as the demon yelped in agony, his body shrinking down like a deflated balloon until it was swallowed up by the sea.

What had I done? I had killed something that was alive, even if it was evil, even if it was a dark monstrosity—I had killed it. I felt sick. I felt faint. I knew I had to get out of the water before I passed out.

I was the girl who had trouble squashing a mosquito. I certainly never intended to become such a devastating witch, turning water into deadly ice spears. My kind did not use elemental energy for such purposes unless at war.

Maybe Winter had seen my potential for destruction, maybe that was why he showed up in my world. Or, maybe, it was not me at all. I had to, at least, consider the possibility that dark magic had infiltrated my core.

I dragged myself to the shore and fell to my knees, exhausted. Out of the corner of my eye, I spotted the man with the mask running for his life.

I brushed away wet strands of hair from my eyes. I got up and trudged back to the pier, my teeth beginning to chatter.

I found my white cardigan and wrapped it around my shoulders. With my luck, I'd probably catch my death of cold.

A different kind of shiver ran through me. There was a disturbance in the energy fields around me.

It had to be Winter.

"Show your face!" I called out. "Well, here I am, you bastard."

He had taken everything from me. He had taken my innocence, my life's plan and now he had turned me into a killer. It was just what he wanted. How he must have loved watching my moral defeat from the shadows. I wondered if he had popcorn as he enjoyed my despair and delighted in my unhinged fury as he pushed me beyond my limits.

I spun around, again and again. "What are you playing at?"

Silence was the only response. He was not here.

And it made sense. Who was I kidding? He would never recruit a basic to do his dirty work, *for fuck's sake*, not Winter, not a Chief Magistrate for the Seventh Council.

It didn't make me feel any better. If not Winter, then some other renegade wielder of magic was in town, training basics to channel energy, teaching them rudimentary spells. Not only that, he had them work alongside those lemon-eyed death dogs for which I had no reference at all—and that was far more disturbing than anything else.

It did stand to reason that this new player didn't want me involved in Winter's mysterious plans. We had that in common.

Screw Winter. It's not like he was an innocent bystander. It was like the Frankenstein thing, only I was the monster. I was Winter's monster. Fuck. He helped to create this new side of me. And this other bastard showed up right after Winter found me. I put this on the Immortal Magistrate.

Why did it have to be my life that got hijacked?

I fell back onto my knees. I heard myself laughing like a madwoman as if I were outside my own body. How did I ever think I could escape to Sweden, or that I would be allowed any free will whatsoever? Winter had connections everywhere. I had nowhere to run. My old life was gone.

And my tears tasted like saltwater.

Chapter 15

WINTER WALKED A CIRCLE around me. "What the hell happened to you?"

The tiniest quiver of energy leapt forth from his aura and brushed against mine for only a moment before dissolving away into mist. It had a soothing effect, almost nurturing, but I wasn't so easily fooled. He sensed I was teetering on the edge of something from which there might be no return.

I raised my eyes to him, unblinking. I'd spent the night on my doorstep, unable to sleep, not wanting to go inside and leave the moonlight. The lunar energy replenished me, body and soul. After the fight at the pier, I had begun to lose myself. I had expended so much energy. I did not like who I had started to become or what my destiny might hold.

Winter found me like this, my clothes wrinkled and my hair tangled. A plush *Doctor Who* blanket hung over my left shoulder.

"I'm fine," I said. "It's a lovely morning. Why are you out so early? Is there another torture victim on my block? Is morning abuse like your cup of Joe?"

"Cup of what?"

"It means *coffee*," I said, suddenly tired. "It's a thing people say."

Winter started to say something but changed his mind. He reached down to take my hand, gently pulling me to my feet.

He put his hand in my hair to remove a twig, or maybe it was seaweed or demon debris.

"You're always looking for answers," he said. "Today, I have some."

"That's great, can you give me a moment?"

I locked him outside and jumped immediately into the shower, letting the hot water wash the mud and salt out of my hair and off my body.

The hot water poured down my face and I felt nothing. I was in a state of emotional overload. I felt numb. My sense of what Winter truly wanted was all over the place. I avoided telling him what had happened at the pier. I also was in no hurry to hear his so-called answers. He knew way more than he would ever tell me and I would always be at a disadvantage.

I slid into worn jeans and an old sweater and let Winter in. This time, he had no snide comments about the messy state of my life.

"Let's hear it," I said. "What do you have to say?"

His face was streaked with hard lines, more so than usual. He was obviously fatigued. It seemed I wasn't the only one who hadn't slept.

"You will be meeting with the Seventh Council soon."

Well, roast me over hot coals and slice me sideways.

"That's the big reveal?" I asked.

Seemingly, this man would never stop testing my patience.

He grinned. "Disappointed?" And there he was, sarcasm and lack of empathy oozing out of him like bad breath. Vintage Winter.

All that smugness vanished from his face as fast as it came, replaced by stone cold gravity. "You can't face them unprepared. There are things we need to discuss."

I drew in a slow breath.

There is nowhere to go, I might as well listen.

"Chaos and his legion grow stronger," he continued, "but he needs more manpower. He doesn't have time to convert more Immortals, so he has turned to shapeshifters. Sources tell us he has gathered an army of shifters numbered in the thousands."

"Shapeshifters? They can't possibly be a match for Immortals."

I didn't know much about shifters except that they were loners and rarely formed connections outside of their factions. They were not allowed in the Deep Down because they were violent, volatile and completely clan driven.

The most powerful among the shifters could transform

into two or more different species and a rare few had supposedly mastered human form shifting, or so the legends went. They had beastly strength, they could heal fast from severe injuries and lived long lives, but they were not immortal and they did not channel elemental or earth magic. That's all I knew.

Winter took a step closer. "It's true that it's very hard to kill an Immortal, but there are other things that can be done to us. Vile, horrible things. Things that would make us prefer death. Chaos knows well of these unspeakable offenses and he is out there teaching shifters those dark secrets."

"Sounds charming," I said, sinking into my couch.

"No," Winter said, "they most assuredly are not charming. These are not standard shifters he recruits. They are the most fiendish shifters, rejected even by their own hierarchy. They are not typical pack wolves or honey bears. These killers can shift into grotesque monstrosities you would never want to witness with your own eyes."

I threw my hands up in the air. "Tell me about it."

He stopped to read my expression. "Have you seen such a creature?"

"I don't know if the demon animal that followed me around was one, but I can tell you I never want to see that creature again or any other grotesque monstrosities."

"They don't wait for invitations. No one wants to see one, and few survive the encounter."

Except maybe a bad bitch like myself.

"I'm going to take a big pass on that," I said. "If they can fuck with Immortals, can you imagine what they would do to me?"

"Or your grandmother? Or your mortal friends? We must take a stand now. Immortal rule is the only thing keeping them in line."

My heart quickened. "What do you people expect from me? I hate to be the one to tell you this, buddy, but if you're counting on a single San Diego coed to win your war, then you've already lost."

His tone softened. "Luna, you're not expected to fight them, if that's what you're asking."

I'm not going to lie, a huge jolt of relief rushed through me. "What then?"

"We believe you can prevent them from shifting."

Their belief made little sense, but I decided to play along. "That's it?"

"That's it. If they don't shift in time for battle, they'll slink back to their holes and Immortal rule will be restored. Then all returns to normal and you can go back to your trivial existence among the basics."

"And what about Chaos? Why wouldn't he come for me?"

"That won't happen."

"How can you be sure?"

"Because he doesn't even know you exist."

Okay, maybe I should have told him about the fight at the pier.

"You're not convinced," he said.

"If it's too good to be true…" I stopped talking literally a fraction of a second before I called him by his name.

"But it is true. I'm always forthright."

I shook my head. "There is a big… no, there's a huge hole in your plan."

"The plan is perfect."

"I can't help you," I insisted. "Last time I trained was eight years ago. I made the choice to cut off my connection to the Deep Down when I turned fourteen. All lunar witches are given that choice. I took it. I chose a normal life in a world I could understand. That meant no more trips down below, no classes, no substantial use of magic. My knowledge and skills are limited. You're asking that I control the shifting of thousands of people. I can barely get through a session of spin class. You need a more experienced witch."

Seriously, the more sincere I got, the more I amused him.

"You don't need to control the shifting, just the Moon."

I rolled my eyes. "Oh, because that's possible."

"Isn't that what the lunar part in your Order's name is all about?"

"No, *oh my god*. We absorb power from the Moon, we don't control celestial bodies. We're not Greek gods. How do you not know that?"

"I know many things, young witch. For instance, once a century, we go through a metamorphic Moon, a moon that morphic shifters depend on. When midnight strikes on a metamorphic night, they can shift into anything they wish, be it real or imagined. All they need to do is visualize a form and it comes to life for two moon cycles, forty-eight hours. Only a lunar witch can interfere with the metamorphic phase of the Moon so that it loses most of its magic. I know this, Luna Mae. And, as I can see plainly in your eyes, you are remembering a time when you knew that, too."

He wasn't wrong. We were taught that in school, but it went in one ear and out the other. No one had even seen a metamorphic Moon in almost two centuries. Nor had anyone seen a metamorphic shifter.

Winter's story was like Halley's Comet meets the bogeyman.

Reasonable minds assumed the phenomenon had run its course. Strange magic usually derived from waves that waned and eventually ceased to exist.

Nothing stayed forever in the preternatural world.

"Morph shifters?" I said. "I thought they were a thing of the past. Where have they been all these years?"

"Waiting."

"That's terrifying. They can really change into anything?"

He nodded. "Chaos has gathered most of them. They are deranged, bitter, hungry and, when they shift, they will be almost as strong as the most ancient Immortals. They hunger for blood and power. They've been waiting for the morphic Moon for a long time. As you well know, it's exactly this moon that makes lunar witches most powerful."

The hairs on the back of my neck stood on end. I didn't want to imagine what Chaos had promised those blood-thirsty shifters to win their allegiance. Almost certainly, it would begin with a feeding frenzy of human flesh.

"So, let's hear it. When does this morphic Moon happen?"

Winter stared at me soberly, almost human. "In two weeks, at the midnight hour, the Moon enters the metamor-phic phase," he said. "At peak hour near the 33rd parallel North, the epicenter of the transformation will not be far from where we stand, right here in San Diego."

Two weeks? In my mind, sand was racing through an hour-glass.

Winter reached out and took my hand. My first instinct was to pull it away, but I let it linger in his grasp. "You're necessary. That's why I'm here. There are no other lunar witches in the area, and you are fresh magic, your connection will be primal, instinctive. That's good. Also, older, more steadfast witches would have been harder to bend to my will in a short time frame."

"I'll assume there is a compliment in there somewhere," I said.

"I do not waste time on charm. If you do not help us stop those beasts, our world will fall."

I felt like I was shrinking. "And I thought finals was a lot of pressure."

"There is but one test that matters, Luna Mae," he said.

"I was attacked," I said in a burst. "I know I should have told you."

He let go of my hand. "When?"

"Last night by what I think was a basic trying to cast spells and some kind of scent monster, a wolf, or baby morph, I don't know."

He grabbed my shoulders, pulled me to him, then took my head in both his hands. He could have killed me in an instant. "Are you sure about this?"

"Yeah, they weren't Gaslamp district drunks, that's for sure."

"Have you been contacted by any others with power?"

I shook my head. "I'm not sure what you mean."

"Where did this happen?"

"At the pier down at Ocean Beach."

"Take me there," he said. "I need to hear everything that happened."

He led me to an old red Honda Civic parked across the street. I wasn't sure I'd ever seen anything more shocking than Winter's shit Civic. I would have sooner expected him to drive a sky chariot pulled by enslaved phoenixes.

Winter held the passenger door open and I slid in, biting my lip. I somehow resisted complimenting him for his bitchin' battle tank or his epic cruiser or his badass pussy wagon. Jokes were wasted on him anyway.

It felt like an aberration that he would drive a car at all. Did it mean he had a driver's license? A social security number? Did he live in the basic world? Did he have a girlfriend named Candace who worked at the Gap?

Somehow, such thoughts had never crossed my mind. I always imagined he lived in an underground mausoleum or a torture dungeon with the rest of the SoCal Immortal squad, spending every second practicing his scowl.

By the time we stepped onto the pier, the rising sun was working at its morning Monet. The sea was calm, but my heart was not.

"This is where the wolf went in the water," I said, finding fresh claw scratches on the railing.

Winter examined the marks, nodding. "And you just went after him?"

If I didn't know better, I would say he was impressed.

"Had to scare away the masked guy first," I said.

"Right," he said, bending over the railing to sniff noisily.

"Could it have been one of those morph shifters?"

"No, it would have turned human when you mortally injured it. This is an unclassified creature. Species unknown." He bent his face. "The scent it left behind is quite pungent, but unfamiliar."

"More than pungent, it's straight up nasty. Maybe it was one of those scent demon things."

"Scent demons do not have a scent, they follow scents."

"Okay, but how about the mutant wolf look... with the burned patches on the fur... any relatable creatures in your Immortal field guide?"

"You're being funny, but there actually is such a guide. There is nothing in there at all like this strange hunter."

I followed him to the beach where he examined vague disruptions in the sand, which might have once been footprints. He kneeled and scooped up a handful of sand.

He watched as it slipped through his fingers, then quickly picked up more sand and did the whole trick over again.

I crouched down next to him and did the same—the simple ritual looked so calming I had to try. "I did things last night I didn't know I could do."

"Here, at the seaside, with the metamorphic Moon coming, you are formidable."

"But I felt like I was channeling unspeakable sources."

"Dark magic, you mean," he said as if he expected my questions.

"Yeah, and that's not a pool I want to be swimming in."

"Better to swim than to drown," he said, abstractly. He tired of our conversation and moved to another spot to test more sand.

"Don't I have any choice in all this?"

"Your powers are growing, Luna Mae. The energy is already shifting due to the cycle to come," he said. "Your magic will swell in ripples at first and then waves. And when your powers crest, we must be ready."

Out of nowhere, Lucia entered my thoughts. I knew I should not keep secrets from Winter, but I didn't want her or Lily on anyone's radar. They had no part in this war and I meant to keep it that way.

"I want out," I said. "I know that I can't get out, but I just want out."

"You and me both, Luna Mae," he said, "but the way out is perilous."

"Don't you love this stuff?" I couldn't help but ask.

"No, I do not," he said. "And I am going to assume you knew that."

Chapter 16

As soon as Big Rob took over the evening shift, I sat down with Faion at one of the four tables in the empty patio outside the coffee shop. A thick line of carefully trimmed bushes hid us from the busy street, but that manicured divide worked both ways. Anything could be hiding on the other side.

Every muscle in Faion's face was taut as his attention seemed focused somewhere inside him.

My paranoia reared its nasty little head again.

"What's up, Faion?"

"Let's leave tomorrow," he said. "Let's go back to Oregon."

I would love nothing more. "We've been through this. I can't leave."

"I'm talking a day or two. We'll talk to our grandmothers. They have insight and perspective that we don't."

"I'm a marked witch, Faion. I'm under constant Immortal surveillance. If I leave town now, they'll think I'm running."

Faion balled his fingers into fists. "I had another premonition, Sophie."

Big Rob strutted through the door. "On the house," he said, setting two large vanilla lattes on the table.

"Thanks, Rob," I said, wanting to hasten his departure.

Rob crouched down next to Faion. He was a big guy, obviously, but his face possessed the innocent wonderment of a ten-year-old. There wasn't a single mean bone in his body.

"Sophie's a good egg," Rob said, tilting his head toward me.

"Rob?" I said, fearing where this was going.

"She's not all chatty, driving you crazy all day with details about microblading, celebrity couples and keto dieting."

Faion raised an eyebrow. "She's a good egg, huh? Sophie, I think this dude likes you. *Good egg* is Gucci level hetero male affection."

Big Rob cracked a smile. "I'm just saying, don't get her in any trouble, she's like my little sister."

Enough testosterone already.

"Rob, what's this about?" I said. "We're just having coffee."

He shrugged. "Okay, this dude, he's been acting like a stalker. Hangs outside, checks you out through the windows. And I'm not talking just once."

Oh boy.

"Thanks for looking out, but it's not like that," I assured him.

"Yeah, she too skinny," Faion said.

I rolled my eyes at Faion. "Rob, I can handle my own friends. We're good. You better check on the counter. I'm sure Maura could use the help."

Big Rob shrugged, unconvinced, and went back inside.

"He calls *me* a stalker?" Faion said. "That boy is all about your business, Sophie, for real. He's all about your *biznass.*"

"He's not, it's just boring working here. And you, buddy, have obviously got to stop hovering."

"Somebody's got to," he said.

"Apparently, I already have Rob."

"Yeah, you do."

"Shut," I said. "We're co-workers. I know his girlfriend."

"He must be tired of that old stuff," Faion said.

"Don't be vulgar."

"I'm done," he said. "Let his basic ass worry about you. He'll just pour hot coffee all over them devil dogs and Immortal assholes. No worries."

"I thought you said you were done?" I said, glaring. "Can we get back to your premonition? Please!"

Something changed in Faion's eyes. "It was the worst. It shook me, to be honest. Deep purple sky, dead bodies everywhere. People gasping their last breaths, guts spilling, and heads rolling down the street in slow motion."

I felt a cold shiver. "People we know?"

He lowered his gaze. "People we know, people we don't know. The old, the young and even... us."

My blood froze. Diviners had very precise visions, but their significance, at times, was up for interpretation. "You saw us dead?"

Faion held his breath. "We were beheaded," he said as he released it, "so, technically, I just saw our heads, just rolling and rolling."

Oh shit. There's no good interpretation of that.

"Your premonitions are not always literal, right?"

"That's the thing, usually, yeah, but it's not like I have experience with shit this heavy, apocalyptic savagery and what not. I need my gran's guidance. This *end of days* business is most definitely not my jam."

"We're in this, okay? All options are bad. Pulling our grandmothers into this would only complicate an already fucked-up situation."

Faion was spiraling downward. I knew the feeling. I had two choices. I could try to distance myself to protect him a little while longer, or I could share all I had learned and hope he could somehow pull it together.

In the end, I needed his help and if I were him, I'd want to know the world could be coming to an end while I still had time to do something.

I told him everything Winter had told me. I told him about Chaos and the morphs, as well as what had occurred at Ocean Beach Pier. I told him I had killed the beast and that confession shamed me to my core.

He had no reaction to any of it. I had never seen anyone so completely stunned. He could have been one of those wax figures at Madame Tussauds.

"Faion, did you hear what I said?"

"There is a hell," he said. "We're living in it."

He stirred his latte with a plastic spoon. He seemed almost like a different person—everything about his personality had reversed completely. I became mesmerized by his methodic stirring motion until I glimpsed a fresh bruise around his wrist.

"Your wrist," I said. "Did you get into a fight?"

"I wouldn't call it that..." Faion looked off into the distance. "Your boy Rob is not alone in thinking I'm odd."

"Did someone hurt you?" I said.

"Fuck those dudes," Faion said. "I foretold their futures before things got ugly. I almost feel sorry for them. Their next twenty years will not be kind."

"Don't feel sorry for those assholes," I said. "I hope they all—"

"Luna, don't say it. We should have the empathy they lack."

I sighed. "Now you sound like my gram."

"Exactly," he said. "I learned that from mine."

"Our grams are awesome," I agreed, "but we can't go to them this time."

"I know," he said, but his attention had moved elsewhere. His eyes became stone cold as his gaze fixed on something over my shoulder.

My head spun. I heard his voice before he stepped into view.

"Luna Mae, the girl who will not learn."

Winter glided to our table. He wore a black t-shirt and blue jeans. His hair was spiked up and darker, a result of the wet look provided by a hefty dose of styling gel.

"How long were you spying?" I said.

"Long enough."

His hands were in his pockets, his head leaning toward me. Then he rolled his neck so that his focus shifted to Faion.

"Mr. Trice, I just can't get you out of my head," Winter said.

"Have we met?" Faion said, weakly.

"Let me give you this warning," Winter said. "My mind is not a safe place for you to be. And what is seen through these eyes would destroy you."

Holy shit, he knew?

Faion cleared his throat and swallowed hard.

Winter slid the latte out of Faion's hand and poured it into a flowerpot. "Enter my head again and the price will be absolute," he said, lowering his brow.

"Never," Faion managed to say, barely.

I sprang to my feet. "Listen, you bully, leave him alone. He was trying to help. If you got a problem, take it up with me."

I grabbed Winter by the shoulder. "Leave my friends alone!"

He wiped my hand away as he reached out to Faion, but right before gripping him by his skinny neck, he dropped his hand. "Keep your diviner on a shorter leash or I'll have his head."

Faion's face betrayed that we were having the same thought—his premonition of our heads rolling in the streets.

"Were you not held as a baby?" I hissed at Winter. "Control yourself."

"No, it's cool," Faion said, standing up. "Big dude's right to be salty. This was all on me. Hundo P. I'm the bad guy." Faion grabbed his backpack, nodded compulsively and vanished into the dark street behind the bushes.

A tiny spark of blue energy sizzled on my left palm. I took a deep breath to extinguish the flame before it turned into something I couldn't contain.

Winter took Faion's seat, somehow satisfied.

I stood by the table, seething inside. "Do you always have to be a dick?" I said. "I mean, is that absolutely necessary? God."

He tapped his fingers on the tabletop. "Manners are a deception."

"Oh... my god," I said and reluctantly took my seat.

I needed a moment to compose myself. I didn't want to detail the whole stupid plan Faion and I had put in motion, especially the embarrassing *exploding a water cooler over his head to get him out of his shirt* scenario.

I was in no mood to be humiliated.

"When did you figure it out?" I finally said.

"Try the moment you decided to strip me of my shirt."

Humiliation commence. At least it explained why he had decided to open up about the rebellion the next morning. He knew I had heard everything.

"The thing I don't understand," I said, "is that if you knew, why did you let it happen?"

He chuckled. "It's astonishing how little you understand. I've been waiting for you to call me by my name. Call it a test of your self-control. Twice you almost failed yourself."

"And yet you say my name willy-nilly," I reminded him.

"I like your name," he said. "What I don't like is you not owning your story or your truth. Secrets among allies become harbingers of doom."

I felt blood rushing to my ears. "You're the harbinger of doom," I said. "Don't you have anything better to do than stalk me?"

"I'm here to escort you home."

I laughed. "No, you're not."

He looked at me as if I was unwell. And I really wasn't.

"You are no longer safe here," he said.

"I can take care of myself."

"All incidents indicate that the demons come out after dark. I will be your escort on nights you work late. You will find me here at the opportune hour."

"Hard pass."

"I thought you might say that," he said, strangely pleased. "Which is why there's a plan B."

His face told me that plan B was going to be worse. A lot worse.

"You suck," I said.

He shrugged. "Either I chaperone your nocturnal commute or I must report to the Council that hostiles are pursuing you. Your life has great value to the Magistrates of Eternal Beings... for the moment. I'm sure they can arrange for you a cozy but heavily guarded little den at the Court until the metamorphic night in question."

I didn't even roll my eyes. Why bother?

He stood up, offering me his elbow. I stuck my tongue out and rose with a deep sigh. I gently folded my arm around his and a tender jolt shot up my spine.

His manners were so dusty—they were from hundreds of years ago.

Being in direct contact with an Immortal apparently created energy flow. The buzz in my arm raced around my shoulder and tickled my breastbone.

When we reached his dingy Civic, he held the passenger door open. With a grunt, I broke free from his warmth and sat down in the car.

I slammed the door shut, the only way I could express myself.

Chapter 17

THERE WAS A TALL shadow dancing on my door. I hadn't noticed until I took out my keys and Winter drove away. I stopped on my first step, noticing the shadow moving. I readied to strike swiftly if necessary.

The shadow turned out to be Emmet-shaped. I took the final step up and saw him to the right, swaying to a beat only he could hear.

Emmet was grooving with his back to me. I reached out to tap his shoulder. He spun around, startled.

"Sophie," he said, taking his earbuds off for me to see. "Jamming to the Lumineers. Forgot where I was."

"Does one jam to the Lumineers?"

"What?" he said.

"Nothing, what are you doing here, Emmet?"

"I texted you. I have the evening off."

He showed me a white paper bag from Buca di Beppo.

"Thought you might want to eat," he said.

"Oh, you texted," I said. "So that's all it takes."

"Did I overstep?" he said, suddenly mortified. "I can go."

"It's fine," I said. "I know your free nights are rare."

"It was all of the sudden," he said. "I texted you a few times. I just felt inspired, so I showed up."

"Inspired? For more Italian food?" I said, rummaging through the contents of my purse to find my phone.

"Not just any Italian food," he corrected me. "Baked rigatoni, penne San Remo, tiramisu... Food for gods."

"Hungry gods," I said.

My fingers fumbled through old receipts, empty gum packs, lip balm tubes and scattered coins, but not my phone.

"I must have left my phone at work," I muttered.

"You didn't see my texts," he said. "And I show up like a creeper." He dangled the food under my nose. "Take the manicotti. Forgive the man."

I gave him a half-assed smile. "*Aww*, that was almost a pun."

Emmet's smile turned upside down. He was cute when disappointment made him look like a boy. I didn't have the heart to send him away.

"You can come in, but only if you leave the puns outside."

It was one of those nights and times in a girl's life where it would have been easy to jump into bed with a good man like Emmet and forget the world.

I had to be careful. Simply knowing me had become

dangerous. If I had any sense, or at least concern for others, I'd stay far away from him.

My vanity was not dead. I studied Emmet's face to see what he thought of my apartment. Nothing. He took no notice. Was I comparing him to Winter? *That's crazy.* For what point? I wasn't going to psychoanalyze myself during such dire times. Clearly, Emmet was familiar with the disorder that persisted in cramped college apartments after graduation. Winter was not.

I fell back over the arm of the sofa, kicking off my shoes. "So, Groshek, why are you trying to fatten me up?"

Emmet shrugged.

"Is it like a primal caveman thing?" I continued. "You hunt the food for the woman in hopes she'll be grateful enough to lie back on your furs?"

He sat down next to me. "Wouldn't a caveman just beat you over the head with a club and then drag you by the hair?"

That would not have gone well for you, Emmet.

The impulse to touch him was very strong. Here was this hot guy, a *normal* guy, who'd come all this way to see me, patiently waited outside, and was happy for whatever crumbs I threw his way, no questions asked.

Any girl would fall head over heels for this dude.

"I've been thinking," he said. "About you and Sweden. I could come visit. Heck, maybe they have an exchange program where I could spend a month or two there, training at their superior sports medicine facilities."

I was speechless. My eyes slowly widened.

He nodded. "Too soon?"

"Emmet." I really didn't know what else to say.

"If you were staying here," he said, "I wouldn't be acting like this. I wouldn't be moving so fast. I'd have the proper amount of cool guy patience, you know. Wait three days to call and all that."

"It's all good. You're busy and I'm leaving. Shit timing."

Part of me wished I could confide in him, but to do that in even the smallest way would include me telling him I was really a witch. I would not insult him with a veil of lies about a sucky day at work and I would not tell him the truth that the face rippers and soul swallowers were on their way.

"Shit timing," he repeated.

The only sane thing to do was to tell him I was not interested in a relationship right now and send him away. It did not matter how much I liked him. I had to cut him loose, period.

"So, fuck it," he said. "Romance be damned. I needed to see a friendly face and I think maybe you did as well. No worries about the future."

His fabricated energy quickly faded. He seemed very tense.

"Emmet, what's up? Did something happen?"

"Yes," he said, reluctantly. "At the hospital, we lost someone."

I took his hand. "I'm so sorry."

He nodded. His eyes moistened. "She was ten. Just ten years old."

I took up his hand in both my hands now.

"You can train for every possible medical scenario, but you can't train for this feeling," he said. "Textbooks teach coping strategies and how to shift your focus to the death's impact on the family, but there is no method to forget the light in a little girl's face or her mother's face when that light goes out. I can't just tuck it all away and go back to being same old Emmet Groshek."

He held his face in his hands. Emmet was breaking down. I knew it wasn't from a single incident, no matter how horrible, but a totality. Maybe it was the accumulation of years of study and sacrifice and the loneliness of that life, mixed with the terrible things, and even the fleeting things like our friendship.

We can never know completely what causes another's mortal anguish, but we can comfort them as I wanted to comfort Emmet.

I draped my arm around his powerful back. I touched his sad face and wiped back his hair so I could kiss his temple softly.

"Emmet, I'm here. Let me hold you."

He sucked in a sob. "That's all I need."

His forehead nestled against my neck. I ran my fingers through his hair. He released a lifetime of tension in one long breath. His big hands fell onto my thighs. My mind lost all desire to form coherent thoughts.

You've gone too far, Luna Mae.

My whole being lost the will to resist. His mouth found mine. We kissed passionately as he drew me closer. He gently bit my lip and then forged a path of tiny kisses down to my neck, causing shivers that ran to my very core.

This went against every decision I had made in the past forty-eight hours, but I found it impossible to pull myself away from Emmet.

"Do you want me to stop?" he whispered into my ear.

He had given me the perfect out, but instead of taking it, I slipped my hands under his t-shirt. The defined, lean muscles along his back and shoulders tensed at my touch. I hurried to pull his shirt over his head.

I marveled at the sculpted power of his tanned chest. My hands eagerly went for his firm pecs, shuddering to feel the frenzied beating of his heart.

I kept telling myself I was about to stop, but Emmet pressed his strong body against mine. It felt so good—*he* felt so good, so warm and exciting.

It wasn't like me to be so impulsive. I didn't know what the future held and if this one night was all we could have, then so be it.

Guys like casual hook-ups after all, acting so desperate for that first time, only to lose urgency once they've had a woman. Maybe this would help him move on.

I lay back on the sofa, my brain turning to goo as Emmet's

hands and lips seemingly traveled everywhere at once.

"Sophie," he said through thin breaths. "I want you. Do you want me?"

"Yes," I whispered, feeling raw need pulsing in my veins. I wrapped my legs around him to pull him closer.

My lips parted as I gasped. My eyes rolled back and closed and then—

The door was loudly kicked in and Emmet and I looked dumbly at Winter standing in the door frame. He stormed into the apartment, wielding a curved katana in his right hand.

His eyes burned like hot coals. "Disentangle from that man," he hissed.

I sat up, quickly. "Seriously, dude? A fucking sword?"

"Luna, get out. I'll take care of this." His words came out intense and deliberate, leaving no room for protest.

Did he just use my lunar name in front of a basic?

Emmet went pale. He took my hand. "Sophie, who is this guy?"

This night... fucking hell.

I faced Winter. "I'm not going anywhere. What's going on? And what do you have against my door? This is getting ridiculous."

He flipped the sword upside down, tip to the ground. "Do you have any idea with what man you are consorting?"

Consorting? What's happening?

"You know him?" I said.

Emmet sprang up, putting his shirt back on. "Why is he acting like he owns you, Sophie?" he said, looking ready to pounce.

Oh boy.

"Nobody owns me. He's just, ah—"

Winter stepped in front of me, cutting me off. "Have you been around a shapeshifter before?"

Shapeshifter. The word hit me like a fist in the stomach.

"Their aura doesn't register, Luna. Not when they don't want it to."

Emmet growled. *He actually-fucking-growled.*

I reeled back, suddenly dizzy. The only thing that kept my brain from turning to jelly was the fear that those two would go at each other and Emmet would end up really hurt—or worse.

"You've finally gone nuts," I told Winter, but my heart wasn't in it. I knew by now he spoke the truth and, besides, I was drowning in memories of the night Emmet and I had met at that sports bar.

Winter fixed his eyes on Emmet. "It's not easy to spot a shapeshifter," he said, "but this one reeks of it."

"I can't feel the slightest trace of magic," I said, avoiding Emmet's eyes, afraid of what I might see in them.

"Their auras are utterly unique. They do not originate from the Deep Down and so do not rely on relatable fields of magic. Learning to recognize them is a lost art."

"Why won't you say something, Emmet?" I pleaded.

He glanced to me vacantly, unblinking as if *I* had betrayed *him*.

"Is it true, *Dr. Groshek*?"

He considered my words. "His mention of shapeshifters does not surprise you in the least. How do you know about such things, Sophie?"

"What do you mean?"

"You weren't surprised in the slightest to hear him talk about shapeshifters as if they're real. Why is that?"

"Wait, you don't know why I would know?"

"No, that's why I'm asking. Please, enlighten me."

"Oh, please," Winter said. "You may have not known what he is, Luna, but he knew what you are, trust me."

Faint golden sparks glided over Emmet's irises. There was a belligerence in those eyes and not a speck of fear. He either had no clue what Winter was or he really believed he could take on an Immortal.

"Emmet, just go," I said. "This is my apartment, not a battleground."

In a single breath, he was by my side. "Will you be safe?"

"She will. When you're gone," Winter said, swinging the sword forward, stopping the blade inches from Emmet's throat.

Emmet laughed a little as he stepped back and circled to the door. His gait was incredibly light and flowing. How had I missed that? And where had my sweet, uncertain Emmet gone? Vanished out of existence? Had he ever existed?

The walls closed in. Everything I had felt for him, everything I believed he felt for me, were lies.

I sensed Winter standing behind me. "Let me guess," he said. "He was too good to be true. Your first encounter had a flair for the dramatic."

I stayed silent, feeling more and more like a complete fool.

Winter walked to the fridge. "There's another fucking task on my plate. I'll have to investigate this playboy shifter to see who he is and, more importantly, how he found you. That's all I needed."

"You could just kill him. That's what you do, isn't it?" I regretted the words the second they had escaped my lips.

If he heard me, he didn't react. "I don't have time for this shit."

I laughed. "Wouldn't time be of little concern to Immortals?"

In one stride, he stood inches away, breathing down onto my face. He clutched a can of root beer in his hand. *My* root beer. "Good idea," he said. "Upon your suggestion, I might kill him after all."

I realized I didn't want Emmet dead, not even if he had been playing me from the start. Not even if he was a morph operative. "Don't you dare, do you hear me? Leave him alone, whatever he is."

"Oh, is that love baring its teeth?" he said, quite amused.

"Leaving him alone is a new condition of my cooperation."

His eyes narrowed into his trademark, mocking squint. "The perils of working with a witch, known love mongers, crippled by sentimentality. What is that humans say? Ah, yes, I remember, *there's one born every minute.*"

"Better than feeling nothing," I said under my breath.

"Makes sense. You're both moon creatures. The lunar witch and the wolf shifter. Both so weak, so fucking predictable."

A wolf. Dear god.

"Promise you won't hurt him."

"That creature does not matter to me," he said. "It's you. If you forget him, then I can forget him. From now on, you will do exactly as I say."

"Fine. For how long?"

"For as long as necessary," he said. "First edict is that you will no longer mate with that wolf boy. If he shows up, you come to me. If he calls, you let me know immediately. If he sends you a letter, you hasten to deliver it to my hands. If you dream about him, you wake up and call me."

Geez, drama queen much?

I didn't dare to ask, but I deemed it obvious that Emmet wasn't a morph shifter. There was no way Winter's Immortal ass would not have gloated.

Now my turn. "Fine, I'll listen and whatever, but stop busting down my door, for one, and you do not have the right to stalk me, follow me, barge into my free time like a crazy clown invader. I have a life, even if it's about to end."

He reached inside his back pocket. "I was returning your phone. I heard it jingle in my car. When I got to the door, I sensed the wolf. I feared you were in danger. It didn't cross my mind it was mating season."

"Not funny."

"On that we can agree."

"You're infuriating," I said. "Has anyone ever told you that?"

"Yes," he said. "Throughout all the ages of man."

I tried not to smile and failed.

"Enough trifling banter," he said, firmly. "You will stand in front of the Council on Thursday."

My head spun. "In two days?"

"Clearly, you need a directive. The sooner you speak the oath the better."

Did he say oath? What type of indoctrination were they planning?

He rubbed the back of his neck, pensively. "If you have any sense at all, you won't willingly offer information to the magistrates unless they have asked for it directly." His voice turned into a raspy whisper. "And you won't repeat anything that I have told you or shown you."

"What dark secret are you hiding?"

He raised the sword so that it hid half of his face. "My leniency."

Holy shit. Winter is a gentle Immortal?

He stepped through the door but stopped on the top step.

"Don't you think of bailing out, Luna Mae. The ones you love are not on my kill list yet, but you'll find that I am very practical at getting what I need."

I shut the door gently, then leaned back against it. My heart had not stopped racing since I had first touched Emmet. His kisses lingered on my lips while Winter's words lingered in my head.

If I was a shifter, I would have changed into a rock.

Chapter 18

My eyes stung. I blinked incessantly as I adjusted to the intense orange light after being in the dark for what seemed like hours.

Someone had removed the hood from my head, blinding me for a moment. I was in a large room. I straightened my hair. I was wearing it in a high ponytail, but the forceful removal of the hood had pulled out a bunch of strands from the hair band.

Everything came into focus. The walls were wood paneled. The carpet was overly plush and very art deco. Two golden statues of double-headed eagles, the Immortal heraldic symbol, stood on pedestals on each side of wall-to-wall and floor-to-ceiling burgundy drapes.

I could not find the source of the bright light. *Strange.* I turned, expecting to find guards behind me, but I was surprisingly all alone.

Winter had disappeared a moment after we entered a black limo. He had slipped a brown hood over my head and told me not to take it off for any reason.

I had sensed some presence in the limo besides the driver but quickly fell into a haze. I had no memory of how long the car ride had been or who had helped me out of the car and into a never-ending maze of staircases.

The Seventh Council was the most powerful secret society in the history of the world. They were extremely lethal and calculated. They had held actual rule over many regions and countries in the past under assumed personas.

From Nebuchadnezzar II to Darius the Great, there had been plenty of members of the Seventh Council out in the open world running the show.

Even among Immortals the Seventh Council was feared.

In the modern era, the Council worked mostly in the shadows. The growing prevalence of technology and now universal surveillance had caused a new mission statement and near complete withdrawal from public life. Technology and weapons of war were easy enough for Immortals to defeat, but that would mean the basics would learn of their existence. The Earth would become a warzone and billions would fall, mostly basics. The Immortal imperative had always been to control the billions, not eliminate them.

Now this new foe, Chaos, and his bloodthirsty morph legions, threatened to make a mess of the very world the Immortals had spent millennia building.

The light dimmed. I felt my chest rise and fall as I tried to stay calm.

The burgundy drapes slid open with a faint hiss, revealing a dark, slightly elevated stage. A pressure squeezed my throat as a soft glow sprang forth and lit the stage. Six magistrates sat on ornate, red-velvet chairs.

A seventh, taller chair sat unused in the middle. A chill filled my lungs when I realized the throne-like seat must be reserved for the fabled Grand Magistrate, whose name alone evoked fear in all the souls who dwelled deep and all the charmed souls who walked the Earth.

I searched for Winter's face among the magistrates in vain. Instead, I managed to draw the attention of one of the female magistrates who fixed her gaze on me like a hawk on a field mouse.

Tall, blonde, with a straight nose and sharp features, it'd be difficult to guess her age if she was basic. Most would place her somewhere in her thirties. Her blue eyes had penetrating power, making me feel like I was shrinking like a drying sponge. She might be considered attractive, if you could get past that look in her eyes that she'd gladly eat you alive.

This was bad. Being at the mercy of six, maybe seven, members of the Seventh Council usually meant your life was past the point of no return. I was literally sitting in the worst seat in all the worlds. As crazy as it sounded, I desperately craved Winter's presence.

Better the devil you know and all that jazz.

A gong sounded somewhere deep below. Two guards arrived at my sides. They wore heavy black armor and carried wide-blade swords. Their big hands landed on my shoulders, immobilizing me.

The magistrates rose to their feet.

"His Majesty Grand Magistrate and Eternal Ruler Supreme Düsternis," the guards announced with one voice.

Oh god.

Düsternis. They might as well have called him the devil himself. An Immortal so powerful he let his true name be known across factions and clans of the magic world.

I clutched onto the amulet around my neck, hoping that Faion would be able to witness and document everything. We had opened a connective path between us last night, exchanging amulets infused with our own blood.

If anything were to happen to me, Faion was to warn the Lunar Order.

I felt a sudden, insatiable panic that everything would go wrong. My magic felt small and subdued since stepping into the Immortal realm.

Even so, frail sparkles lingered beneath my skin, shimmering like thin breaths on a cold day, waiting for a chance to reassert their full force.

True to his nature, Düsternis made a dramatic entrance. A white spotlight shone on him. His long, red cape floated across the stage, giving the impression his feet never touched the ground. His straight hair reached his shoulders, dark brown sprinkled with silver. His trimmed beard had more salt than pepper. He was built like a bull.

In his left hand, Düsternis held an eagle-headed scepter made of gold with silver detailing. It was rumored that he was six thousand years old and one phase away from becoming Eternal, but his ambition was a better match for the temporal world than it was for the mystical halls of the Eternals.

Düsternis hungered for power and control, hardly god-like.

His voice boomed. "Are we now in the presence of the low-level servant of Selene?"

No one answered. *I guess that was a rhetorical question.*

His godly eyes latched onto mine. I swallowed even though there was no spit left in my mouth. I somehow knew it was not an answer from me that he wanted.

The female magistrate who had been scrutinizing me now leaned over to whisper into another magistrate's ear—a hairless, severe-looking Immortal with sparkling bronze skin.

The hairless magistrate stood immediately. "Grand Magistrate and Ruler Supreme, I present to you Luna Mae, born of the Lunar Order, currently self-exiled in the mortal enclave of San Diego, a recruit of Chief Magistrate Winter. She is, by all measures, a recruit of little substance."

Okay, my hype man totally blows. Sheesh.

Düsternis sat and raised his forefinger. A wave of unbridled power crashed into me, draining me of every speck of energy I possessed.

By his sheer will alone, the Grand Magistrate invaded my blood cells, blocking my vital functions and shutting down my energy core. I clutched my stomach with both hands as it twisted with burning, suffocating pain.

I thought I'd faint. His force clamped down on my skull. I feared it would crack and shatter, but as a scream formed on my lips, the force seeped down my neck, then spilled onto my shoulders and dove down my back, like sharp, jagged knives jabbing into my flesh.

The pain in my belly burned like the flames of hell. I crumbled to my knees and vomited green bile all over their plush carpet.

It serves you right, assholes.

Two black boots stepped in front of me. *His* boots. Winter. I raised my eyes, doing my best version of a fearless stare. Rage bubbled inside my skull. I could kill him with my bare hands.

Except, I can't.

The bastard winked at me.

Who does that?

I closed my eyes and shook my head to make sure I wasn't dreaming. Nope, he was there, smiling and apparently in grand spirits. His back was to the magistrates, so they probably missed the whole rousing show.

Yet, there was no gloating in Winter's smile, no arrogance for a change. Should I have been encouraged? Were we playing this game together? Were we somehow, beyond my understanding, winning?

He spun back and with one leaping step cleared ten feet of stage to bow to Düsternis, then took a seat behind the other magistrates. There was a whole second row behind the first that I hadn't noticed.

The tall blonde turned back and whispered to Winter. He nodded twice, then whispered back. She stole a glance at me. Her face had become even more sinister. She nodded after Winter said something else.

Are they talking about me?

The pressure inside my skull and stomach intensified again, emptying me of all pointless thoughts. The swelling agony was so overwhelming it would cut me in two if I didn't find a way to push back.

My eyelids fell shut and did not reopen. Winter's face found me there in my private dark, smiling, winking, trusting. Even if it was a trick, it was good to think he had some faith in me and in *us*.

Gathering every particle of energy that I had left, I focused on a tiny pain-free spot on the top of my head. I guided my feeble reserves to that very spot and willed it to expand.

My teeth clenched as I began to tremble, the effort forcing me down onto all fours. A blazing heat oozed out from the top of my head all the way to my toes, gradually cooling my sweating body and relieving the internal pressure.

I had held the Grand Magistrate's power in check, freeing

my body from his viselike possession. His terrible hold ebbed and shrank as my own power built itself up slowly but surely.

Düsternis motioned me with his right forefinger.

I stood up, meeting his gaze.

"Adequate," he said. "Your pure energy control and training in the sorcery arts of the under realm are sufficient to fulfill the task at hand."

Immortals and their goddamned tests.

"I am Magistrate Argos," the bald one said. "Chief Magistrate Winter has briefed you on the nature of your cooperation. On the sixth day of the month of October, Selene will enter her metamorphic phase. You shall be present at the epicenter to exert your power in order to diminish the impact."

"Are the particulars clear, child of Selene?" Düsternis asked.

"Yes, Your Majesty," I said.

I feared I came off sarcastic, but he just nodded, then drew in the magistrates to form a circle around him.

"Excuse me," I heard myself say. "There's just one thing."

Their heads turned so slow I thought they all shared a single brain.

Winter would not be pleased. He had specifically told me to say nothing unless asked a question, but to hell with him.

I put on my innocent face. "Will this have to be done every century?"

The Grand Magistrate's eyes turned into tiny slits,

burning with disdain.

"What is your meaning?" Argos said.

"I mean, in a hundred years or so, upon the next metamorphic Moon, wouldn't the morphs be in hiding somewhere waiting to give it another try?"

Argos jolted back as if punched in the chest. "There won't be another try."

No, there won't. It dawned on me that the plan was to kill all the morph shifters when they were at their weakest, in mid-morphing, and probably capture, or kill if they could, as many rebel Immortals as possible.

They wanted me to be the catalyst for a genocide. Or, at very least, extreme wartime atrocities.

The end justifying the means is bullshit logic in my book.

I chose my words carefully. "You will slaughter the morphs and my magic is needed to facilitate the slaughter." Winter was about to burst at the seams, but there was no stopping me. "You tell me they're evil, that they must be stopped, but how do I know you're any better? Why should I take your word?"

"They kill for sport," Argos said, his face turning into a red ball of rage. "They are not charmed, not even human nor beast. They are flesh rippers."

The look on all their faces was the same.

"You are afraid of them," I said. "Why?"

I stole a glance at Winter. His face was unreadable, revealing none of the fear that the others, even the Grand

Magistrate, revealed. He, no doubt, expected my insolence. Already, he knew me too well.

Winter stepped in front of Argos. "Once they shift, if they shift, the morphs will have a forty-eight-hour feeding frenzy to spread like wildfire, eating every basic they see until they sniff out the other realms, including the Deep Down. Their hunger will not cease. Does that answer your question?"

Winter does not play. Should have remembered that.

I had a compulsive defiance that kind of felt like a death wish just then with half a dozen or more magistrates glaring at me.

"Dare not test our patience, lunar witchling," Düsternis hissed. "You will do as commanded or you will die and then many others will die because you did not assist us. If you comply willingly, our magnanimity will allow you to return to your San Diego. Your name will be erased from the Eternal annals. You will have the basic life of the sickly human, as you desire."

Magnanimity? Ha! These people were accidental comedians. If only he knew I had heard with my own, well, with Faion's ears, that their first impulse was to murder me.

"What about my Order?" I said.

"What about it?" Argos said.

"Will you stop hunting us? If I help you, will there finally be peace between us?"

There was a long silence. Not a popular question.

"That depends entirely on the Order," the blonde said.

Her voice was deep for a woman but melodic and with a strange accent, almost Nordic. "We can only stay out of your Order's way if they stay out of ours."

Okay, that Immortal bitch was spinning some fake news right now. The Lunar Order would have happily stayed out of the Immortal way if they had not caused so much death and destruction over the last thousand years.

The Lunar Order would never turn a blind eye to the tyrannies of man no matter who was behind it and the Immortals probably knew that.

For now, the fact they had negotiated with a lunar witch was better than nothing. It was a definite first. I'd take it.

"Bind me to the oath," I said.

All magistrates stood. A cone of red light flooded down on me, trapping me inside its blinding glow.

"The light burns in your heart," Argos said. "Break the oath and both will be extinguished."

He walked to me and pressed on my temples with both hands. "You are bound to the Seventh Council until the end of your days. You will not speak of the Eternal Beings, you will not profess deceits to the Magistrates of the Council, and you will not run or hide from us."

"Yes, I so pledge," I said, my voice barely audible.

The ancient words of the oath spilled forth from his mouth and then I repeated each word three times.

Herrat.

Laiman.

Forethor.

Manghas.

Ferom.

When the blade pricked my left palm, I screeched. Argos bent over and licked the blood clean off my hand.

WTAF!

"You are bound to the Council of Eternal Beings," he said. "Your blood magic flows inside me now. You shall return to this spot to be released upon completion of your task."

THE GUARDS LED ME to a room with a small table, two chairs and a lamp.

When they left, I let out a sigh of relief I had been holding back since Düsternis stepped onto the Court stage.

I held onto my amulet with both hands. "Faion, if you're listening, I think I might have just made the biggest mistake of my life. On the bright side, I may have seen the last of that egotistical ass, Winter."

Too late did I realize that he had stepped into the room behind me.

I was not the same frightened girl he had first met. I refused to even acknowledge he was in the room.

I would tell him to go to hell, but we were already there.

He reached from behind and grabbed the amulet. He brought it to his mouth and spoke into it like a microphone.

"Mr. Trice, we will speak soon of your impression of today's session. As for your friend, she will never stop seeing me, for I am not a man that any young woman can ever forget. Each night she will find me in her dreams."

My mouth gaped wide open as he sauntered out of the room.

Chapter 19

THE IMMORTAL BASTARD TOLD Faion I'd find him in my dreams and took off without a word. I needed to speak to him while awake, not dreaming, regarding the details of the upcoming night of the morphs just nine days away.

Better him than that uptight Argos dude.

Three days had gone by since my oath and not a word from Winter or Argos or any of the magistrates. Every day I grew a little more furious.

And what about Winter's promise to escort me home every night to protect me from those gnarly beasts and their sordid handlers?

It wasn't like him to pull a disappearing act. Could he have made a misstep? Had something gone wrong? There was no way such a calculated sonofabitch would leave a college girl to her own devices when it came to subduing the metamorphic Moon.

No, something must have detained him. Maybe Chaos led his renegade army of Immortals straight to the heart of the Magistrate Court and all hell broke loose. At least that would explain why Winter (and the entire Council for that matter) had lost interest in me.

That would not, however, explain why the Deep Down had yet to issue a warning to all magic users. A brutal insurrection among Immortals would not stay hidden from witches, sorcerers, diviners and telepaths—not to mention the insane reverberations that would have disturbed the orbs.

A new clarity dawned on me. This was yet another test.

Fucking Winter. You need to grow up.

My heart jumped when I heard a muffled sound outside. I *hoped* it would be him. How pathetic.

The sound got louder, feet running on pavement and then stumbling into something, a rubber trash bin maybe. That ruled out Winter. Tripping over his own feet would not be a thing of which he was capable.

Perhaps it was Emmet, trying to grab my attention without having to knock on my door. So many conflicting emotions surfaced. That whole Emmet thing was so messed up. I didn't want to think about all that.

Whatever we had going between us was based on a string of half-truths and omissions—if not downright lies. If he was a shapeshifter, he probably knew I was a witch. And now he knew I hung out with Immortals. There was no way he'd knock on my door. It'd have been nice to get some answers from him, but then again, the fact he hadn't reached out was probably the only answer I needed.

And he claimed he'd move to Sweden to be close to me. Men.

Another sound outside—*thump, thump, thump*—like fingers tapping glass or hard plastic. I caught a glimpse of movement outside the window, flapping wings whizzing by in a flurry.

Shit. I felt it now. There was an unfamiliar etheric field outside, circling my home.

Filling my lungs to steady my nerves, I opened the window and leaned on the windowsill to have a peek outside.

A knock at the door startled me, causing me to jerk my head up and smash the back of it against the window.

I rubbed my head and walked to the door. Something warm wet my fingers. Blood. I had cut open my scalp. Perfect.

Magic hissed in my ears. "Calm down," I whispered. "We got this."

The peephole framed Lily's lovely face like a renaissance painting.

I let her in. She strolled to the sofa with the casual assuredness of a girl who was not being asked to fight against flesh rippers anytime soon.

"Hey, baby girl," she said, taking off her peach, zip-up hoodie.

"Hey, Lil, what's up?" Before she took notice, I managed

to wipe the blood off my fingers with some brown napkins that came with a Panda Express takeout last night.

"Did you lose your phone?" she said with a pout. "Or is it your plan never to text me again? I blew up your phone with messages. And every text was extremely important in the moment I hit send."

She wore a blue skater skirt and a black and white striped tee that highlighted her striking curves. Her radiant skin gleamed with lightly applied bronzer and aqua-blue eye shadow.

In contrast, I was still wearing the old San Diego Chargers shirt I had slept in and it was past noon. I hadn't showered or brushed my teeth yet, even though I had to be at work in less than an hour.

"That's exactly what happened," I said, sitting next to her. "That and I'm just buried lately. Look at me. I'm just tired."

"You do look like the hottest of messes right now," she said, studying all my *ratchet* qualities. "I thought you'd be shacked up with Emmet the Frog."

Not a frog exactly, but you're in the ballpark, Lil.

"That's done," I said.

"Sophie..." Lily looked worried, and she really was, because she wanted good things for me. "What happened?"

"Another time," I said.

"Wait, did you chase him off?"

I rolled my eyes. "Why do you always think I chase them off?"

"I don't always think that," she said. "I might have maybe once or twice mentioned that you should let them fall in love before you make it clear you are the funnier and smarter one. You know about the male ego."

"It was nothing like that. Not this time."

She studied my face with suspicion. "You sure this has nothing to do with that tall drink of muscle milk I saw here last week? Uncle Viking?"

"Gross. Lily, no. How about we talk about your love life?"

"Thought you'd never ask. Rocco asked me out."

Wow. I didn't see that coming. "Holy amazeballs, Lil. How? Why?"

She bent her face. "Did you just ask *why*?"

"You know I didn't mean it that way."

She smiled ear to ear and hugged me. "You totally should have meant it that way, because I'm not worthy. Rocco's a fucking god!"

"You're totally worthy and I'm happy for you."

"First things first." She pulled out an antique jewelry box from her purse. "Lucia went shopping. She found deals and thought you would like this."

She offered me the box. I scooched back on the sofa, feeling dizzy. Lucia buying me a gift was strange—accepting it would be crazy. Even if Faion was wrong about her, I couldn't be too careful. The fate of the world and all.

"What's the matter?" Lily said with a frown.

"Um, I... whoa, your mother bought me a gift."

She shrugged. "People buy people gifts, yeah. I'm the delivery girl. Gifts are often thought of as a good thing, Soph. A friendly gesture to make our days a little bit brighter. It's Lucia, she's very impetuous. Zero clue what she's thinking, your guess is as good as mine."

"It's kind of surprising."

"Yeah, I think that's the point. C'mon, open it. Lucia said she immediately thought of you when she saw it and had to get it."

She had me cornered. No witty way out. I took the box. My fingers fumbled with the bow wrapped around it. Seemed harmless enough. It'd be hard to fit anything truly evil in such a small container.

I untied the bow. Inside the box, there was a colorful llama brooch made with bread dough and glue according to the label.

"It's really... nice," I said, biting my lip.

Lily took the brooch out of the box. "Ah, it's Ecuadorian bread dough art. Lucia has good taste. Here, let me pin it on you."

The moment she clicked the safety pin on my shirt, an aggressive wave of power streamed through me, crashing against my magic. My body shivered as my elemental energy fought back, pushing out the intruder.

Quickly, I ripped the llama pin off my shirt and stepped on it, again and again, until it turned into a gooey mess.

The hostile magic got severed from me like a broken

string, but my magic still whipped around in my veins, shocked and threatening to tear my body apart and strike out at everything in sight.

I picked up the mangled llama and set it on fire inside the kitchen sink, then washed the debris down the garbage disposal.

"What the hell just happened?" I heard Lily's shaken voice behind me.

She had been saying my name over and over before that, but I had heard it faintly and from a great distance away, as if in a vacuum.

I didn't dare turn and face her. "You have to go now, Lil," I said with a quiet growl. "I have not been feeling well. Don't come back here. It's best we don't see each other for a while. Don't ask me to explain."

"I'm just—" There was concern and fear in her voice.

I sensed her hand reaching for my shoulder. I spun away. "You need to go. Trust me on this, Lily. Please."

Her lips trembled. She was breathless, heartbroken. "First you don't text back for days and now this? And you ask for trust? You're looking at me like I'm the devil. What the hell is happening? Talk to me."

I opened the door for her, my eyes watering. "Just go."

The tears on her cheeks almost brought me to my knees. She snatched her jacket and walked out without a word.

Oh shit, oh shit, oh shit...

I paced the room, belligerent mutterings spilling out of

my mouth. I turned away my best friend. My heart felt like it was being torn out of my chest, but I had to push her away. Violent days were ahead.

A chill spread over me. Lucia was knee deep in forbidden magic. She knew I was from the Deep Down. Why else would she have sent that evil charm, loaded with an obstruction spell?

To be honest, I was mostly pissed she had risked her own daughter and my best friend on such a dangerous undertaking.

Could I even trust Lily again?

I swatted the troubling thought away. Lily was an innocent bystander. I had to believe that or, what was the point of anything? I would protect Lily no matter what, even if that meant leaving her life for good.

And where the hell was Winter? I needed him. The only person I could count on I had to chase away. And now what was I left with? All these ugly souls who couldn't care less if I lived or died.

If they even have souls.

I tapped my fingernails on the coffee table. I had managed to summon him before with a powerful ritual that almost destroyed me. But now I was under a blood oath that restricted use of my magic. And my free will, really.

I picked up the phone and texted Faion.

Need u to help me find W. IRL ASAP.

Sitting on my couch, waiting for Faion's text, I wondered if I would ever again be allowed to walk free with my friends in the basic world.

Chapter 20

THE LOCK MADE A clicking sound when I tried the handle. A fraction of a second later, an electric jolt pulsed through my fingers.

With a yelp, I spat on my hand to cool down the burn. I pushed gently against the door and was shocked again, but this time I was better prepared as I formed a thin barrier of elemental energy to guard my skin.

I had come to the right place. It wasn't electricity or fancy tech that had knocked me back—it was a protective ward, powerful enough to repel a small army.

The place was boobytrapped. I sensed wards, protective spells and energy shields strategically placed in layers to reinforce their effectiveness.

It would take hours, if not days, to break the wards, but, luckily, all I had to do was bypass them and I was pretty sure I knew the cheat code.

I lowered myself to eye level with the lock to use my secret weapon, the true name of the man who owned the condo and had installed the magic that sustained the ancient wards.

"*Winter*," I whispered, followed by a disyllabic spell that was as potent as devastating when used in conjunction with a ritual name—UNSEAL.

The magic ward on the door hissed and smoked before it split in two and retreated to allow me entrance.

I stepped into a dense quagmire of protective spells and wards connected to each other through elaborate witchcraft patterns. A thief would be striped with burns before they took a second step in here.

Some of the spells used to bind together the crisscrossing elements were simple spells I recognized—others were beyond my skill. It would take me a lifetime to defuse them, and even then, they'd renew themselves almost instantly as that was how they had been designed. Only their master could truly shut them down. His name alone would not protect me. The wrath of the ancient guards slithering about the condo would erupt if I disturbed their balance in the slightest.

I switched on a lamp and walked about the living room on tiptoes. Unlike the shitty car he drove, this place must have cost a small fortune.

Situated on the waterfront in the most hip area of La Jolla, it featured an open floor plan with cherry hardwood flooring and huge sliding glass doors that provided stunning views of the Pacific Ocean. Contemporary art hung on the walls and the kitchen set the standard for state-of-the-art.

The wards shadowed my every move, unsure of my intentions, white lines glowing inches away from my feet but not daring to touch me.

Winter's name was a weapon like no other in my hands.

But it shouldn't be. When I left the Deep Down, I vowed to live a magic-free life in the basic world. In the span of a few weeks, I had violated that promise to my Order a hundred times over.

I had basically twisted Faion's arm to get him to help. He used a series of scouting spells to locate this condo, despite his certainty that I was going to get him killed, or worse, if Winter found out.

And now I had used the etheric essence of an Immortal Magistrate's name to commit an act of territorial invasion.

I managed to sit down on his couch without triggering the wards.

Minutes went by, then an hour and another. Sunset came and went, the soft rosy heavens turning into a dark palette sprinkled with silver specks.

What if Winter didn't come home tonight or ever? The condo was immaculate—in fact, it looked untouched, possibly for days. On the other hand, I had smelled fresh soap and aftershave when I first entered. He had likely taken a shower that morning.

I became bored. I'd love to go through his desk drawers,

but I doubted his wards would allow it. I took my phone out of my jacket and jotted down some random thoughts in the notepad.

It was close to one in the morning when I jolted awake after dozing off in the fetal position on his couch. I heard steps outside the door. I sat up and straightened my hair, making myself look alert and totally chill.

The door swung open and Winter walked through it. He saw me and stopped, all the color draining from his face.

It was then I noticed the sword in his hand. He sensed his wards had been disturbed, but obviously did not think me capable of the feat.

Insulting.

I stretched and yawned. "Hi, Jonas," I said, grinning.

He shut the door, locked it, then regarded me with a heavy glare. He was not one bit amused.

"Jonas Sandell," I went on, pleased with his frustration. "Sounds like a Viking or at least a major shareholder of IKEA."

"Are you finished?" he said, placing the sword on the table.

"Yes, Jonas, I'm finished."

"I bet Mr. Trice regrets the day he met you," he said. "The things you've been forcing him to do are not healthy choices."

"Anyone could find out the name of a property owner," I said. "I hardly needed help."

"Not the name, the location," he said as he set a pile of junk mail on his counter. "But I am too tired to discuss. We both know the truth."

"Do Immortals get tired?"

"Only if they have to deal with you."

"That was a joke," I said, almost proud of him.

"It really wasn't," he said, sitting down in an armchair. "There is, however, something we need to discuss."

"I agree."

"You used my name," he said, punching each word. "You have violated my trust at the highest degree."

"*Trust*? Did you say *trust*? That's most definitely a joke. You take me to your freaking Council of prehistoric bullies, you force me to take a blood oath and then you vanish, leaving me to fend for myself. Boom. Trust broken."

"You used my ritual name to find my home and to break my wards. Not only violating our bond, but your bond to the Council and your bond to your own Order for that matter."

"You should talk, you've always used my ritual name."

"And I retained respect for your name. I honored its ancient line of magic. You spat on mine. Give me a good reason I shouldn't inform the Council."

"Hmm, I don't know, because then you'd have to admit all the secrets you have knowingly allowed Faion and me to witness?"

We were at an impasse. Neither of us were willing to accept fault.

"You are more than expected," he said. "You're not as naïve as you appear, you're not a victim, you're a..."

"A witch?" I put in. "Damn right I am. Never forget it."

"I was going to say a worthy opponent, but yeah, you are a witch, or at least something that rhymes with it."

It was my turn to glare at him. "What did you just say?"

"I thought you liked jokes?"

"Maybe that's not your thing," I said. "*Mean* is more your thing. And *manipulation*. And even when you were sort of supportive, it was all a big, fat act of deception and psychological violence."

"You'll soon be rid of me. One week and that's it."

"If I make it out alive."

He flared his nostrils, then took off his jacket. I was surprised to see he wore a tight, olive t-shirt and slim-fit charcoal chinos. He looked like a normal guy—a ripped, streamlined, drop-dead gorgeous grown-ass man, but he'd totally blend into the world of basics.

"You'll be fine," he said. "I'll make sure of it."

"Dude, you're so all over the place. First it was like, '*You will help me, or I'll kill you*', then it was like, '*I'll protect you. I'll boil hearts for you.*' Oh, wait, and that totally weird thing you said about me finding you in my dreams."

"I warned you not to get close to me."

I locked on his eyes. "Maybe you're having dreams about me."

"I rarely sleep."

"Daydreams, then. And you totally lose it when I'm with guys."

"I've been with the beauties of the ages, Luna Mae, your modern flair and schoolgirl charm is fine for the day, but hardly registers with a man like me."

"Oh, so it does register," I said. "I didn't expect you to freely admit it."

"Clever, but I neither dream nor feel jealousy," he said. "And when you say you were with *guys*... you mean a shifter and a man who prefers men?"

"Is that it, Mr. Ikea, you prefer men as well?"

I did love getting under his indestructible skin.

He took a moment. "To you, I prefer almost anything," he said.

"Keep telling yourself that," I said, tired of the topic.

I walked over to grab a heavy hardback off a shelf. I leafed through it, not to read, just to enjoy its weight and old-book smell.

Winter snatched it away and put it back on the shelf.

"Don't touch without permission, Luna."

"Sophie," I said, raising my voice.

"What?"

"When we're in the basic world, I'm Sophie and you're Jonas."

"Sophie," he said, "you're quite the... witch."

I glanced side-eyed at him. "I see what you did there."

"Perhaps, you see too much," he said. "Wisdom has a sharp edge."

"That's kind of true," I said, moving about his living space. "Hey, that ice queen at the Court, was she one of those *beauties of the ages* you've been with? You know, the ones who are so much more than me?"

"I do not submit to gossip," he said, frowning.

I had touched a nerve. "I saw the way she looked at you, like all her ice might melt away with one touch of your fingers."

"You want to question me about my love life?"

"Do you have one?"

"I do not have time for such dalliances. The world is at stake."

"Hmm, maybe I should speak with her next time we meet."

He exhaled, his eyes serious as hell. "If you know what's good for you, you'll stay away from Chazona."

Playing with fire was never my forte. Literally and figuratively. I never messed with fire. And yet... "Chazona? Really? That doesn't quite roll off the tongue, does it? I bet it's distracting as hell to say while in the throes of passion."

He walked to the kitchen, ignoring me. I followed him.

"I received a basic's evil spell while you were out screwing *Arizona*. My best friend delivered it unknowingly."

I regretted my words immediately. Winter had been acting reasonable. There was no reason to provoke him.

His cold blue eyes calmly found mine, freezing my soul. "I have every confidence you handled it accordingly. If you cannot shatter a silly little spell by now, then we are all doomed."

"Oh, okay, yeah, I'm good," I said, wondering if I had overreacted with Lily and perhaps was too quick to link Lucia to Chaos and the morphs.

"Today's our little secret," Winter said, equally eager to erase our conversation and my misdemeanor break-in from our memories forever.

"Great. Agreed," I said. "I really needed to see you. It's the only reason I broke the rules."

His shoulders tensed. "I come on too strong, I know, but that is not without reason. My responsibilities are great."

I held his stare for a moment. "I guess I know how that feels. I want to explode all the time, too. We're deep in this thing."

He hesitated, then grabbed his jacket. "Yes, we are, indeed. Come with me, I'll show you what I've been working on."

Chapter 21

THE NIGHT HUMMED LIKE a living organism as Winter and I climbed a steep bluff just south of the border. We stayed low when we reached the top. Down below in a small clearing, a dozen tents surrounded a stone fire pit. Through binoculars, I zoomed in on the eight shifters gathered around the high flames.

Five guards were in human form and two were in beast form (one wolf, one cheetah), and the final guard was in a state of mid-shifting: half-human, half-beast, and dripping with some sort of wet membranes. Horrific.

"They set up camp last week," Winter said. "They bring in a few human captives every night. I want to find out what they do with them."

"This feels like a trap," I said.

"Possible, but unlikely. Only the Grand Magistrate and I know this location. It's doubtful Chaos even knows we know about his plans for the morphs. Only the Council has that privileged information and each magistrate has proven over many centuries to be extreme loyalists."

"Here in the dirt world, we call that extremism."

"Exactly," he said. "They will do what's necessary."

Okay, so he missed my point.

"So why did we climb up here?"

"They're hiding something vital. I'd bet my life on it."

I smirked. "Tough time paying that bet since you can't die."

"Then I guess we'll pay with yours," he said with a grin before pushing my face against the ground.

Immortal horseplay sucks.

"I'm a girl," I said, spitting dirt from my mouth. "Save that crap for your Immortal buddies."

"Quiet, girl," he said.

One of the men below swung his axe and bludgeoned the wolf's skull. The wolf yelped achingly before going suddenly silent.

"That's the alpha," Winter said. "He's displaying his authority."

The alpha shifter was a massive man, at least six foot six, and he had a neck like a bulldog. He ranted at the fallen wolf who lay whimpering.

Two other men lifted and then escorted the wolf away.

"Does the Seventh Council always meet in the SoCal Court?" I said.

"We move as needed. There is no base."

"The gypsy life," I said. "Do you pack up and leave when it's over?"

He thought for a moment, which was unusual. "You'll miss me?"

I shrugged. "So you keep saying."

"I am aware of my unpleasant side," he said, "but it would be far worse with any other magistrate."

Was that a Winter apology?

"Definitely better you than *Chazama.*"

"The alpha shifted," he said, "he's on the move."

I glimpsed a wolf the size of a Kodiak bear run off into the night.

Winter quickly formed a misty cocoon around me. "No matter what, stay here and stay inside the shield," he said and took off before I could protest.

Of course, he'd hunt the alpha and leave me alone. What else was new?

I kept my head down, occasionally taking a quick peek below. The shifters that were in human form disappeared into tents. When they came back out, they had two children with them.

I looked through the binoculars. Two young girls, around seven years old, looking lost and worried. There was no way to tell if they were basics or shifters with all the auras floating around, but the fact their hands were tied told me all I needed to know.

The cheetah circled the girls while the mid-shifter twirled a large knife. The blade reflected the dancing flames in the fire pit. Somehow, the mid-shifter had kept his human face and human hands while the rest of him had shifted into a huge panther. I shuddered, knowing he had designed himself just for this moment of horror.

My heart pounded in my throat when a shifter kicked the terrified girls down onto their knees and forced them to rest their heads on blocks of wood.

Magic raced to my fingertips like an avalanche of hate. I surged to my feet. A ball of energy escaped my right hand, racing down to the fire pit.

Tongues of fire exploded out in an expanding circle, blasting two shifters off their feet.

They bounced off their backs instantly and landed back on their feet.

Now they all sniffed the air and turned in my direction, like a single beast with multiple sets of eyes.

There was no way I could stop them from up here. My energy would not strike at full power from such a distance. They were alert and quick as hell, they had brushed off my strike like a mosquito bite, and now they knew where I was. They'd duck and leap over every blow I delivered until they got to me.

Panic rose in my chest. Not for me but for those little girls. I charged down the bluff, magic raging in my blood, blindly hurling energy jolts.

All seven morphs formed a defensive line at the bottom of the hill, baring their teeth at me. Everything blurred as I ran faster than ever, trying to get to them before they all shifted.

I blasted the first morph that got in my way, setting him on fire like he was made of paper. The second shifter I targeted leaped aside to avoid the blast, then spun on the spot and grabbed my arm. Claws dug deep inside my back, ripping skin and flesh apart—the cheetah shifter.

I screamed so loud I hurt my own ears, the pain cutting across my back like a hot iron.

Winter's shield. I'd walked straight out of it, forgetting to form any protection of my own. He was right. Anger was my worst enemy.

The shifters piled on. I collapsed, hitting the ground like a rock, their weight suffocating the life out of me.

Blood pounded viciously in my head. Elemental energy streamed out of me, producing an electric current that grew fiercer than I could control.

The unruly power consumed my limbs. Underneath me, the earth shook. My body began to hum like I was about to explode. The energy spilled out of my hands in dual torrents.

Multi-colored currents of raw energy expanded above the shifters. Gritting my teeth, I concentrated until my skull ached. The unbridled power suddenly condensed into itself and imploded with a sonic boom.

Instinctively, I spun a shield around the girls to keep them from being incinerated alongside the beasts.

Everything detonated at once. The raging force skipped over the girls' shield and tore through morph flesh while vaporizing the tents, leaving me and the children untouched.

I stood stunned as the shifters squealed, their bodies melting and falling to pieces like they were made of wax.

My senses returned to me slowly. *The children.* I scrambled over the mutilated morph bodies to get to them. With a thin line of magic, I cut the ties on their hands. I used my body to shield them from the gruesome dead.

A distant sound of hollering and galloping reached my ears.

I wheeled around and crouched down, taking both girls in my arms. Their little faces were covered in dirt and ashes, lips trembling.

"Listen to me," I said. "You girls have to run now. Run up that hill and down the other side. Go to the road, you'll see a red car. Get inside, lock the doors and stay low. I'll come for you."

They ran. *Good girls.* I turned to ready for more morphic shifters materializing from the darkness of the canyon.

Shit, oh shit.

There were a whole lot of them, too many, maybe fifty. I hoped someone would find the girls. I would be lucky to hold these beasts back for more than a few minutes, but I had to try... the girls had to have a chance.

The morphs ran at me at irregular speeds. Some fast, some slow, some in straight lines, others circling around.

They began tearing the clothes off their human bodies as they transformed one-by-one into an army of oversized beasts—wolves, bears, cougars, even bulls and an eagle.

Claws and snouts pumped forth, fur and horns and a hundred yellow eyes came charging as they were being born into existence. At least the Moon had not gone completely metamorphic yet, limiting their beastly forms to species of this world.

I was struggling, rapidly losing my vigor as a good chunk of energy had spilled out of my body already and I'd had no time to replenish my core.

Gathering whatever I had left, I tried to create a shield.

The morphs crashed against my shield like rabid dogs, lusting feverishly for my flesh. One-by-one they were zapped by the energy in the shield but wouldn't give up despite their scorched hides. Their rage grew ever more maddening and reckless.

They kept chewing on my shield even as gums bled and snouts sizzled.

Their paws and hooves banged down like giant fists, rattling the shield until pain radiated through my arms and neck. I felt my body shutting down, unwilling to exert so much energy to sustain my shield.

My head spun about, trying to avoid the horrific faces of the sinister predators that wanted nothing else except to eat me alive.

Then I felt him.

My eyes blinked and they found him in the distance.

Winter... running to me.

The tall, majestic, fierce Jonas Sandell racing to my rescue.

He pounced on the morphs like a thunderclap, rage taking over his features, killing all that stood in his way. He twisted necks and ripped off heads with his bare hands, crushed windpipes and blew knee joints.

His clothes were being shredded by desperate claws and fangs. His flesh tore and bled, but somehow mended nearly as fast like a video game.

He was reducing their number as he turned red from blood and exertion. No force on Earth could defeat him when he had that fierce look on his face. The morphs figured that out. They had not survived this long by being slow learners. Those that yet breathed retreated, quickly, as if it was all a dream.

Winter chased after them. He'd not rest until they were all dead.

I dropped, gagging for air, unable to sustain the shield one more second.

A blade burst through my back, slicing right through me. Shocked, I looked down to see the blade's tip sticking out right above my stomach.

Fluid spilled out of my mouth. I touched my lips, feeling the sticky warmth of blood on my fingers. A thunderbolt of energy split the morph in half as he dragged the blade out of me in hopes of stabbing me again.

Two other morphs scurried away. The dull echo of their retreat rang loudly in my ears. The world spun. In the distance, running back to me, there was Winter, naked, covered in blood, muscles twitching like a god.

A nice final image before fading away.

Chapter 22

STRANDS OF MOTHER'S AUBURN hair danced on the sea breeze. Her fine hair was always dancing and shining and kissed by sunshine. She smiled that slow-rising smile every time she looked at me, and my small heart rose with it, up to the golden red magic of her breathtaking, windswept hair.

I am the Sun and you are the Moon, she always said as the waves rolled in and the sea crashed against her legs and wet the hem of her yellow dress and made my beautiful mother shiver with nature's pure joy.

I wanted to go there, return there, to where my heart was bursting and my soul was as beautiful as mother, but copper and salt clogged my throat.

Mother faded when the void swallowed the Sun.

My eyes opened to his dirty face. I coughed blood onto his bare chest.

Winter dropped to his knees, slipping an arm under my

neck. My weary head fell against his shoulder.

"The Sun is gone," I whispered. "Time to sleep."

He took my face in his hands. His eyes were full of panic.

"That look," I said, "it's that look when someone's dying."

He did not deny it, he just turned away.

"You'll have to heal me. I'm not immortal, you see," I said with a smile. "I break."

"I can't heal you," he said. "Your heart. The damage is severe."

I was too tired to cheer him up or find a lovely thing to say. What a sad life and even sadder end.

Sad, but not pointless. I saved two children.

I struggled to breathe. "Go... find another witch."

"No," he said. "I can't heal you, but you can."

I couldn't laugh or move. I had cast my final spell.

"Concentrate. Use your core," he insisted.

"I don't heal. I'm not immortal."

His eyes burned red. "Yes, you are, Luna."

"No."

"Then why do you yet live? Your heart and lungs were punctured through with a rusted blade. And here you are... breathing... talking."

His strange, metaphorical pep talk did nothing for me.

He raised me up. The pain nearly blinded me.

"I'm serious," he said. "You've done this before. Heal yourself."

My Immortal handler had lost his shit.

I curled my fingers behind his neck, my head resting on his shoulder. My eyes grew heavy. Dying wrapped in those strong arms was a good end. Good enough.

He shook me. Roughly, violently.

Yep, stark, raving mad.

My chest stung as if he was ripping it apart. My blurred vision took on black spots now. I was falling into an abyss from which I would not climb out.

Winter stuck his fingers in my wound and opened it wider. I could only see white now and feel absolute pain. He reached inside my chest. He squeezed my mangled heart.

I was gone now. The pain was all there was—just one eternal scream.

"Now," he yelled. "Activate your eternal core."

My lungs stopped. Oxygen drained from my blood. My heart stopped. I knew it with absolute certainty. Yet, my mind grew more lucid... my hands buzzed with magic and energy.

I could see again. I could see Winter's bloodied face. I choked on air, gasping and spitting as oxygen refilled my lungs. My chest rose and fell again. The pain diminished as my hand found my wound. Tissue and flesh met, bonded and sealed. I became whole.

"The witch that heals," Winter said. He kissed the top of my head.

My god, he was naked. I was in his arms and he was as nude as the day he was born, but with quite a bit more muscle.

"Put me down," I said, sternly. Then it hit me. "The children!"

He raised an eyebrow. "Children?"

"Yes." I staggered off and began to run up the bluff, adrenaline taking over completely. I couldn't believe I was both alive and running.

Winter caught me in full stride—yes, still... native. "What's going on?"

"Two little girls," I said, short of breath. "Those assholes were about to sacrifice them. I had no choice. I had to attack."

We reached the top in time to see an ambulance driving away. Two women in a sedan also drove away. They were probably good Samaritans. They must have called 911.

"I can't imagine what those babies went through," I said and exhaled.

A small beam of light flashed in my palm. I quickly scanned Winter, then the state of my own body. We were both covered in blood, sweat and dirt.

He read my mind. "The Tijuana River is just over that foothill," he said, pointing east. "Five-minute detour."

We did not exchange two words while walking.

What exactly does one say to a naked Immortal?

Winter dove in the cold stream headfirst. He came up for air, wiping water off his face with both hands.

"Jump in, witchling," he said. "You smell like morph guts."

"Turn around," I ordered him.

The moon's pale light shone down on me as I removed my shredded, bloodied clothes and dipped my toes in the water. Cold yet refreshing.

"You survived a punctured heart," Winter teased. "A little cold water isn't going to kill you."

Said the Captain of the Titanic.

"Stop peeking," I yelled.

Water and temperature were not things that usually gave me pause. My body felt new somehow. My resurrection had staggered me. The whole mad reality of what was to come staggered me.

I plunged into the water, holding my breath. It felt like the first time I had ever felt the cold on my skin. Elemental energy rushed into me, bathing me in its soothing flow even as I shivered. I rubbed my face and hands clean, then worked on my hair. I pressed down on my breastbone. The ravaging wound had vanished—not even the slightest scratch or redness remained.

I caught Winter's gaze on me. His eyes looked almost tender, shadows and moonlight alternating on the beautiful lines of his face. I sensed a hurricane swelling behind his calm composure and I bit my lip.

"You go first," I said.

"I have clothes in the car," he said, stepping out of the water.

Don't look, don't look, don't look.

"A bit oversized," he went on. "I'll leave them at the foot of the bluff."

Considerate bastard.

Of course, he'd have extra clothes in the car. Winter was like the Immortals' own Eagle Scout. Prepared for anything.

I caught an unintended glimpse of his corded thighs and butt flexing as he dashed into the trees. I counted to ten before I followed.

WINTER TURNED ON THE car engine. "Your place or mine?"

I stayed silent, still processing the insane night we had had, the morphs clamping down on me, the little girls, my improbable revival. In hindsight, going out of my way to find where Winter lived was one of the worst decisions of my life.

"You must have a lot of questions," he said.

"Yeah, but do I want to hear the answers?"

He pulled out onto the highway. "How do the basics say it? This isn't Kansas now."

I tried not to smile. "We're not in Kansas anymore," I corrected him.

"Point being there's no turning back."

"Don't I know it," I said, looking out the window.

He touched my hand. "They can conquer who believe they can." He turned to me. "An old friend of mine said that."

At the condo, I lay down on his couch. He covered me with the softest blanket in the world. He brought me a cup of green tea and a warm honey biscuit. He treated me tenderly, like I was a child. His behavior was simultaneously comforting and deeply disturbing.

He sat across from me. "The element of surprise is lost," he said. "Two morphs escaped. By now, Chaos will know."

"I'm sorry, Jonas, I couldn't turn away from those girls."

"It's not your fault. I put you there."

"I don't understand," I said. "If we were there for information, why didn't we grab a stray morph right away and make him talk?"

He shrugged. "A morph is a pack creature. They would kill themselves before betraying their master. Both the Grand Magistrate and I believed we should stay in the shadows and observe. Knowing how they were preparing would be all the intel we'd ever need."

"Any luck with that alpha you followed?"

He shook his head. "Vanished."

We fell silent. I knew that he was waiting for the real question, the one that had hung in the air between us the whole time.

I also knew he had urgent matters. Time was not on our side.

Ever the one to accommodate, I asked the damned question. "Earlier tonight I was dead for a moment, but now I'm here, breathing. What the hell am I, Jonas?"

He raised his eyebrows, almost apologetically.

"You said I'm an Immortal," I insisted, "but I know I'm not."

"I didn't say that."

"It's exactly what you said."

"I did not say you are an Immortal, Luna. I said you are immortal. There's a difference."

"Are you high? I've been hurt before. I don't heal. I mean, I heal, but like mortals do, there's no accelerated cellular regeneration happening."

He sighed. "I'll try to explain."

"Do more than try."

"I was asked to find a young lunar witch in the San Diego area. When I found you, I sensed something more in your etheric field. I followed you. I stayed in the dark. I observed, trying to determine your mystery."

"Yeah, and we can assume you did. So, let's hear it."

His intense gaze unsettled me. "You are *nata in caligine,* born in the mist. You are a child of the rains."

I swallowed. My dry mouth could use some of that rain.

"Luna Mae of the *Ordre Lunaire,* you have descended from the morning people, thought lost to the world. You are a mist rider."

Excuse me?

I sat up, dropping his expensive blanket to the floor. "I don't believe you."

His eyes hardened. "I tell only the truth. You know that.

It has been many centuries, but I have stood in the presence of mist riders before."

I pushed away the hand he offered me. "It's too much. This whole night has been entirely too much. You're too much. Ever since I met you, everything, it's just been too much, Winter, do you understand?"

I felt tears welling and it pissed me off.

"You have lived like a basic, Sophie of Astoria, I understand all of this must be difficult for your young, human-spoiled mind."

"It's you who are spoiling my mind," I said without any conviction.

"I'll explain a bit more," he said. "Your regeneration capacity could be activated in two ways. Through hypnosis, which I tried the first time we met, and through constant physical aggravation." He moved closer—his breath smelled like figs and olive oil. "Nobody can know what you are. Mist riders are not easily discerned or activated, as my necessary abuse has made you painfully aware. We two will know and none other. Not the Council, not the Order, not your diviner, and not your fucking wolf. Do you understand?"

"I am sure other magistrates have known mist riders," I said.

"A few have, yes, but they must test you by fire to be certain. I will not let that happen," he said. "I've already shielded the atypical parts of your etheric essence."

He was either telling the truth or he had gone mad. I

wasn't sure which option scared me the most. "I need time to adjust, not long ago you were an abusive monster."

"There are monsters of many types in all the realms, to some I may be one, but I'm not *your* monster, Luna Mae. I never was."

"And yet you use my full Order name like a trophy."

He sighed. "I know you feel it. I know you have always felt it." He took my hands. "Someone went to great lengths to hide you, even from yourself. Their motives might have been pure but remain unknown. Until you are strong enough, keep your legacy hidden. The abundance of your energy core makes you a target. Even people you think you can trust would want to gorge you to death to inhale all your rare magic, and they would feel no remorse. There will be no enemies, there will be no friends, just hunters."

"And why not you? Here I am. Weak, unable to resist."

"I am strong enough and want to be none other than myself," he said. "I've fought at the side of great riders. I have only respect for the bloodline."

"I want to sleep and wake up a nobody," I said. "What a joy it was to be a nobody, just to wait patiently in the Starbucks drive-thru. Citizen nobody."

"Mist riders do not hide, Sophie. When they accept their calling, they are majestic and more powerful than any magic creature, but some are susceptible to extreme mood swings and try to refute their nature. Once fully mature, they can even decide to drain their own essence and become mortal."

I pretended not to hear him. "Something sweet and dark, a Caffè Verona."

"Why Starbucks?" he said. "What about your shop, have you not sworn an oath to them?"

I laughed. "You're dumb."

He laughed. "That was a joke, so, in fact, it's you who are dumb."

"You're so old," I said. I was getting tired.

"And wise," he said. "You need rest. Your incoherence is very distinct. Tomorrow we will speak more on your chance to restore the magnificence of the mist riders. It's a choice only you can make."

I lay down, becoming drowsy. "I'm a lunar witch, dumb-dumb," I said. "I draw strength from the moon, from the elements, from the sea. *I'm a LUNAR, baby, so why don't you kill me?* All us little witchlings sang that back in school."

"Not all little witchlings are created equal," Winter said. "One could have been anything she wanted. You were cast as a witch, but you could have been anything, a telepath, a clairvoyant, a demon, an Immortal, even a basic. Your choices were endless. They still are."

"My parents were regular magic," I whispered, falling asleep.

"Yes, probably. Mist riders are unique, sometimes even to their families."

"They are legends, not real," I said, peeking up at him. "Like dragons."

"There is much that defies logic in the worlds above and below."

"You're making it all up."

A steel grip grasped my right wrist, pulling me hard. The short tip of a dagger sliced through my left side, right under my ribcage.

I stared at Winter in disbelief as both of my hands found the knife stuck in my side. I pulled it out. Blood spilled onto the couch.

"You think that I healed you," he said. "The truth is I couldn't. Those I cared about have died in my arms. I was helpless. You're not helpless."

Through my bloodied fingers, through the hole in the shirt that Winter lent to me, the wound fused back together quicker than you could zip a coat.

"Nobody can kill you, Sophie. Only you can kill you."

"If that's the case, then why am I here listening to you?"

He grinned. "It's finally dawning on you."

As a girl, I had read the stories about white horses turning into mist, infusing their riders with potent magic and the gift of invisibility. The horses were the true source of a rider's infinite potential.

"Without a mist horse, I'd only scratch the surface of my potential," I said, "but the legend says the last of them disappeared centuries ago."

Winter rubbed my shoulders, then let his hands run down my arms. "Stay alive long enough, Luna Mae, and a horse will find you—it's part of your destiny. Until then, I can train you. I'll teach you everything I know."

"Oh, goody," I said. "Sounds positively nightmarish."

Chapter 23

Sitting at home and keeping my mind off what happened would have been impossible, so I went to work. I hoped the familiar faces of my coworkers and the regulars would help. Instead, I ended up wondering if any of the faces were shifters in disguise.

The violent memories flashed back in waves. I had a hard time sustaining small talk with anyone. Between customers, I stared off into space, struggling to come to terms with what I had learned about myself.

When I saw Emmet pacing outside the coffee shop, I wasn't surprised. Shapeshifters were master scouts. Of course, he was pacing outside my shop.

I hid behind the counter all the same, cloaking my essence with an etheric shield. I hadn't decided how to feel about Emmet, and I wasn't ready to decide.

Big Rob crouched down next to me. "What are we do-ing?"

"Nothing," I said. "Stretching my hip. Doctor's orders."

He looked down and then back into my eyes. "Is that your doctor walking back-and-forth outside?"

"I don't know," I whispered. "He is a doctor, but my hip's fine. I'm hiding."

"Sophie, I guessed your hip was fine," Rob said. "I can ask him to leave."

"No, just shush. If he asks, I'm not here."

"He knows you're here. He's been there a while."

The counter bell rang. Rob stood.

"Sophie, will you please hear me out?" Emmet said.

Rob looked down at me. "I think you should hear him out."

Shit, essence cloaking doesn't work if they see you first.

I stood, stared straight into Emmet's apologetic face, then gave Rob an accusing look as he walked away.

"Give me a chance to explain," Emmet said.

"Turn around, Emmet. I'm not interested."

"Let me say my piece and then I'll go. I promise."

"Oh, a man's promise," I said, "that's so valuable."

"I get your anger, but I owe you an explanation."

I shook my head. "I don't want your explanation."

"I didn't mean to mislead you..."

"Oh my god, dude, can't you hear? I'm not interested. Shoo."

He crossed his arms on his chest and stood his ground.

Very well, Emmet, have it your way.

I stomped my right foot and leaned against the counter. "Out with you."

Emmet stumbled, fighting against my spell that had enveloped him and pushed against him with an invisible force. He grabbed the counter with both hands.

I increased the pressure a notch, making sure I didn't go overboard. I didn't want to trigger the wolf in him, nor did I want the customers to witness a wolf flying out the door.

Emmet fought to keep his grip on the counter, barely hanging on. The spell forced him to let go and he stumbled backward, unnaturally. I hoped no one would get in his path.

There was fire and determination in his eyes, but we both knew who won this round. Before crashing back against the door, he turned quickly, opened it and walked out.

"That was a little rough," Rob said from behind, startling me.

I turned to face him. "Don't even start with me, Big Rob."

Rob raised his arms in surrender. Of course, he defended Emmet. The good doctor had an easy smile and a naturally chill demeanor. People were drawn to him, his likability was through the roof and he was completely unthreatening—until the fangs came out, and by then it was too late.

His schoolgirl crushes had probably written poems about him, the nurses at the hospital for sure swooned over the young intern and his infectious smile—*yes, doctor, how can I be of help, doctor, I feel something strange in my chest, doctor, could you examine every little inch?*

By the end of my shift, I could hardly stand still. I wasn't about to underestimate a wolf's persistence, so I snuck out the back door.

I'd forgotten he knew I liked sneaking out the back. There he was in front of the tobacco shop across the street, leaning against a pole. He seemed so basic drinking an energy drink and eating a beef jerky stick.

Such a lazy predator. Shifters these days.

I hesitated. I couldn't outrun him, but I could do worse. He cleared the distance between us with a few loping strides.

"Not wise using your magic in public," he said, happily. "But I'm not going to lie, it was incredibly sexy."

"My god, Emmet," I said, trying not to blush. "We're not at *that* place right now and my magic is my business."

"Okay, fair, but I did note you said *right now*, which is awesome."

"You're so frustrating," I said. "It was not meant to encourage you."

"Not at all, I get it. Same page."

He is most definitely not on the same page.

"You have two minutes, but only if you promise not to stalk me at my work ever again."

"Right. So, in a nutshell. You've decided I'm a liar, but you're wrong about that, Sophie, all due respect. I just liked you because you're hot, I mean you're hot because you're cool and your eyes have wisdom and I just like looking at your face and talking to you and this two minute thing, it's a lot of pressure and now I'm sounding undatable, but I hope you get the underlying message that I just like you, a great amount."

Asshole. It was hard as hell not to smile and laugh right now.

"I get your act, Groshek. You do this pathetic, unrehearsed stream of consciousness thing to seem unpolished. But, no, you're hardly unpolished. You're clever and smooth and I'm sure the ladies line up for you."

"There's no line, Sophie. Just you."

The two-minute egg timer better be buzzing.

"The wolf shifter thing, what is that, an after-sex piece of information, or a before meeting your parents thing, or a never thing?"

He didn't answer. He conveyed a sadness so deep I felt it in my gut. I knew he had lost people, we both had. And now we had lost each other.

"Telling that to someone is a burden for them," he said. "Do you go around telling people what you are? Or do you know about hiding that side of you? About trying to be basic with everything that's in you?"

Only last week, I had felt I could eventually open up to him, but he was right. I had never done that with anyone before. And I very much doubted I would be telling anyone about my recent killing spree or my immortality.

"Listen, Emmet—"

"Since when exactly do lunar witches hang out with Immortals?"

What did he just say?

Winter was right. Emmet knew everything. "I rolls with who I rolls," I told him.

His face went red. "I bet the caveman's an experienced lover."

Oh, the nerve.

"Yes, Emmet, that's exactly right. In fact, after I kicked you out of my place, I jumped his immortal bones. He's a little rough, but he makes up for it."

He closed his eyes and sighed. He knew he fucked up. I saw that spark again, the unmistakable golden glint deep inside the wolf's eyes, usually a sign of hunger or curiosity. His stance betrayed agitation, as if he had just been delivered a deadly blow and couldn't recover.

"I deserved that. My temper sometimes," he said. "I am territorial by nature and I hate that about me."

"It's not a good time, Emmet. In about a hundred ways."

"Will he come for me?" he said, feigning fear. "Should I hide?"

"You can't hide from him, but he won't come for you, because I am not his and even if I was, killing my ex-boyfriends is a deal breaker."

Emmet nodded and for once searched for the right words. "I wish I could go back and do things differently. For the record, everything I did tell you about my life, my work, it's all true."

"Well, that's something at least," I said, completely losing interest.

All I wanted was to go home, get in my jammies, binge my favorite season of Charmed, and eat copious amounts of ice cream. I loved inaccurate *basic* speculation about magic. It relaxed me for some reason. And now that I had discovered I could eat as much ice cream as I wanted and still live forever, it's on, baby. *Oh, yeah.*

Emmet rubbed his neck. "Don't let him pull you in, Sophie."

Was that a low growl I heard in his voice?

"I'll do what I want, Emmet."

He glanced at the road. Muscles flexed in his neck. Had he heard a sound only a wolf could hear?

"I'm watching out for you," he said, distracted.

He passed his hand over his hair. His eyes blazed. He leaned in, his lips barely an inch from my ear. My brain short-circuited. He was too close.

"You're in over your head, Sophie. Don't get caught in the middle."

He sniffed the air, spun and raced off into the night. His feet barely touched the ground as he became a distant blur.

Emmet knew. That sexy sonofabitch knew.

And even as I wanted to strangle him with my own hands, I hoped he would survive whatever was to come.

Chapter 24

Faion had taken one look at me and determined I needed a break. That's how we ended up at the very crowded AMC Mission Valley multiplex on a Saturday night, watching *Colette*, even though Faion had already seen the movie twice.

Two hours later, we crossed the street to the bus stop. Faion kept going on and on about Colette being fierce and *we got to struggle to find our voices* and *everybody needs to define themselves* and *fuck gender roles*, but my attention kept drifting away.

In three nights, the Moon's metamorphic phase would reach its peak and I'd have to stop the morphs from shifting into bloodthirsty monsters. Having witnessed what morphs would do to small children, I had little choice, but I was still a long way from processing my role in the pending massacre.

Faion snapped two fingers in front of my face. "Earth to

Sophie," he said. "You're still battling in your brain space, come on out into real life."

I shrugged. What did he expect? That I'd take one look at Paris of the past and all my problems would disappear and my schoolgirl hopes return?

"We have to get some food in you," he said, shaking his head. "They got a Yard House in the mall. They got a nice menu and all the beers."

We walked back across the street. I was not in the mood for people or music or a sports bar to remind me of Emmet. I came to an obstinate halt, pulling on Faion's hand to get him to stop.

"Not feeling it," I said, ready to collapse.

"When's the last time you ate?" he said, arching his brows.

"I just want to go home."

He nudged me forward again.

"Faion, I mean it. Go have dinner if you want, but I'm calling it."

He leaned back a little to get a good look at my eyes. "Stop yelling."

"What? I'm not yelling."

"Yeah, you are. That's whisper-yelling and it's ugly."

I chuckled. "You're funny, but the answer is still a loud NO."

A mini-sized puppy with pointy ears ran up to us, frolicking, and gently tugged on Faion's pantleg with its tiny teeth.

"Hey, little man," Faion said, crouching down to pet the dog.

The puppy raised a paw as if to high-five Faion, then backed up, decided to play bite again, then got on his back to have his belly scratched.

Both Faion and I obliged, then the little devil barked and ran off. He had no leash on and no owner in sight and was headed towards the busy street.

"Poor little dude will get run over," Faion said.

We took off after the dog. A few seconds later, we were following him down into an underground parking garage. The place was empty this time of night and big enough to fit a hundred cars. According to the entrance sign it was corporate parking and closed until Monday.

The puppy saw us, wagged his tail for about half a second, pretended to lunge forward, turned and sprinted deeper into the garage, tripped on his feet and skidded across the concrete floor.

And it was at that very moment that the lights went out.

"Damn," Faion said in the total darkness.

I reached out for Faion's hand. We could barely see each other.

The puppy barked.

We switched on our phone lights simultaneously to search the garage.

The puppy was gone.

"That's strange," I said.

Metal roller shutters clanged down behind us, blocking our exit.

Someone stepped out from a cement support column. I squinted as the murky figure stepped right into the faint light from my phone.

I could not believe my eyes.

"Lucia?" I said, incredulous.

"Hello, dears," Lucia said with a wide grin. "What brings you by?"

It was as if she had just rolled out of bed. She wore a pink sweat suit. Her hair was wild with frizzy curls and her eyes were puffy and bloodshot.

"What are you doing here?" I said, stepping in her direction.

Faion grabbed my hand and pulled me back. He shook his head as if to say, *stop talking*.

To the right, a tall man came into view from behind another support column. His face was concealed by a black mask, just like the man casting spells that night at the pier.

I looked closer. It was the same man. His eyes were hard to forget. He was beefier than I remembered, his muscles stretching the sleeves of his shirt. He shifted from foot to foot as if preparing for a boxing match. Out of his pocket, he produced a gem-studded dagger.

White, glyph-like markings suddenly appeared on Lucia's cheeks and hands, glowing.

My God. She had been branded by powerful magic. Some

great and terrible force had subjugated her.

"We need to bounce," Faion said.

Lucia began to chant.

The light will die
The moon will drop
The witch will cry
Her power STOP!

A wave of icy air encircled me, making it hard to breathe. A red glow sparked against the far wall of the garage. Fire.

Don't do this, Lucia, please, don't.

The overhead lights zapped back to life with a sizzle. Strange wailing sounds swooshed across the garage. My eardrums throbbed in pain.

Faion stepped back. I felt his energy trembling.

Lucia's eyes rolled back into their sockets, turning a sickly white.

"Lucia," I said. "It's me, Sophie. Lily's friend. Your daughter's friend."

She laughed, then chanted again.

The crow will swallow
The witch's flesh
Her bones will hollow
And her ashes mesh

Lucia was lost in a trance-like stupor. Her incantation was blocking whatever elemental energy remained in the parking garage. The old curse even ate away at my connection to my own core energy. Curse spells like that could briefly strip a lunar witch of her magic.

In capable hands, the curse could even make my heart stop.

Faion pulled me close. "She salty as fuck, let's work on that door."

"Stay in place and face the curse," the masked man growled. His command of the paralyzing spell had improved. Both Faion and I felt it crawl up our legs like we had cement boots on.

Lucia moved forward and hissed, "Areika!"

A sorcerer's fire curse. My blood froze. How could she know an outlawed word that had been banned from being spoken since 1666 (*sorry, London*)?

The blaze from the back wall spewed forth. Someone had been tipped off about my aversion to fire sources.

"Mankara!" Lucia chanted, opening her arms wide. The glowing markings on her skin went from white to scarlet as the blaze behind her leapt higher.

Wonderful. A curse I didn't know. I readied the energy that was available to me, hoping I wouldn't have to use it.

Lucia moved forward. Her voice echoed off the concrete walls.

"Pyrrha!"

Please, Lucia, I don't want to hurt you, I don't want to hurt you.

"No elements to draw from, witch," the masked man mocked. "What will you do now?"

Oh, but I am not only a witch.

Information is king. And what they did not know was about to become a painful lesson. If I had initially rejected the truth of what I am, if I hesitated to embrace my fiercest voice—well, that was about to change.

The flames raged, stirring a hot wind that would make the temperature unbearable. With a wild scream, I freed myself from the paralyzing spell.

I stomped my right foot hard. The ground shook, chunks of concrete broke off and fell, but I controlled them. I sent the debris straight for the masked goon. He ran but the concrete pieces swept him into the air and launched him. He hit the wall with a thud.

"Luna!" Faion cried out.

I turned. Faion fell to his knees. A circle of fire formed around us—the flames roared, getting hotter by the second.

Faion's translucent aura fizzled into a thin veil of smoke. The extreme heat must have knocked him unconscious. Great, now I had to use energy to keep him protected from the fire on top of everything.

Lucia's eyes had gone blank, like there was no life left in her, no thinking mind. Her lips kept moving but no sound came out. She looked possessed.

My head ached as I tried to find a way to stop her without hurting her. She was way more powerful than I ever thought she could be.

The masked man surged to his feet. His scream sounded like a roar inside the burning concrete tomb. His resolve was impressive. He glared through the flames at me, dagger in hand.

Lucia gasped, clutching her chest. She stumbled down to sit on the cracked cement, folding her arms in her lap like a school kid. Her eyes were wild, like she didn't know where to aim them.

Faion's eyes snapped open. "Yes!" he said, in an almost celebratory voice. "I'm in Lucia's head. I have her contained! Somewhat... I think."

I leapt into action. Balling my hands into tight fists to control my energy, I jumped out of the fire ring. The flames licked at my jeans and sneakers and I felt the heat roasting my skin.

I came face to face with the masked man. "Extinctus!" I said. Instantly, the fire ring was dissolved. The flames creeping alongside the garage walls shrunk down into a flicker and died.

The man stared into my eyes, bewildered. Spells like the one I had used to control the fire took an enormous amount of elemental energy. They could only be cast when an elemental witch had an abundance of resources at her disposal. I had none.

Faion stepped next to me. His eyes held the same curiosity.

Out of nowhere, the puppy ran at us, ears pointed to the

ceiling. Twenty feet away, it started to shift—body expanding, legs elongating, fur sprouting from its back, huge claws sliding out of paws, crooked jaw gaping wide open like it came unhinged, with rows of serrated teeth sprouting.

"The fuck?" Faion yelled as the demon was on us.

No time to think. My magic reflexes just reacted.

I grabbed the beast by the neck and hurled it against the wall. The thing howled in a savage, bone-chilling way and vanished into tendrils of vapor.

Damn.

That second of wonderment cost me. The masked man came at me from behind and planted his dagger in my left thigh.

I sighed and turned to him slowly. I watched as my maniacal grin quickly erased his resolve.

You fool. Your basic weapons are no threat to a mist rider.

His hand came for my throat. He was a foot taller, yet my hand blocked his attack with a speed and ease that blew my own mind. With my other hand, I raked the mask off his face.

The unmasked man let out an ear-splitting growl before he fled. He pulled out a remote control to open the roller shutter. He had to tuck and roll on the ground in order to miss colliding with the rising shutter.

I watched him run in shock. He was famous for running. The unmasked man was none other than Lily's jock crush, Rocco Barnes.

My hand fell to my injured thigh to apply pressure. Some

pain registered briefly, but the healing process had already begun. My previous enhanced recoveries had activated an automatic regeneration in my cells. Winter mentioned that might happen. I was a self-cleaning oven of sorts.

It was then I noticed that Lucia had not recovered. She did not have the benefit of immortality. She had collapsed.

Faion dropped to his knees to check her pulse. "Heartbeat's stable."

I inhaled, filling my lungs with the fresh oxygen pouring through the now open entrance. Lucia would survive. She would wake up in her own bed. That was the important thing.

I placed my hand on Faion's shoulder. "Let's take her home."

Faion nodded. He was shaken. He had never come that close to a hostile entity before, let alone a scent demon disguised as a cute puppy.

"Faion, I need you to do me a favor."

"Yeah, okay, as long as it's basic."

"As soon as we take Lucia home, I want you on a train, bus, plane, whatever we find first, to Astoria."

His two stunned eyes locked on mine. "You want me out of the way."

"Out of harm's way, yes," I corrected him. "You did your part, my friend. The rest is up to me now."

"I'll go to Oregon if you go to the hospital," he said, motioning to my leg. "Here, let me take a look."

I twisted away before he could get his eyes on my wound. The last thing I needed was for Faion to discover my healing powers. "It's not that bad, but I'll go to an urgent care near my place, I promise, once we take care of Lucia."

He grabbed my hand. "Luna, I'm not afraid to fight."

"I know, but this is the wrong kind of fight for you."

He relented, reluctantly. Faion Trice was one of the kindest and purest spirits I had come upon in my two worlds. Though we had not known each other long, his friendship already meant the world to me. He had been there when no one else would or could and it was time that I returned the favor.

After getting Lucia home safely, we took an Uber to the train station.

Chapter 25

I walked away from Old Town Station worried about Faion, Lucia and Lily. To survive the upcoming days, I would need to forget about them. Knowing Faion would be with his very capable family in Astoria helped. He'd be safe there.

When we put Lucia in her bed, Faion and I had combined forces to wipe her memory clean of the events at the parking garage. We also attempted to implant an impulse spell to convince her she had a bad virus, hoping she'd stay home for two days. We couldn't be sure it would work.

My brain processes were on overload. I had no clue why Lucia would come after me, or how she acquired intimate knowledge of sorcerer curses and banned fire spells, or how Rocco, the football player, fit into all this.

There I was again, trying to rationalize for Lucia. I had made excuses for her before and it cost me. Her dealings with magic weren't some middle-aged woman's lark. She had a demon animal with her, for fuck's sake. Whatever was going on, she was knee deep in it.

I stared at Winter's number on my phone with shaking fingers. It was five minutes after ten. My stomach growled. I was ravenous after skipping dinner and burning through my energy reserves. I was hungry like a wolf.

I know, bad word choice.

Winter's phone rang. One... two... three times.

Nada. Maybe he was with the magistrates. Did phones even work down there?

He answered on the fifth ring, after I had already given up.

"Problem?" he said.

"Yes. How soon can you be here?"

Twenty minutes later, his tires screeched in front of Perry's Café, a block from the station. I'd grabbed a tuna melt and a chocolate shake. Funny how much worse my food choices had been since I found out I was immortal.

"You're hurt," he said when I got in the car.

I'd borrowed some of Lily's old clothes but hadn't wiped my leg clean. Blood had seeped through the gray skinny jeans, forming a small brown stain at the spot where I had been stabbed.

"Another ambush tonight," I said.

I told him everything, except for the part where Lucia was the woman who attacked Faion and me. He listened silently. I kept stealing glances. He was especially unreadable tonight, but I noticed his biceps flexing as he squeezed the wheel tighter and tighter.

"You're staying with me," he said when I was done.

I knew he'd say that, and I was cool with it. That's why I had called him. There was no reason I should go about my business as usual until we fought off thousands of morphs and survived. My place for the next three days was by Winter's side. I would soak up whatever he wanted to teach me.

"I have information that might cheer you up," he said. "The girls you saved have been reunited with their families."

His words gave me the greatest feeling of relief.

"Luckily," he continued, "the paramedics and good Samaritans did not mention my red Honda Civic to the authorities."

I furrowed my brow. "What did you do?"

His eyes grinned. "Me? You saw me, I bathed in the river."

"That's not what I mean. And I can assure you I saw nothing."

"And I can assure you that nobody got hurt."

"Maybe not physically..."

"Luna, it's different in Mexico. And I would be a fool to ever leave my car without cloaking the license plates with a blinding spell."

It made sense, but the truth was I didn't trust him, not completely. I knew there was a roaring ocean of history behind him, a long, dark past I wasn't sure I would want to know or could even understand.

Winter never lied, but the greatest dishonesty wasn't lying, it was omission, leaving out all the things that mattered.

"Could Chaos be the one sending demons after me? Maybe he knows you're planning to use a lunar witch to stop his morphs."

A grimace wrinkled his perfect face. "I don't think so."

"How can you be certain?"

"If Chaos wanted you dead or captured, it would be done the first time, faster than you can take a breath."

I shuddered. "That's a comfort."

"Yeah," he said, switching lanes. "That very fate awaits countless others if we don't succeed."

"Okay," I said, "then maybe he's sending you a message."

"That's not Chaos, that's not his MO. He doesn't tiptoe around things. He blows them up. He attacks head on. He was a soldier, an enforcer, not a diplomat. He cracks nuts with a sledgehammer."

"You sound confident. How well do you know him?"

"Chaos is well known amongst our ranks. He's been a thorn in the Council's side since Marco Polo was in Sumatra."

"That's oddly specific."

"Oh, no, there's nothing odd about it," Winter said. "Someone was using Marco Polo to destabilize two regions. We didn't know it was Chaos at first, but until we found out, a lunar witch aided us in creating monsoon winds to keep Polo stuck on that island for months."

"Ah, so when you need us, we're fine," I said. "Other times we're totally expendable. That's so fucking typical of tyrants."

That pretty much ended the car conversation.

We reached the condo and he parked the car inside his spacious, three-car garage. His wards hummed like kittens before a saucer of milk when they sensed him. A soft glow framed the door like a silver aura when his fingers hovered over the lock. The door popped open without a sound as the wards ebbed, letting us in.

Winter took out his phone and plopped onto his couch.

I planted myself in front of him, hands on hips. "If not Chaos, then who?"

"I don't know," he said, completely indifferent. "Some renegade who has sensed your power and wants to challenge you—some unsavory beast exiled from his realm, seeking revenge. Maybe the woman who attacked you has lost her mind. Unauthorized use of chants and curses often drives basics mad."

He seemed to have stopped in mid flow.

"What?" I prodded.

"It's a stretch, but it could be someone among my kind who wants to challenge me through you. As Chief Magistrate, I often bring other Immortals to justice and that has made me enemies among my kind."

Hold the phone... Chazona.

"It's Chazbona," I said. "Makes total sense. I saw it in her eyes, total disdain, pure hatred for all that I am, a witch of the Lunar Order."

He flared his nostrils. "You're reaching."

"Am I? If you had seen the way she looked at me. Trust me, girls know when other girls hate them. She's like a mean girl of the Immortal kind."

"It's not Chazona."

"How do you know? She's all about you and your muscled vibe. She wants to get with you and make a bunch of mean babies. And when she noticed you have taken an unusual interest in me, her claws came out."

"Do you hear yourself, Luna Mae? You sound like a basic. Female intuition does not exist. That's just paranoia rebranded with a more noble name."

"Okay, answer me this," I said. "Did you two ever... commingle?"

"Luna, that's enough." His voice was authoritative and harsh, like he was chastising a spoiled child.

It stung. Time to change the subject.

"Were you ever going to tell me what I was?" I said, doubtfully. "I mean, if I hadn't ended up on the brink of death, would you have even bothered?"

He shrugged. "Everything's a bother. It is what it is."

I lowered my eyes. "I'll take that as a no, Eeyore."

"You often make references I don't understand," he said.

"You literally just told me a whole thing about Marco Polo."

"He's very famous."

"Yeah... in swimming pools."

His whole face contorted. I loved how confused he looked.

"I might have told you," he said. "I very well might have. I did think about it. And if not me, I am sure someone would have come to you eventually."

Someone... but who? My long-lost bastard of a father? Another mist rider in hiding? Or someone waiting for me to get stronger before they sank their teeth in to drain my gift and, possibly, my life?

My eyes watered. What in effing hell was wrong with me?

"Immortality is a bitch," I said. "I don't know if I can handle it."

"We don't get to choose the load we're born to carry." He let his guard down for the first time. The Immortal took a backseat to the man. "The higher the power, the higher the stakes. The greatest danger for you lies with the Immortal gods, the Eternals. If word of your existence reaches the Eternal halls, they will want to test you. We must make sure you are ready. I don't want them to break you before you even know what you can do."

He stood. A twitch above his eye told me he wanted to reach out and touch me, but he quickly managed to control that temptation.

I wished he would have touched me. I wished he would wrap me in his arms again like the night I almost died, so I could fall asleep without fear and not wake up until

I felt the sun on my face.

Get it together, girl.

"Chaos knows about our night at the morph camp by now," I said. "Isn't it likely he'll call off the whole 33rd parallel North transformation tea party?"

"He gets this chance once every hundred years and there's no guarantee the morphs will survive another century. He'll follow through. Believe me."

"But if Chaos sees me, why won't he just kill me in a single breath like you said?"

"Because I won't let him," he said. "You can sleep in the master bedroom. Make yourself at home."

He wanted me to sleep in his bed? *I don't think so.*

"With you?" I said. "Don't you have a guestroom?"

Winter chuckled. "I have an errand to run."

"You're leaving me alone?"

He opened the door. "You are hardly helpless," he said with a wink. "And don't worry, my wards like you. They will protect you."

"Jonas," I said. "Be safe. I'd rather you were here."

He closed the door and was next to me in an instant. There was this sudden darkness in his eyes, hungry, fathomless, demanding darkness.

His intense gaze mesmerized me. We said nothing. I instinctively put my hand on his chest to get him to move. Instead, he took my wrist.

The darkness in his eyes turned into something different,

more savage and desperate. He pulled back, letting go of my wrist.

"I'm protecting both of us now," he said. "Try to remember that."

He left, the door locked, yet I could still feel him. His wards closed around me with a gentle *swoosh*, eager to keep me safe.

Chapter 26

TO MY RIGHT, A thick line of purple-trunked trees, covered in leaves so big and soft they looked like small cushions, rose five-hundred feet above my head. To my left, a deep crater the size of a football stadium gaped open, gray sand rolling at a snail's pace down the slopes. In front of me, a vast flower garden stretched beyond my vision in a cornucopia of dark colors and sweet fragrances, divided in the middle by a melodious stream.

Winter and I had squeezed ourselves through a transparent fae wall, put in place many centuries ago in order to separate the enchanted valley from the basic world, so it could serve as temporary shelter for magic beings who tired of the Deep Down and needed a place to rest and contemplate.

Immortals sealed the entrance to Serenity Valley when disputes erupted amongst guests of different factions and clans, which led to conflicts and even skirmishes that reverberated all the way to the ears of the Eternals.

Not a soul had visited this ethereal paradise in over three hundred years, but here I was, the first of my line to experience the unmatched beauty and splendor of a fairy-tale land created in a time before recorded history.

The metamorphic Moon had crested in this very spot several times over the centuries. It would do so again tonight, at midnight.

Big snowflakes swirled and danced in the silver moonlight that shone so bright the evening could be mistaken for an overcast day in a forest.

I took an uncertain step, holding out my hand to catch snowflakes. They did not melt in my palm. They resisted my warmth and, instead, grew a little bigger. These weren't snowflakes at all.

My mouth opened and I laughed joyfully. The round, white, furry flakes flocking to my palm were ice flies. The tiny mythical creatures had very limited consciousness, but they were drawn to agents of good and had an uncanny ability to spot malevolent intentions.

A flurry of the white bodies landed on me, clinging onto my skin and hair like I was an ice fly magnet. I felt the soft energy emanating from the tiny creatures and a soft melody reached my ears.

I looked to Winter, bewildered. His eyes were warm on a strangely pacified face. He reached out to gently brush ice flies off my eyelids.

"They know you," he said, fascinated.

Strange, since I didn't know myself all that well.

The fae wall burst open, sending a rainbow of shimmering colors to light up the evening sky. A group of sixty Immortals in light armor stepped inside the enchanted valley. Their marching was almost soundless—the only thing I heard was the settling of their swords against their armor when they came to a halt in front of the crater.

I watched in awe as they leapt down the crater, one by one. I marveled at the sleek elegance of their precise moves, the absolute focus on their faces.

The Immortal Argos broke from the group to address me. A red dagger shone in his right hand. Looking closer, I saw that the red was his own blood gathered from his slashed left palm.

"Your oath binds you to the Court, lunar witch," he said, pinning me down with two unfeeling eyes.

He set my left hand in his, slowly, ceremoniously.

I winced when the blade carved my skin and dug deeper into my palm. Blood spurted. Argos quickly covered it with his own wounded hand, our bloods re-bonding inside the oath. He bowed to me before vanishing behind the giant purple trees.

The magic gathered in me until I felt sick in my stomach, spinning into a tsunami of energy that I would struggle to control.

Winter's eyes went steely. "Your hand," he said.

I glanced down. My hand had already healed. Not good. A witch could not heal so fast. All this energy from the swelling Moon and the enchanted valley had accelerated my cell regeneration.

Argos could not know. I panicked.

Winter grabbed my hand. I caught sight of the switch-blade a second before it touched my skin, reopening the wound.

I clenched my teeth. "It will heal again," I said. "The magic overflow is impossible for me to contain."

"The blade's been soaked in charmed danshen and fever-few," he said. "It will delay the blood from clotting."

Argos returned with a woman at his side. She was tall and looked young, a little older than me, but with Immortals appearances were always deceiving.

She had toned arms and legs and wore the armor of the warriors and a silver helmet. A sword was sheathed behind her back. She bowed to me. "I am Kirsi," she said. "I am here to assist and protect you."

A Valkyrie. A warrior goddess who shepherds souls through battle or into the afterlife. Or, at least, a very old Immortal posing as one.

The Moon reached its zenith. All eyes rose to the shimmering pale disc as it became encircled by an orange halo.

We moved closer to the crater, away from the enchanted trees.

The final battle was about to begin, a confrontation that

would decide the fate of an entire generation of magic beings.

There was nothing to do but wait.

Argos, Winter and Kirsi positioned themselves a few feet apart, forming a triangle of which I was in the center facing Kirsi. All at once, they planted their swords in the ground. Kirsi closed her eyes at the Moon, then opened them at me. I nodded. My three protectors were about to make me invisible.

They began chanting in a feverish way, their words blending together in an incomprehensible song. I was not familiar with the spell nor its origin. It didn't sound like anything I had been taught.

A dome of thin mist began to form around me. At first, it flickered weakly, its vivacity ebbing and flowing, but gradually it stabilized, like a halo of finely threaded silk.

Kirsi cleared a part of the halo and stepped inside it. The halo closed again behind her.

"You will stay here," Winter said. "Kirsi will stand by your side. She won't allow anything to get to you. We will all sense it if the dome is breached."

With that, he and Argos leapt into the crater.

Stay safe, Jonas. Please.

The invisibility halo sizzled when I attempted to touch it. The spell didn't quite turn you invisible, more like it made you very hard to spot by those outside the dome.

People's attention glided over you, the dome deflecting

their eyes from seeing inside.

I sat down to turn my focus within, relaxed by Kirsi's watchful gaze.

Six minutes to midnight, a subterranean thunder shook the ground. My eyes flew open. The time was at hand.

The enchanted, giant trees trembled, their tops swaying as if giant hands knocked them to-and-fro. A few trunks snapped and crashed to the ground with a dreadful, dull thud.

The morphs burst forth like a sea of huge, brain-sick monsters. They growled and howled at the top of their lungs, baring their teeth at the Moon.

They shrouded the land like giant locusts. If I failed, if they shifted into dragons or dinosaurs or flying yetis or whatever malformed fiends they had in mind, they'd be impossible to stop.

As one entity, they started to rip their clothes off their bodies, a raging madness taking over their bloodthirsty faces.

I glanced at Kirsi, my heart pounding. Her face had gone stone cold. With one knee on the ground, she unsheathed her sword, preparing to pounce.

The rabid horde stampeded, maddened with anticipation. Most of the morphs in the field were male, but there were females among them, as deranged and hyper-charged as the males.

One of the morphs wailed loudly. Fangs and claws sprouted as he fell on all fours, exploding into a hyena form, impatience getting the better of him. The morphs closest to him stopped, perplexed, before they came down on the hyena, wildly punching and kicking.

They might have killed him in their rage. I couldn't really tell as more morphs stepped in front of the first line, hiding the hyena.

I took in the whole grotesque melee, but something didn't feel right. The morphs were on their own, exposed, unarmed, unbridled completely. Where were the renegade Immortals? Shouldn't they be commanding the morphs while the ecstatic beasts' mental capacities diminished?

As soon as I thought that, the morphs stopped, becoming very still. A bolt of lightning cut across the sky, setting the orange halo around the Moon ablaze. The beasts erupted into some sort of demonic dance, howling as one.

The Moon dimmed, its silver essence collecting into a frantic swirl that compressed its surface glow. The Moon now appeared a sparkling diamond.

The witching hour was upon us.

My turn.

Lunar energy coursed my veins with a lulling hum. I dropped all my defenses, abandoned every shred of control over craft and my body, every bit of training, every fevered impulse—gone in a split second. I surrendered to Selene's dominion. I was intoxicated by her raw, uncontained power.

The metamorphosis triggered. Fur, claws, beaks, crests and fangs rolled along backs, arms and distorted faces like a wave over a stadium crowd.

My muscles slackened. My eyelids dropped. I had to create a profound connection between my nervous system and the metamorphic Moon.

The uniting path stretched wide between us. I felt dazed, shocked, as the lunar energy raged through me. I vibrated from head to toe. My fingers tingled and sparked, over-whelmed conduits for the metamorphic storm.

A torrent of images attacked my brain, sand grains shrink-ing down to molecules then atoms. My mind expanded, riding sonic waves of energy, piercing the Moon's surface, drilling through layers, lusting for the Moon's core.

The geothermal energy boiled and hissed like red lava. I began to soak it up, every cell spasming as the absorption of the lunar life force brutalized my body with a million volts of magic.

I burned and bled and healed in a thousand different ways. I fell onto my back and screamed but I could barely process the pain.

The morphs shrieked, suspended in mid-shifting, half-human, half-monster, as the morphing effect weakened, and their mutating cellular structures were pulled in every direction.

Suddenly, my core emptied as quickly as it had been filled, all energy escaping through my pores as the Moon rejected our connection.

Selene had been fooled for a time, but now she resisted.

She would not be so easily invaded and plundered of power.

I gasped, barely able to breathe.

"What happened?" Kirsi said as she helped me sit up.

The morphing resumed. The beasts started to grow, stretching out to terrifying proportions.

"Nothing I can't fix," I whispered, grinding my teeth. *Watch me.*

I attacked Selene head on, capturing every drop of Serenity Valley's lavish elemental energy. I cried out as my cells sucked in the etheric essence of an entire enchanted kingdom.

It all was within me, the sorcery, the witchcraft, purple tree energy, the charms of the blossomed gardens, the songs of the stream water, the magnetic fields of the stars—it was all mine.

I feared I would swallow the world whole.

Cradling everything into a single impulse I hurled it at Selene.

You will bend to my will. You will succumb.

The Moon quaked. The morphs got caught in the middle of this battle of wills, half transformed, going crazy with their desire to shapeshift.

The attack of the Immortals was sudden and swift. They charged the morphs, taking them by surprise, blades shining above their heads. Axes and swords whistled as they fell with such speed, chopping down the morphs.

The beasts recovered some of their wits and lunged at the

Immortals, claws and jaws snapping, eyes fevered with rage.

The air was heavy with the scent of sweat and blood. Immortals and morphs collided until they became one big expanse of flesh.

Despite superior numbers, the morphs were both weakened in states of mid-shifting and unable to think as a pack with their minds severely impaired. Their healing powers were low in such conflicted states.

They had been seconds away from tasting their triumph, the full realization of a hundred-year dream, to be at the peak of their powers, finally, but a single witch put an end to all that. Now they were dying.

Deformed, mangled, legs spotted in fur, jaws protruding unnaturally, unable to close, mismatched limbs, skin mixed in scales and feathers, all too grotesque, not for this world, the stuff of nightmares.

I turned away. I was done. Everything had detonated within me and now I was hollow. It was no longer a matter of my control.

Out of nowhere, a demon dog trotted my way. I rubbed my eyes to purge the apparition. The terrible beast had a scarred, long snout and ruined fur like the other demons that had hounded me before, but it was huge in comparison, taller than a horse and thicker than a bull.

Its nostrils flared, sniffing the night air. It sensed something.

Me.

Another demon materialized out of thin air, a gigantic wolf. Then another and another and another. They kept coming—dogs, wolves, bears—sniffing, drooling, circling the dome they couldn't see or understand.

Were they scent demons after all? A strange result of interbreeding with morphs, maybe?

Kirsi gripped her sword, her face losing its certainty. I stayed still.

The smallest sound and they'll know we're here.

I had nothing left in me, nothing. I searched again and found no energy other than the heart's electricity which supported my mortal, human life. If those things saw us, Kirsi was completely on her own. I didn't have the energy left for a yoga kick.

One of the demons came so close I could smell its foul breath. It scratched at the thin halo with a terrifying shriek.

Kirsi pounced, driving her sword into the demon's neck. I shivered as the thing choked and gagged trying to scream. The rest of the demons flocked to their dying mate.

A figure blurred past, taking down two more demons with a single swing of his sword. Winter.

The other demons pounced on him all at once, six, seven, no... eight. Eight hellish fiends digging into every exposed inch of his flesh. His pale skin turned red as he bled out everywhere at once, but it didn't slow him one bit.

The sword of my Immortal protector kept coming down again and again, his powerful legs kicking demons off him with ease, his body spinning like a dervish as he ducked and jumped.

The monstrous bodies began to fall as Winter hacked them down, until they became a pile of flesh and fur drenched in blood.

Luckily, I didn't have the energy to throw up.

Winter nodded to us, then hurried to rejoin the battle.

I took a deep breath. The ranks of the morphs were thinning—the Immortals clearly had the upper hand. I just wanted to go home and soak in a hot tub for two hours.

A man emerged from the distant carnage. An Immortal. He walked with long strides, at a leisurely pace, toward the crater. He was very tall, all sinewy muscle, dressed in light golden armor and a long, scarlet cape. His skin shone bronze under the robust moonlight. His steps were measured but assured—each one of them bringing him closer to me.

He was not like the other Immortals. His origins were impossible to place. He was certainly a mix, but something else, too. It felt like every charmed and every basic race and ethnicity had blended together to build his DNA chain.

His gaze never left me. His eyes were hard to hold—two black stones burning with the intensity of celestial space. Eyes that could stop a heart.

With every fiber in me, I knew the name of this Immortal, as I knew that he should never learn of my existence or my name. *Chaos.*

He studied me carefully, his face touched with a quiet

curiosity as if he had refused to accept that I might be real. He could see me as clear as day. Things like invisibility spells held no dominion over his vision.

I was unable to look away. It was as if the Sun was falling to the Earth. His blood called to me. A primeval connection hummed inside my chest, urging me to abandon the protection of the halo dome, to abandon all logic, and meet this true and ancient enemy on the battlefield.

He raised his hand in front of his chest. Kirsi fell to the ground, grabbing her throat with both hands. I froze.

The Moon hung in the sky above, a yellow disc trimmed in blood orange. My heart fluttered. I knew I should do something, help Kirsi, summon my magic, run... anything would have been better than standing there, waiting for Chaos to choose whether to kill me quick or drain my insides.

Winter broke from the fight. He raged across the field to get to Chaos.

To get to me. *Again.*

Chaos sensed danger and spun around, drawing an enormous sword.

The two Immortals clashed, blade on blade. When their swords met, it was deafening. I had never seen or heard anything like it. They fought with unnatural strength and speed, muscles bulging and glistening, legs leaping to incredible heights to defy the laws of gravity.

The passage of time came to a halt. All that had existed, since the beginning of all things, was there in the thirst for blood on the faces of these two ultimate warriors. Their swords moved like hypnotic pieces in the violent machine of life and death. Their bodies became drenched in the sweat of all creatures big and small. They lunged, swung, spun and sliced with a lust for survival inherent in all living things in all worlds.

I thought this fight would last forever. I thought it was the eternal struggle of life coming into being before my very eyes.

Maybe I was just in shock and denial.

Three Immortals stepped away from the battle to gather around the titanic duel and watch. Kirsi climbed to her feet, coughing, as Chaos released his hold on her throat to focus his power solely on Winter.

"Help him," I told her, gripped by fear.

"When two Shadows fight, no one can interfere," she said, darkness spreading inside her eyes.

My stomach turned. Winter's face was distorted under the weight of the colossal effort, a shimmering rage rising from deep within.

Chaos's face, on the other hand, registered neither fatigue nor concern. In fact, there were times I thought this whole damned battle amused him.

An invisible whip lassoed around my waist, yanking me forward. I barely had a moment to catch the wicked grin on Chaos's lips as his superior force dragged me to him like I was a ragdoll.

Winter's attention divided for a fraction of a second. He

lifted his left hand to block Chaos's force from hurling me right into the middle of the fight.

It was all Chaos needed. He dropped me a few feet away, wheeled around, jumped high and came down hard, sinking his sword inside Winter's shoulder blade near the neck, pushing the sword all the way down until all I could see sticking out was the grip.

The thrust took no more than a single breath. Winter fell to his knees, blood spurting out of him like a red fountain.

My breath caught in my chest. The three Immortals moved behind Winter, emotionless, doing nothing. Chaos yanked the sword out of Winter's body. The sword went up again. From the angle, I knew that when it came down, it would sever Winter's head from his body.

Not his beautiful head!

With a scream so piercing it hurt my eardrums, I collapsed to my knees and slammed both palms on the damp earth. My fury split the ground open, the gap growing with incredible speed, instantly separating Chaos and Winter.

In the distance, morph bodies stumbled and rolled into the gap, while others made a sudden, panicked escape.

Kirsi was on the Winter side of the gap, while I was stranded on the other side, *the wrong side*, alone with the nightmare known as Chaos.

It would take everything in me to even make it back onto my feet. Would anyone dare come to my rescue now that I had served my purpose?

Chaos grinned. He was so close I could smell the musk off his perfumed skin. He brought two fingers to his lips and blew me a kiss, then turned away and vanished, leaving nothing but a blue smoke behind.

Without Chaos, the rest of the morphs would soon be slaughtered.

I was weak. I was alone, unprotected. Winter lay in a pool of his own blood, barely breathing. Why hadn't Chaos killed me or thrown me into the gap or at least taken me with him? He just left.

Attempting to stand, I suddenly got vertigo and fell hard. The enchanted realm was spinning, wildly, out of control. My heart pounded in my chest. I felt nauseous. My head started to pound.

I wanted my mother.

It's been so long.

Instead, Kirsi was there, wrapping me in her arms.

Chapter 27

I DRIFTED IN AND out of consciousness for hours—or perhaps days. Every time my eyes opened, I flinched, a crushing headache squeezing my temples until I couldn't take the light and closed my eyes again.

Voices reached me from afar. They were different every time, some deep, some austere, some melodious, some worried.

Gradually, the fog in my mind cleared and I was able to make out a few coherent words: *one more day, still unresponsive, she's a fighter.*

I tried to sit up and fell back onto the pillows. The severe pain had subsided, but now I was experiencing insurmountable fatigue. The soft sheets felt so good on my skin. I let out a long sigh.

"There she is."

A face bent over me, kind, lovely, concerned. Big,

almond-shaped brown eyes, auburn curls, bright pink lip gloss.

I knew that face. She looked very different from the Valkyrie goddess who had fought by my side, but it was her: Kirsi.

"Where am I?" I said. "What happened? Is this the afterlife?"

She had an easy smile. "Not quite, this is the guest quarters of the underground keep of the San Diego Magistrate Court."

Guest quarters? What a lovely name for a prison cell.

"You were barely hanging on when they brought you in," Kirsi continued. "Throwing yourself smack in the middle of two battling Shadow warriors is not good for a lady's health. Those high-intensity Immortal etheric fields colliding... not fun. It won't just mess up your mascara, it should have killed you, Luna Mae. Consider yourself lucky. The impact emptied your core out completely. It's a miracle you're alive."

Except it isn't.

Kirsi was in a strangely talkative mood. "I'm not sure why the Chief Magistrate was there," she said. "Winter should have never accompanied you to Serenity Valley, being the one magistrate that Chaos can challenge and ceremoniously execute. Not even Düsternis could intervene."

"What? Why is that a thing? Why can Chaos kill Winter?"

Kirsi bit her lip, possibly having said too much. "Chaos and Winter are Shadow warriors. Within the Umbra Order, a Shadow is granted the ability to steal the life force from other Shadows in a duel. When that much energy is thrown around, mortals nearby almost always die, and even an intervening Immortal would lose part of their regeneration capacity. In other words, you have to stay clear."

I wasn't sure what any of that meant, but now it made sense why nobody interfered during the fight. It also made sense that Chaos left me behind. He would have assumed I was mortal and already dying.

"Who brought me here?" I said. "Why? Compassion is not exactly an Immortal's first instinct. No offense."

Kirsi smiled and nodded. "Your honesty is poorly timed, but not wrong. But really, I don't believe you're that ignorant. No offense. I think you already know why."

It hit me that she had just told me Winter was mortal, or at least fighting to the death, when he faced Chaos.

Did he survive? Did I save him, or was I too late?

I took her hand. "Jonas?" I said, my mouth dry as sandpaper.

Her big eyes studied me. I sensed a curiosity and a disapproval behind her hesitation, almost as if she felt my question was inappropriate. Maybe knowing his real-life name betrayed an intimacy that was not allowed.

"See for yourself," she said.

She moved aside. Winter stood in the doorframe, broad shouldered, strong, healthy, his blond hair freshly cut.

He picked up a chair and set it next to the bed.

With great effort, I managed to sit up. "You look good as new," I said.

He didn't smile, but there was tenderness on his face. "I'm not new at all," he said. "I'm quite old."

I smiled for him. "You're supposed to say I look good as new, too."

"You know already, Luna, that I never lie."

"Maybe not, but you are full of shit," I said.

Now he smiles. Maybe he likes to be insulted.

Kirsi set a glass of water on the bedside stand and left.

Winter squinted at me. "You're a badass, as the basics call it."

"What do you call it?"

"Warrior of virtue," he said.

"I like yours better," I said. "But really, I was saving my ass as much as I was saving yours. We all just did what we could."

"It was a field of valor."

"Did we win?"

"The battle was won, but war will continue. Chaos lost most of his morph army. We gained time. Net win, yes, but he will have a new plan soon enough."

Winter was not the only one who was honest to a fault. "Chaos almost killed you. I've never felt more powerless in my life."

His expression hardened. "He saw you. Chaos should not have been there. We do not know how he materialized out of thin air. I failed you, Luna."

I didn't want him to apologize. We already had enough awkward moments between us. "Yeah. So? He thinks I died, and he obviously did not know what I was. He'll never see me again. And if he does, I can handle him."

"One does not handle Chaos, certainly not you—not yet. You have a repressed survival instinct. Your compassion makes you think twice before hurting anyone and he's a two-thousand-year-old Immortal, a Shadow warrior and an eager assassin. Killing's not only what he does best, it's what he does for a good time."

"But I'm also immortal and I have my tricks, too."

He took my hands. "Luna, he will have you for breakfast if you give him the slightest of openings. You need my experience."

I shook my head. "Jonas, it's done. Killing me wouldn't change a thing. If he even knows I'm alive, I'm no longer a threat. He had his chance. He didn't take it. I'm insignificant now. Besides, we can't be joined at the hip for eternity. And I won't run to you every time I have a problem."

"No, you need to run to me," he said, matter-of-factly.

"*Bah*, it's a non-issue. Tell me, what's a Shadow warrior anyway?"

"To the one who saves your life, a warrior must always be true," he said, reluctantly. "But what I tell you now, must stay within these walls."

"For sure," I said. "I can keep a secret."

"Umbra is the highest order within the Immortal Councils. After a thousand years on Earth, an Immortal has the option to train and compete in the most grueling ways for the great honor. Very few take the challenge. Even fewer succeed. I can't reveal more."

"Both you and Chaos pledged to this fraternity and got in?"

"We did. Long ago."

"He's two thousand years old, right? How old are *you*?"

"Age is a number. An Immortal Shadow is ageless."

"Evading a question and/or not answering directly are forms of dishonesty where I come from, just an FYI."

"Oh, well I didn't say I was *Oregon honest.* That is a level even beyond Immortals."

"Are you having a go at humor again? It's honestly not that bad."

His eyes glimmered. "It is time you rest."

I put my hand on his wrist. "How long have you lived alone? It must get so lonely when you live forever."

He took a deep breath and then let it out. "Loneliness, like anything, is something you improve at. It's a skill you must and will learn."

"I'm not sure that's a fun lesson. The thought of living forever, losing those I care about over and over, is not appealing. Like not at all."

He leaned in and kissed me. I didn't see that coming. The world stopped. My senses went berserk. His kiss was light years away from anything I'd experienced before, there was nothing safe or comforting about it, it was fierce and hot and wet like a forest fire or a sudden storm. It shook me.

I pulled away, bringing the back of my hand to my lips. "Why?"

"I didn't want you to feel lonely."

"I don't. I didn't."

He grinned. "At least now you won't have to wonder."

How did he always know what I was thinking? The last thing I needed was a *boyfriend* who could read my mind. And we were not age compatible, not even a little. He probably went to the University of Babylon or Jericho Tech or the Cave Institute.

Deciding not to say any of those jokes, I just stared.

Someone looked in from the door—the ice queen herself, Chazona.

If I had balls, they would have shrunk.

"The Grand Magistrate would like a word," she said.

For a moment, I feared she was talking to me, but then I realized she wouldn't stoop to being a messenger girl to summon me. No, the only reason she'd deliver a message herself would be to pull Winter away.

She might be Immortal and a magistrate, but she was also a woman, and she could not fool me. I'd know that deriding look anywhere. She was telling me I wasn't worthy of Winter's attentions and she'd make sure that I'd never have another opportunity.

Shots fired, but it was not necessary. I never intended to see him again.

Winter looked at me, raising an eyebrow.

"Go," I told him. "We're cool."

He nodded. "The Council has released you from your oath, as well as any and all future obligations," he said. "You're free to go."

Wait, what? Just like that? I wanted to feel relieved, if not happy, that I could resume my life, hang with Lily again, spend the holidays with Grandma and then pack for Sweden, but something didn't feel right.

Whatever, that was above my pay grade. Chaos seemed like a hot mess who could not plan a vacation, let alone an uprising, but I would not let the nagging feeling that it all had ended a little *too neat* ruin my freedom.

I was sure I'd find a way to forget that Chaos was still out there, and I was sure I'd eventually stop feeling Winter's uninvited lips on my lips.

Chapter 28

I HAD BARELY BEEN home for two minutes when Lily texted me. Lucia was unwell, she said, and Lily had to take her to the hospital last night. Seconds later, I was back out on the street waiting for my Uber.

I had stayed in the Magistrate Court guest quarters for three days and I still didn't feel like myself. I was plagued with the impulse to take long naps and binge eat between naps. There was no food I turned away: clams, octopus, liver pâtés, brussels sprouts, everything that would have made me turn up my nose only days ago, I gobbled it all down while recuperating at the keep.

"Lily," I said, trotting down the hospital hallway. "How's Lucia?"

She took my hand to lead me to a small sitting area. "They don't know, they worry she might be catatonic."

I stopped walking. "Catatonic? Lil, how is that possible?"

Lily opened her arms wide, frustrated. "You tell me. One moment she thinks she has the flu, the next she just checks out. Unresponsive."

So, the little flu spell Faion and I had cooked up worked. I hoped we were not somehow responsible for her current state.

"She just sits there," Lily went on, "awake, looking at... I don't know, the wall, the window, some phantom? She won't talk, she won't move, she won't eat unless you feed her and then only soft foods."

We sat down. I listened quietly as Lily went into the details of how she had found Lucia on the floor the night before and called 911, the tests the doctors had ordered, the inconclusive results.

"What are the odds?" she said in the end. "I mean, you went through the same thing with your mom."

I knew Lucia would have a price to pay. I just hoped it would be later rather than sooner. Seeing Lucia and Lily like that broke my heart.

"Lily, about the other day... I don't know what that was about, I've been a little out of sorts." I paused, picking my next words carefully. "I had this irrational idea that there was an evil spirit in the house."

She wasn't as stunned as I thought she'd be. "Huh, that's weird. That's exactly what Lucia said before she stopped talking. She was like freaking out about how she'd been possessed and some dark spirit had come for her soul. *La*

Llorona had stolen her soul, she kept saying." Lily's voice cracked. "I shouldn't have made fun of her, Sophie. I'm the worst daughter."

I took Lily's hand in mine. "Lil, do me a favor. Stop going out with Rocco until Lucia is back to her old self. It's not good to overload at a time like this."

"That's not even a problem, the jackass stood me up. His mom said he left town yet again."

Lucky for him, because I was about to pay him a visit. I'd have made the bastard give me some answers about Lucia.

"We'll get through this," I told Lily, holding her hand. "Lucia just needs a rest. That lady overworks herself, getting involved with too many things all the time. She'll be back to busting your butt in no time."

I was bluffing. I had no idea if Lucia would ever recover, but I was determined to find a way.

"Sophie?"

A man's voice. I turned. Big Rob, in a wheelchair. Big elastic bandage wrapped around his head, black eye, left arm in cast.

"Shit, Rob, what happened?"

Rob gave me a pained grin. "Two masked dudes kicked my ass."

This couldn't be happening. No, it had to be a coincidence.

"OMG, dude. Where?" Lily said.

"At the shop," he said. "It happened so fast."

I went to Rob and touched his right arm which seemed to be fine.

Rob winced. "That's still a little bruised as well."

"I'm sorry, Rob," I said.

In more ways than one.

"I'm fine. Can we possibly have a word in private, Sophie?"

"I'll check in on Lucia," Lily said, smiling to Rob before she left.

Rob's face went pale. "Sophie, those men came for you."

"When?" I said.

He studied my face. "That's all you have to say? You look completely unfazed right now. What the hell?"

"No, I'm fazed, Rob, but I'm having a day. Lily's mom suddenly fell into a catatonic state. You're all beaten. It's just a lot, you know."

I was getting really good at bullshitting.

"Yeah, okay, now I'm sorry, Sophie. I'm having a day, too, a couple of them actually and, I don't know, crazy shit is happening."

"Tell me about it."

"Last night," he said. "That's when they came in."

Just as I thought. Same time Lily found Lucia on the floor. Someone had gone to great troubles to drag me out of seclusion and get me to the hospital.

"Thank god your friend showed up," Rob added. "I might not be here today if it wasn't for him."

"Friend? What friend?"

"The tall guy, that dark-haired dude you chased out of the shop. He was still out there, stalking. Turned out to be a good thing for me."

"Emmet," I said.

"That's him. Right, *Emmet*. I need to remember his name, but those thugs knocked my noggin pretty good. Good-looking man, that Emmet, you need to reconsider and give that homie another shot. He's straight legit."

I put my hand up to stop him. "Okay, Rob. He has his strengths. I'm glad he was there. Not for the stalking part, but the *saving my friend* part."

"Lots of people showing up asking for you lately," Rob said. "Including the manager. He really wants to talk to you."

"That's not good," I said, knowing my excuses wouldn't fly this time and I would soon be out of a job. "What about Emmet? Is he okay?"

"Okay? Are you serious? He's like a black belt. If he shaved his head, he'd be a young Jason Statham. Totally handed those goons their asses. They ran out of the coffee shop like their hair was on fire."

Sounds like Rob should date him.

A psychotic affinity for violence with unmatched strength and speed? Sounds like my wolf shifter. I'd like to chalk it all up to courage and good timing, but it was just as likely Emmet was in on the whole thing. My gut told me Emmet was not capable of such deception, but I really hadn't started off on the right foot with shifters in general.

And it was entirely possible that this was all Chaos. Winter said he might show his hand again soon. I didn't know, but what I did know was that whoever was behind sending my friends to the hospital would be arriving any minute.

"Rob, feel better," I said, kissing his cheek.

"Sophie, are you leaving?" I heard Lily's voice behind my back.

I turned but kept moving. "Baby girl, I'll call you. Hugs."

Chapter 29

A LIGHT SHOWER BEGAN to fall as I stood outside the hospital. I walked around the building, careful to stay under the awning to keep dry.

"Such an enchanted day, don't you think, buttercup?"

A man's voice came from above. I stepped out from the awning to see if the man was talking to me. My heart leapt into my throat. Chaos was perched on a second-floor balcony railing, dressed in black. He looked like a well-dressed vulture.

He waved a half-eaten glazed doughnut at me. "Cursed with the briefest of lives, basics still happily eat their way to death," he said, considering the doughnut. "I mean, what's up with that? If they won't value their mortality, why should we?"

I steadied the magic stream under my fingernails, ready to strike.

He dropped the rest of the doughnut, then licked his fingers clean. His eyes were filled with mischief. My blood began to ache.

Staring into his eyes, I stepped on his discarded doughnut, squashing it.

He chuckled. "The answer to your question is *NO*," he said, "you cannot outrun me."

"What do you want, Shadow?" I punched that last word to let him know I was way ahead of him.

He stared at me, unblinking. "I see my old friend shares much with you, but not everything. Did he, by chance, tell you exactly what must be done to become a Shadow Warrior?"

I raised my arms like I was losing patience. "Is talking people to death one of your powers, because so far I'm impressed."

His eyes brightened, sending a shiver down my spine. "I do hope you enjoyed your larks with my little interbred friends. They might have come out of the oven a little early, with faces only a father could love, but their undying loyalty was inspiring."

Damn, I was right the whole time.

"Do you hear yourself?" I said. "And, dude, not a surprise that those demons were your science project. Now that I know you better, I get that *sick and twisted* is kind of your brand."

He feigned modesty for comic effect.

This psycho thinks he's funny.

"They weren't meant to hurt you," he explained. "Just an exercise in quantitative analysis. I wanted to know exactly what level of command you now possessed. They were to prod a little and report back. You didn't have to destroy them, honeybunch. It will be an effort to make more."

What the hell is he on about?

Sounded like madness, pure and simple.

"If you knew I had the power to stop your morphs from shifting, why did you send them to Serenity Valley without cover? Do you enjoy slaughters?"

Chaos hopped off the balcony and landed in a soft crouch. He stood up and towered over me. His face appeared younger than his voice and reputation promised. He emanated the raw sexuality and masculine intrigue common in violent men and athletes. Women would line up for this dude if it wasn't for the crazy in his eyes and the arrogance in his words.

He trapped my nose between two of his knuckles and pulled. I slapped his hand away and took a step back. He wanted to play.

WTF?

"There are important matters to discuss," he said, casually. "The rebellion was a mere blip in the bigger picture. Your job, bunny rabbit, is to help me stop the fucksticks of the Seventh Council from taking over the world. To do that, I needed you out in the open and ready to play, but I couldn't have found you without Winter's help. He has access I do not."

Gradually, the truth dawned. "You set him up. Both of us."

He grinned. "Smart girl. I just had to hand feed him information about renegade Immortals and morphic shifters. I had to make it all sound plausibly terrifying." He made a scary face, jumped up and down and yelled, "Boo!"

His unhinged behavior hurt his plausibility.

Then he got serious. "Winter would never have brought you out of hiding unless it was something big."

Things began to fall into place. "You betrayed Winter's trust. That's it, isn't it? At some point he trusted you and then you betrayed him. And now you sacrificed all those morphs to manipulate him."

Thank god, Emmet was not one of them.

"Guilty as charged," he said.

"I have to say, he underestimated you. Winter said you always went straight at a thing. You never played the long game."

He was pleased. "They all underestimated me, sugar pop."

"What's with all those annoying nicknames? Stop it."

His face turned dark. "Düsternis and his insipid crew of clowns have plans to take over the Deep Down, reign over all magic factions, then bring the basic world to its knees."

"I don't believe that," I said. "No, you're playing a game."

"I wish I was, little dove, but they have gathered

indestructible power. A great and terrible power beyond anything the planet has known. They are done hiding. They will be able to alter climate to bring forth an ice age, they will be able to disarm or control nuclear weapons as well as nuclear power plants. Life as you know it will be forever lost. You will submit or die. And they will profess that they are doing it all for humanity, that they will save the planet. You've studied social anthropology, Sophie, if you listen to them, very carefully, you will hear that they use the same words that tyrants and dictators use."

"And why should I believe a word of this?"

He circled me. "Because you sense the truth. It might take years, even decades, but they will make this happen. Their control of technology will be absolute. And, in the Tech Age, if you control tech, you control the world. Why do you think they banished me? I was the opposition vote, and dictators don't like opposition votes."

That was a lot to take in. One thing was certain—whether there was truth in his words or not, he was trying to control me. "Why are you telling me?"

"You should not trust Winter," he said. "He is sublimely clever."

"Oh, and I should trust you?"

"You'd be a fool if you did. Are you a fool, dove?" He laughed. "Consider this thing between us a temporary truce. When the time comes, if necessary, I *will* kill you, Luna Mae. Your kind is one of the most dangerous to ever walk the

Earth. When I come into power, if I doubt you in any way, I will crush you before you reach maturity and full access to your potential."

"I'd like to see you try."

I really needed to quit threatening lethal Immortals. It was a very bad habit I'd picked up lately. I was just over men telling me how it's going to be.

His eyes went predatory. "Oh, yes, you can be killed, button. It's not easy, but I'm a sucker for a challenge and, to tell you the truth, nothing's all that hard if you're willing to put in the time to learn how."

"Oh, did you find a chat room for Immortal cheat codes online?"

"Sometimes funny, sometimes facetious, always defiant," he said. "I can see what my old chum sees in you."

The facts unfolded inside my brain. Chaos knew what I was, *what I truly was*, and he was threatening me. Openly. He must have also known that without a mist horse, I could only access a fraction of my abilities.

For sure he'd want me dead before I found that horse, but for now he needed me for some unforeseen reason.

"As if I care what either of you think," I said.

"If that is true, then you and I can coexist, but I must urge you to watch your back. Do not let yourself be used. Magistrate Winter will not hesitate to weaponize you again as he has done once already. It's his plan, it's always been his plan, ever since you sparkled to life."

Now I knew he was batshit crazy. "What are you talking about?"

"Oh, sweetheart, you didn't know?"

"Know what?"

"Winter didn't happen upon you in a time of need. He didn't just trip over you on the way to find another witch. He's always known where you were. He's your watcher, your true guardian."

I felt like imploding. "Since when?"

He laughed. "Since always, since you played at your mother's feet, since you fell out into this world and gasped your first magical breath."

Damn it, tears started welling. It was too much.

"If you're not going to kill me, I'd like to go."

Strangely, he was surprised, even moved by my tears. "Ah, dear heart, do you know how exquisite it is for Immortals to witness nuanced suffering? It's like art being born right in front of our eyes."

"That's morbid," I said.

"Oh, no," he said. "We are the watchers of it all."

"Goody for you," I said. "Can I go?"

"I don't think you believe me, and after all my troubles creating a disturbance big enough for him to walk you to death's door, to my door. Believe me, I tried easier ways. He was never going to share you willingly. I begged, I threatened, I groveled. We both needed to train you vigorously while there was time. He wouldn't hear a word of it. He is obsessed."

Don't listen to him, Luna. He's a madman.

"He's obsessed?" I said. "Yet, it was you who caused a complete massacre just to have a chat with me."

He nodded, laughing. "Well, when you put it that way... but, seriously, one day you will be grateful that I did. Winter has programmed every step you have ever taken. He will try to use you in the Immortal quest for supremacy. You will never be free, Luna." He winked at me. "Unless you're willing to take a stroll on the dark side."

I turned to go. I had heard enough.

He leapt in front of me like a jungle cat. "Don't break my heart, tulip. We will achieve great things together, save the world and have a few laughs along the way. I can't win this fight without your charms and you can't win it without mine. I know you won't sit back and watch Immortals enslave every last mortal being. That's when they kill you. Sorry to tell you, the girl dies in the end, no matter how it ends. At least I'm good enough to admit it."

"Gee, thanks."

"And as a bonus, I'll even spare the life of that little busy bee, Lucia."

That caught my attention. "What have you done to her?"

"Very little, she was already halfway there..." He spun a finger over his temple. "Cuckoo town."

I shoved him. "Tell me what the fuck you did."

He stepped back, in the most dramatic fashion, as if swept

away by my strength. "Whoa, you're a tough cookie. The woman, she just couldn't resist my many charms. She fell in love. The rest was easy."

"You have charm?" I said, not believing my ears.

He laughed out loud. "Women have chased me through the centuries, shrieking as they go. Poor little things, drawn to power and darkness. They need a master with might. They crave the living lord. When I spot one with certain gifts, I help them along and they are ever so grateful."

Oi. What a load of crap.

"What are Lucia's gifts?"

"A certain naïve optimism is always a good start. Her knowledge of ancient worlds and their rituals did speed the training. She proved to be a willing channel for my telepathic command. Typically works like clockwork, but you are not typical, are you, dumpling? You sniffed it out like a boss, as you kids say. You are, after all, a descendant of legends."

"What happens to the women when you're done?"

He reached for a strand of my hair. My psychotic glare made him change his mind. He returned his hand to his pocket like a scolded child. "The women are killed quickly. I do have something like affection for them, and a quick death is the humane thing once their mind has been scattered. Not unlike the basics do with horses and dogs who have passed certain thresholds of health."

"If you do that to Lucia—"

"I know, sugar plum, I figured you'll go after my head if

Lucia doesn't make it, and I simply can't afford killing you before we save the world."

I closed my eyes. I needed a moment. It was because of me that Lucia and Rocco had been scrambled into instruments for Chaos. No one who knew me would ever be safe again.

"What's going on in that pretty little head, green eyes?"

"Dinner plans, and ways I might kill you."

"A girl after my own heart."

I laughed. Not for him. More because of my emerging insanity.

"You don't give two shits about basics or magic factions. Why this eternal battle against your kind?"

"The million-dollar question arrives at last."

"Well?"

"No spoilers, Loony Luna. You have to wait for the finale."

"Have it your way, then. I'm not helping."

"Time will tell. It holds all the secrets."

I suddenly realized we were having this conversation in the rain. This was hardly how I envisioned encountering Chaos. Soaking wet, wiping soppy bangs out of my eyes while I listened to the most notorious Immortal Shadow of all pitch me on a plan to join forces to save the world.

I mean, c'mon! I just graduated from San Diego State. Go Aztecs!

"This is how it's going to be," I said. "You are going to release Lucia from whatever voodoo bullshit you have over her. You'll allow her mind to heal. You'll leave Rocco Barnes alone and you will gather proof that what you're saying is true. I don't want to see your face or your half-cooked shifter babies before you have something concrete for me."

He kept nodding as if making a list in his head. "Is that all?"

"Yes. No. One last thing. Is Emmet Groshek working for you?"

He squinted. "Is that a real name?"

"Never mind."

I was keenly aware that a deal with Chaos was spotty at best. He could switch gears at any time, break my neck, shatter my windpipe, drag me back to his lair for some all-day torture, or use me to lure Winter. The possibilities were endless. I needed to develop an exit strategy.

"Chaos, next time leave my people alone, you know where to find me."

I walked away, trying to stand tall, but a dark memory whizzed into my head—Chaos wielding his Damascus blade above Winter's neck on the battlefield in Serenity Valley.

"Hold on a second, angel face."

What now?

He ran to catch up. He once again planted himself in my path and crossed his arms across his chest. "Who and what is an Emmet Groshek?"

Give me patience.

I pushed him aside, but he scurried back in front of me.

This guy sucks.

"Hasta la vista, mi niña linda," he said, overcome with glee. He ran off and once again vanished into a puff of smoke.

My life right now.

Chapter 30

THIS TIME, I DIDN'T have to break his wards or use his ritual name. Winter was home and astounded to find me at his door.

"Were you not the girl who insisted we stay out of each other's lives?"

I walked around him to get inside. "Yesterday's news."

"Okay," he said, closing the door behind him.

I tried not to focus on the fact he wore only swim trunks. His skin was tanner and his three-day stubble looked California cool. The past week had left him glowing with health, rest and peace of mind. It all looked good on him.

"I did some surfing," he said, as if reading my mind, pointing to the ocean outside the window. "Just got back."

He grabbed a shirt from the back of a chair and pulled it on, arms first. He straightened the shirt and finger combed his lush, wet hair.

I found a spot on the couch. I had waited two full days after my rainy-day chat with Chaos before bringing my doubts to Winter. Unfortunately, the two days did very little to calm me.

"I have a question," I started. "When you said we were the only ones who knew what I was, did you mean me and you? Or did you mean me, you and fucking Chaos, the sadistic tormentor of the fucking world?"

Totally not how I rehearsed that.

"What are you accusing me of?"

"He knows I'm a mist rider and you know that he knows."

"That's not the case."

"He seems to think otherwise."

Winter's face stiffened. "You talked to Chaos?"

"He did most of the talking, like non-stop, out there, crazy talk."

He walked to the bar and poured himself a drink.

"Aren't you even going to ask what he told me?" I said behind his back.

He turned, glass in hand. "No need. It's obvious you can't wait to tell me."

"I can't even with your smugness right now."

"Forgive me, please proceed."

I stared at him with daggers before taking a deep breath. "Chaos contends that the Magistrates of your Council plan to wage war on all magic factions and to rule on Earth. He said he's been trying to stop them. It's the reason he was banished. Basically, he's the good guy standing between the power-hungry Immortal tyrants and the free world."

Winter rocked back and forth on one leg, not his usual grace. "And did he sound like a good guy?"

I suddenly felt like I was being cross examined. "You know what he sounds like. He could definitely use a PR person."

Winter's slow responses were unusual for him. "Chaos has had good ideas, but always for the wrong reasons. He believes what he's saying, that's the problem. You would be wise never to trust such blind conviction."

"Trust an Immortal! I see you give me no credit."

"You're upset," he said. "How can I help?"

"There's more. He said his rebellion was a smokescreen."

Winter raised an eyebrow. "Smokescreen for what?"

"For me. For you. He claims he needed to get you to reveal me. All of it—the rebellion, the war, the morphs, all orchestrated to uncover my identity, just so Chaos and I could have that chat. Insane."

Winter flared his nostrils, realizing he had been played. His features became rigid. He took a sip of his drink, having nothing to say.

"Does that upset you? That he outplayed you? Is it all a game to you two? Some macho rivalry that has terrorized the ages?"

"Chaos will say anything, he always finds a new angle," he said, coldly. "And if you think he outplayed me, what do you think he'll do with you?"

"You both do that, say anything to get what you want," I said. "How are you any different than him?"

He came to me, grabbed both my wrists and lifted me to my feet. "Why don't you come out with it, Luna Mae? Say what you want to say."

"Fine," I said, shoving him. "You've always known about me. You planned to use me all along. And you'd love nothing better than to command me for the rest of my life."

He pressed a finger to the top of my head. "What have I told you about trusting Chaos?"

"Guess I fucked up that command, Commander. You know what? You're so full of shit." My resentment was no longer hiding itself. "And to think I had convinced myself you couldn't lie."

He moved to the window. He stayed silent a long time, peering outside, the bright sun lighting up his tan face. "You were given to me," he said.

"Given to you? I'm not anyone's possession. I'm a person, not a pawn in these games you Immortals play."

"If I wanted you to be my pawn," he said, staring out at the sea, "why would I have revealed your true nature? Any other magistrate would have taken you young, before you knew who or what you were, they would have trained you, broken you and shaped you. I allowed you to grow up with as little interference as possible, to form your own personality. I let you live, really live, have a life."

I fought back a tidal wave of misery and wretchedness

trying to overtake my heart. He had just confessed to every-thing Chaos had said.

"I can't believe you have sanctified your role in all this," I said, sucking down the desire to sob. "Tell me, what were you hoping to achieve?"

He finally turned to me, his eyes burning with intensity. "You were to submit to me of your own free will as a fully grown, mature adult."

I scoffed. "Well, you fucked that one up."

"That was the plan," he said. "The old plan. It changed."

"Oh, here we go," I said, covering my ears.

"Listen, Luna, after getting to know you, the person you have become, my focus changed. I recognize you as an equal. I have no wish to deceive or possess you. To thrive, you must be in control."

As he spoke, I remembered his passionate kiss, but I also sensed he wanted me in every way. No matter what he said, he wanted to possess me, my mind and heart. He would control me that way, his mist rider, under his thumb. There was a savagery inside his eyes that betrayed him. He'd been fighting the urge to grab me and force me to submit to him, his rule, his body, his idea of the perfect world. The effort must have been colossal. It was not just Immortal men who desired such a total ownership over a woman.

"I will be no man's plaything," I said. "I do not and will not submit to anyone at any time for any reason. You got the wrong witch."

"I know this, Luna Mae, Sophie of Astoria, last of the Mist Riders."

"You forgot future Ethnologist," I said. "At least I chose that one."

Our eyes lingered on each other, unblinking.

"Have you watched me since I was a child?"

Nothing.

My head felt like it was shrinking, trying to make sense of things. "How do you mean I was given to you? By whom? My parents?"

He raised his chin a little, then breathed out hard through his nose. It was clear I would not get one word from him on that subject.

"It's okay," I said. "I'm sure Chaos can answer that one."

"Chaos is toying with you, can't you see? He's enjoying this whole sick crusade," Winter said. "He thinks he's saving the world and he thinks they'll love him for it."

"This is not about Chaos," I said. "It's about you, still keeping things from me, like you have been doing since my birth."

His face softened. "Some things are better left unsaid, Luna. Letting go is not always giving up. If you dig too deep, you'll never find your way back to the surface. I'll stay out of your life. I'll leave San Diego, but you must promise to stay far away from Chaos and his diseased mind."

I impulsively slapped him across the face, delighting in the sound of my nails scratching his cheek and jawline. He hurled a ring of pulsating energy around my feet and I crushed it instantly with my own growing powers.

We faced each other for a moment. Muscles on his neck twitched, the boiling wrath pulsing inside his blue irises scaring and thrilling me. I expected him to pounce, to rip me to pieces. I maybe even wanted that.

Then his face relaxed, all of a sudden, and regained its calm. Winter's transformation was so drastic, it chilled me all the way to my core.

Wake up, Luna girl, while there's still time.

"You know what? I think I'll take your suggestion," I said, walking to his door. "I'll stay away from his diseased mind. In fact, I'll stay away from both your diseased minds."

The immortal bastard didn't know what to say. He started to look like a sad little puppy. "Good," he finally said.

Looking back one last time, I smiled. "It's better than good, it's great. In fact, it's the best idea you ever had."

I left Winter like that and walked out into the California sun.

Chapter 31

TWO MONTHS LATER

LILY AND FAION LAUGHED their asses off. They looked ridiculous in matching Santa hats and beards. The mall was bustling with shoppers trying to get their final gifts on the Sunday before Christmas. Total mall mayhem.

"What do you guys think? Does this scream *Lucia*?" Lily said, throwing a thick, pistachio mohair shawl around her shoulders.

I felt the soft wool, so smooth and cozy. I immediately decided to buy one for myself to keep me warm during the long, cold nights in Sweden.

"Is she a hipster?" Faion said, nose in the air.

"Honey, we are Latin women, our hip game is strong," Lily said.

I loved watching my friends happy together.

Faion picked up a silk, off the shoulder, boho-style blouse.

"That's more like your momma," he said. "She so *bougie*."

Lucia was a little *bougie* and, more importantly, completely recovered. Thankfully, she didn't remember the horrific encounter we had in the parking garage or her mysterious, immortal boyfriend.

Chaos had made good on his promise and released Lucia. The idea of her having been his lover, even for a short time, still made me cringe.

"Silk gets my vote," I said. "Lucia is a summer-all-year type of gal."

Lily shrugged. "You guys should stay here for Christmas. I get that being home for the holidays is a thing, but I'll miss your stupid faces."

"You're going to see this stupid face running, not walking, back to my Gram's yams and ham. Sorry, *chica*! *No bueno*."

Part of me wished I could stay with Lily and Lucia too, but it was time to have it out with Grandma before leaving for Stockholm. Chaos had not returned. That left Grandma to shed some light on who I really was, where I had come from, and how an Immortal Magistrate figured into all of it.

A text flashed on my phone's screen. I blushed reading it.

The fountain below. Can we talk? Emmet.

I leaned over the railing. There he was, next to the fountain on the ground floor of the mall. He had on his wine-red leather jacket that I loved, his hair brushed back and still wet. An older man in his sixties stood a few feet from Emmet, reading a brochure. Their resemblance was uncanny.

Emmet waved.

"Who's the boy toy?" Faion said.

"A friend," I muttered.

"That's Dr. Groshek, I presume," Lily said.

I rolled my eyes. "I'll be right back."

It took me a while to find the right escalator. I tried to speed up the descent by walking as well as riding down. I smiled when I noticed Emmet waiting for me at the bottom.

I was feeling grateful that Lily had dragged me to the hair and threading salon that morning. My brand-new caramel highlights had blended nicely with my dark brown hair that fell to my shoulders in thick curls. I'd had a pearl facial and had my makeup done professionally. I felt pretty.

One look into his welcoming eyes and that boy was forgiven. "Are you following me again, Emmet?"

He raised his hands in surrender. "Total coincidence, I swear. I'm here with my Dad. Christmas shopping."

"I saw him," I said. "Is he...?"

"A shifter? No, that's Mom."

"Is she here?" I said, glancing at the people near his Dad.

"No, she's back in Rhode Island. My parents divorced. When I turned eighteen, she returned to her pack."

"But not you."

"Not one for packs," he said, smiling. "I'm a lone wolf."

"And a clever boy."

He nodded. "Want to grab a cup of coffee?"

"That's sweet, but do you think it's a good idea? We can't

just forget who we are or what happened," I said, as much to myself as to him.

"When I first saw you that day outside the library, I knew you were different, I sensed the magic, but that's not why I liked you. I was attracted to Sophie, the basic girl, not Luna."

"Are you saying Luna's not all that?"

"You know what I mean."

"Yeah, I do, and it's nice," I said. "Anyway, I'm glad you're okay and thank you for being there for Rob. That was really cool."

"There has to be a way to start over, Sophie," he said. "I'm willing to do whatever it takes. A chance, that's all I want."

It was tempting. He was tempting. In another time and place, I might have started kissing him right there at the bottom of the escalator. We would be great together. It would be wonderful to have a strong guy by my side, someone who would have my back, who I could talk to about anything, magic included. That wouldn't be such a terrible thing.

Alas, I sighed. "I don't have time for dating, Emmet."

A fleeting sadness flashed across his eyes. "Then let's be friends."

"I'm leaving. First to Oregon and then to Stockholm." I lowered my eyes. "Getting close to me is not a safe place. I'm not looking to add to the number of people I need to worry about."

"Ouch, that means I didn't make the cut," he said. "You know, I can take care of myself."

We were more alike than I cared to admit. "I know and that's what you should do, take care of yourself. That will make me happy."

"Well, as long as you're happy," he said without conviction.

"You're a great guy, Emmet. I know that now."

"I knew it the whole time," he said. "I have to go. My dad's wandering near the Victoria's Secret shop."

I laughed. I missed him, but I'd made up my mind.

"Go wrangle your dad," I said.

"On it," he said and started walking away. "I won't give up on you."

His stubbornness was a thing of wonder. I stepped onto the up escalator and watched him walk away, a terrible ache in my heart.

Farewell, sweet Emmet.

HERE WE WERE, FAION and I, at Gate 24, waiting to board the plane to Portland. It was the first leg of my trip. After Christmas with Grandma, I'd visit my mother in the Deep Down, then back to San Diego, before taking off for Stockholm in mid-January. It all sounded delightfully normal.

"It won't be the same, you know," Faion said.

"Astoria?"

"No, San Diego... without you."

"What will you miss most? Drooling demons chasing us, Immortals threatening us with bodily harm, or cannibalistic dreams?"

"Well, when you put it that way, you were the worst friend ever."

I grinned. "I'll miss you, too, Faion."

An announcement came through the speakers.

Attention, passenger Sophie Collinsworth travelling on flight AS 1959 to Portland, please report to the information desk immediately.

"Did they just call your name? Faion said.

I nodded. "Yeah, that's odd."

"They better not kick you off the plane."

That would be awful, but I knew it happened. I ran down the steps to level 1 and headed for the Terminal 2 information desk.

I had to push through a group of excited tourists, but then I saw him, leaning against the information desk, elbow on the counter. He was wearing a blue blazer over a cream shirt and casual gray pants. His right hand fumbled with a pair of dark sunglasses. He looked like a 1960s movie star.

No fucking way. Winter.

He spotted me standing thirty feet away. He walked over to where I was frozen in place. "Good, I made it in time," he said.

"In time for what?"

I looked around. We were standing in the last place he

would try to kidnap me, security guards stationed in every direction, a crowd of people armed with iPhone cameras.

"I'm going to do something very stupid..." he started saying.

Oh boy, here we go...

"... and trust you with the whole truth."

Oh, another guy on a truth mission. I was surprised there was no confetti shot out of cannons while sweet music burst forth from the airport's speakers to celebrate the moment. *Men.*

"What Chaos told you about Düsternis and the magistrates preparing to take over the world, it's all true. They have Eternals on their side, too."

An overwhelming urge to bitch slap him till the end of time made my hands itch. "Now? You choose to come clean here and now?"

"It was two decades ago that I came upon the information. I was the one who brought it to Chaos. I suggested we should consider intervening. He shut me down cold. Whatever Chaos is planning, it's not to save the world."

I closed my eyes. "I have a flight to catch."

"You want to know why I chose to shield you?"

"Honestly, I've moved on," I said. "I don't care anymore."

"Hear me out, Sophie," he said, honoring my preferred name. "I stripped you of your etheric essence when you were a child. I found you a home, a safe home, as a lunar witch. I did that to shelter you from the upcoming war."

"Well, now I'm grown up," I told him. "Your babysitting career is over."

"You were too innocent. Your face was like bottled sunshine. I didn't want Düsternis to get his claws in you and consume the best part of you. But now, yes, you know everything, because Chaos duped me, and he duped you. There's no way to run, or I would absolutely tell you to run. We're stuck in this and I wish I hadn't pulled you into it."

"A therapist is more qualified to listen to this, Jonas. I'm going to miss my flight."

"Luna, together we can stop the Council. I can't do it without you."

"I'm sure you can," I said, locking onto his eyes. "But I'm not going to let you suck me into it this time. We're not some crime fighting duo. I'm just a girl waiting for a plane, going home for the holidays. That's all I want to be, it's all I can be, I don't want to become like you or Chaos."

"You have to be trained, guided, so you can resist Düsternis when he comes for you. Luna, we're running out of time. When the monsters and the Eternals and the Shadows come, what will you do?"

"I don't know, kick their balls?" I told him, losing interest. "I tell you what, your best buddy, Chaos, he wants the same thing. You guys should hook up and take care of this. You know, be Epic. Get the band back together. Put your crazy ass evil minds to it. Hey, it might take 100 years, but that's a drop in the bucket for you guys. You're Shadows after all, no mountain too high."

"You're not listening."

"No, you're the one not listening. I'm done with you and your lies. I'm done with raving lunatic Chaos. If you decide to come after me, be prepared for the fight of your life. I know I will be and I'm not easy to kill."

The air clamped around me like a vise. I walked away, cursing under my breath. I stole a glance back to make sure he wouldn't fry the whole terminal with a hissy fit of high-voltage rage.

He did not move—the fire burned in his eyes. I broke into a trot to get as far away from his depressing vibe as possible. This wouldn't be the end, we both knew it, but I wouldn't waste more time worrying about the future.

All we have is right now.

"We're boarding," Faion said, beaming at my return. "Everything okay?"

"All good. Had the wrong name," I said, wrapping my arm in his arm.

We found our seats and buckled up. My story had just begun to unfold, adventures awaited. I would not rest until I uncovered the truth about my birth, my mother, my past, about my lost father.

I was stuck in this thing, but aren't we all? Life's messy and we can never rest until we know that our people are safe, until the basic and charmed folk alike can smile widely in the warm sun of a new day.

Once airborne, I felt free. San Diego blurred into shapes and earth colors, lively like a gathering of dolphins, pulsating, unaware of the magic that sparks in the shadows of its streets, parks, even beaches... unaware of the scattered entrances to the hidden world... unaware of the ancient grudges and the eternal isolation of the Deep Down, that invisible realm full of wonders known only to them in myth and legend, where spells can topple kingdoms and a pale horse runs wild through the mists of destiny, searching for a rider.

About the Author

Stella Fitzsimons was born in Athens, Greece, and lives in Southern California with her husband and two sons. After studying economics and language arts she went on to teach both Mathematics and English before launching *Stella's Literary Bistro*, a bilingual literary journal. Her works include: *Luna, Winter, Silver Dust, Shadow Fall, Moonlight Mist, The Last Rider* and *The Vanishing Tome*.

www.ingramcontent.com/pod-product-compliance
Lightning Source LLC
Chambersburg PA
CBHW020903160726
47993CB00005B/1791

* 9 7 9 8 2 0 1 1 4 5 3 9 2 *